A Complex Journey

Book One

I0591653

Brain Maze

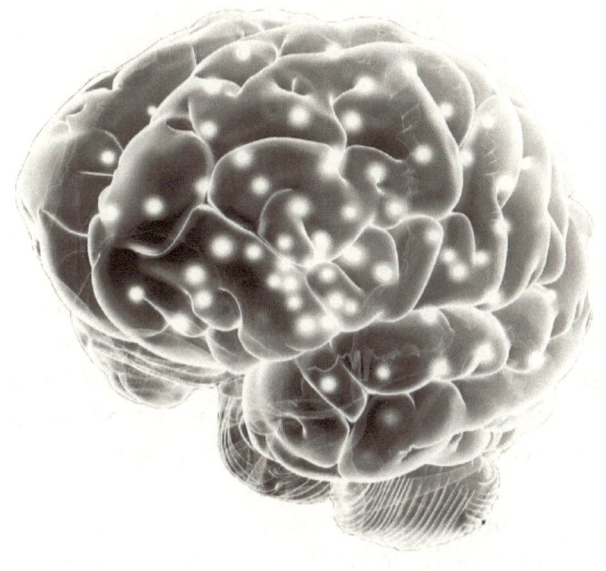

Randy McIntosh

Mouse Gate Press.
1103 Middlecreek
Friendswood, Texas 77546
281-992-3131 TL
www.totalrecallpress.com

ISBN: 978-1-64883-132-4
UPC: 643977-41324-6

FIRST EDITION
1   2   3   4   5   6   7   8   9   10

This is for the folk who go to great efforts to make complicated things understandable.

About The Author

Randy McIntosh is an aspiring fiction writer and established neuroscientist studying brain health and aging for over 25 years. He has an extensive scientific publication record on topics ranging from learning and memory functions in the brain to analytics and computer modeling of brain networks. He has built an open-source brain modeling platform, *TheVirtualBrain* (http://thevirtualbrain.org), in with his two close collaborators in Europe. His first short story, "For the Cost of Steak Dinner" about an interview with a retired hitman appeared in Adelaide Literary Magazine.

Randy is also an amateur musician, enjoying weekend gigs at local cafés in Vancouver, where he and his wife reside.

Preface

I am a scientist who has studied brain networks and complexity for almost thirty years. I want to provide the public with knowledge to better understand the seeming randomness in our world. Climate, economy, genetics, and immunology are complex systems that are inherently hard to predict. If we had a better intuition about complex systems, things like climate change and the recent pandemic might be better appreciated. The subtext of the book is teaching basic ideas about complex systems, but wrap this in fun Sci-Fi narrative.

Table of Contents

Chapter One:
A long slumber

Terry in Prison

Green

Terry's eyes snapped open. He wasn't sure if he heard the word in his head or if it was spoken to him.

GREEN

He realized he was lying down in a sort of fetal position. Why, where, how, and when was not clear.

At the edge of his sight, he could make out a green wall. As he pushed himself upright, he felt like he'd been in a long slumber. Still a bit groggy, but rested. His back and arms were tight. He sat and examined the room.

Chapter Two:
Katya's Speech

Breakfast Discussion

Katya looked into the mirror and felt the familiar nervousness building. She was annoyed that, after all these years of giving presentations, she still felt nervous. Maybe this was a necessary part of the process. She remembered talking with her colleagues in London about public speaking, and each had stories about how they felt before their talks.

- "I honestly feel completely empty, like nothing is in my head. It's rather frightening because there is that moment when I think that's all there is, and nothing will come out when I start!"
- "I try not to think about it until the very moment when I walk up to the podium."
- "I over-rehearse my first few sentences. That opens the floodgates for the rest of my speech."
- "I love the energy before I get up there. It's so motivating, and I can't wait to start."

Oh, please! she thought.

Katya had rehearsed several times and even skipped dinner with her friends to rethink the framing of certain points. She was awake early today, reviewing her presentation and rehearsing her script in her head.

She walked back into her bedroom. Her cats had embedded themselves in the pillows, thankfully avoiding the clothes she'd laid out.

The apartment-hotel was a good choice for her transition after the divorce, but the place still didn't feel comfortable. Things weren't where they were supposed to be — a kind of metaphor for her current situation.

The divorce was amicable, with her and her partner agreeing to sell their property and share the proceeds. The phrasing in the divorce settlement made the entire process feel cold, like you could erase the pain of the past with a few well-selected words.

Katya refocused her thoughts on the speech while she dressed. She decided on "light but formal" attire of her taupe suit to accommodate the persistent heatwave that engulfed Berlin.

There was a knock at her door. Her cats scattered at the unexpected sound.

"Hallo?" she called out.

"Good morning, Katya. It's the stinky boys," Terry's muffled voice rang out.

Katya walked to the door, adjusting her blouse. "One second, please." She paused in front of the mirror to pull her black hair back into a ponytail.

She opened the door to see a sweaty Terry and Logan standing there in running clothes, having just finished a morning run. Terry's grey tank top was plastered to his skin, dense with sweat. He peered over his sunglasses at Katya with a slight grin. Logan, the taller of the two, stood behind Terry, peering over him with a big grin. His beard dripped sweat on Terry's running cap.

"Hi, how was the run?" she asked, stifling the urge to laugh at her friends.

"Excellent. The city is still asleep, and the run along the river is quite beautiful! You would have loved it." Logan stepped beside Terry, placing his hand on his shoulder, revealing a garish combination of a bright orange tank top and silver running shorts.

Katya's eyes widened at the colour combination. "Did you buy that outfit just for this trip?"

"Of course!" Logan smiled.

Terry glanced over at him. "Or maybe he forgot running clothes, and that was all that was available in the shop downstairs."

Katya laughed. "Perhaps tomorrow, we can do the same run. You know how it is with me and presentations. I am nervous, and I need the time to feel prepared."

"No worries at all, Katya. You are the best one of the three of us to give this talk. A bit of apprehension is natural, given the audience," Logan replied.

Terry glanced over Katya's shoulder to look at the clock on the desk. "We're going to grab a bit of breakfast and coffee now. Would you like to join us?"

"Don't you want to shower first? You are all sweaty and," sniffs, "stinky." Katya wrinkled her nose. "That's probably why my cats ran away."

"That would take too long. Besides, showing up like this guarantees we get our own table." Terry puffed his chest out.

Katya laughed again, feeling her anxiety ease. "Okay, I will join you and take another coffee."

The trio left Katya's apartment and headed to the stairs to the main floor. Terry pointed out the direction to the restaurant. "I'm gonna duck into the bathroom, so why don't you two grab a table?"

Katya and Logan approached the restaurant host. "Table for three, please," Logan asked, showing his room card.

The host checked a video screen and motioned to them.

"Certainly, please follow me."

They walked past an enormous buffet that was packed with hungry apartment-hotel guests. There was food from all over the globe, meant to satisfy everyone from those with a conservative palette, to the more adventurous, who wanted to try something exotic.

"You have the option of the buffet, or you can order off the menu. The buffet is an excellent choice because you can try a wide range of foods, and since you might be hungry after your exercise, it's also all-you-can-eat." The host directed the comment to Logan. "We have an option of the booth in the corner or the table by the window."

"Let's take the window, please." Logan smiled.

"Of course, sir." The host walked to the table and pulled out the chairs, "One of our staff will menus in a moment. May I take an order for coffee or tea in the meantime?"

"I would like a cappuccino, please," Katya replied.

"I will do the same, and three very large glasses of cold water," Logan added. "And a flat-white for our colleague whom I see coming now."

"Thank you." The host turned to see Terry approaching. "Good morning, sir. Your companion ordered a flat-white for you. I hope that's okay?"

Terry nodded and showed his room key. "Perfect, actually. Did they order water too?"

"Yes, sir." The host began walking away. "Your drinks will be here soon."

The trio sat at the square table, with Terry and Logan facing Katya. The sun through the window was quite bright, so Katya put on her sunglasses.

"Everyone will think you're a movie star," Terry commented.

Katya laughed. "The way you two are dressed, I doubt that."

"We are your biggest fans." Logan winked.

A waitperson appeared placing three glasses of water and menus on the table. Logan immediately gulped down half of his glass of water.

"I am sure the host told you about the buffet. It's a great deal if you are really hungry. I can also recommend a few things on our menu if you are interested," the waitperson commented.

Terry peered at his two companions. "I think we can order now. Just the two of us will be eating. We'll pass on the buffet today and order off the menu." He pointed to Logan. "Do you know what you want?"

"Steak and eggs, please." Logan looked up from the menu.

"I will do the smoked salmon and poached eggs." Terry closed his menu.

The waitperson reached for the menus. "Very good. How would you like your steak cooked, sir?"

"*A pointe.*" Logan finished his water. "And more water, if you please."

"Of course." The waitperson turned as another waitperson brought three coffees to the table.

Terry turned to Katya. "So, how do you like living in this apartment-hotel? It seems pretty posh."

"Well, it is convenient when my friends come to visit." She smiled, taking a sip of her coffee. "Since I moved after the divorce, it is a reasonable solution."

She changed the subject quickly. "I had an idea this morning that may help to build better intuition for our proposal," she began as she stirred the foam into her cappuccino.

Terry took Katya's cue to change the topic. There would be time later to talk about personal matters. Now they needed to focus their conversation on the task ahead. The Global Council invited them to Berlin to show their brain simulation platform: BrainMaze. Until now, the trio had BrainMaze on neuroscience. They discovered that by extending the core principles, BrainMaze could interact with other intelligent systems to come up with new solutions for hard problems.

Katya continued. "When I reviewed my presentation, I still felt that the concepts around Complex Adaptive Systems might be too hard to grasp. The BrainMaze platform we have developed is easy to explain as a computer simulation platform for your own brain, but I am concerned that linking this to Complex Adaptive Systems will be difficult without some good examples.

"So, I reread an old paper from Warren Weaver on 'Science and Complexity,' and I think I can make a link between 'disorganized' versus 'organized' complexity and what we are proposing to the Global Council."

Terry stirred some sugar into his coffee. "Keep going. We're listening."

Katya sat up and leaned forward. "Okay, here is my idea. Weaver distinguished between 'organized' and 'disorganized' because he felt there was a way to study nonlinear systems that would give you some potential at prediction and control. The idea of disorganized complexity conveyed behaviours that were difficult to predict and seemingly random, like the expansion of gases in an enclosed container. Nonlinearities still drive organized complexity, but there are more deterministic levels wrapped around it so that it is possible to predict outcomes."

Logan looked up. "I like where this is going, Katya, but the language you use is accessible for general audience like the Council members."

"I know, Logan," she continued. "This is my point. I think I can connect between disorganized complexity and the events that led to the formation of the Global Council."

"Ah," Logan smiled. "Please continue."

"Okay, remember about 15 years ago in America when the three branches of government started operating independently? Proclamations came from one branch that had no relationship to initiatives from the other branch. Many actions seemed to be truly random. One branch proposed economic sanctions, then withdrew them only to have the sanction re-proposed from another branch. There was no way to predict government policy, which made it impossible to negotiate. As a result, the confidence in the actions of the US government fell to a catastrophic low. This was not just a problem within the US but also for other countries that simply stopped responding and worked separately to mitigate any large impact of this random behaviour.

"You could say a similar thing happened in the UK, where the governing party employed similar tactics, intentional or not. This played to the fears of many citizens as the random behaviours were seen as a threat that only a more isolationist strategy could fix.

"This is a perfect example of disorganized complexity, which pushed the entire political system to a tipping point. But, rather than becoming even more disorganized, a new structure emerged where local jurisdictions focused on their needs, initially ignoring the need of similar jurisdictions or higher-order jurisdictions."

Katya took a sip of her cappuccino. "For these local systems to survive, they need to be connected, and this is a beautiful example of emergence. Local systems formed small networks of mutually reinforcing interactions. Soon these networks connected with others and formed larger networks."

She raised her spoon to make a point. "Actions that were rewarding for the network were reinforced, and others eliminated. For instance, if an action benefited a local system only at the expense of another, they eliminated it at the larger network.

"The speed at which this happened was impressive. The political bodies worldwide saw the benefit of these local systems. Rather than trying to impose a structure on them, they worked to further connect them across countries and ultimately across the globe.

"The formation of the Global Council was a natural outcome of this. But, unlike the top-down structures of the past, the Council facilitated the interactions of these networks by setting up the infrastructure to make sure the networks communicated rapidly."

"And that's what led to the Global AI system," Terry interjected.

The Global Council benefited from connecting leading scientists and engineers with politicians who were facing the challenge of trying to manage their own jurisdictions, while staying informed of the activities and needs of others locally and nationally. AI systems were more ubiquitous, with an ever-expanding capacity for integrating critical information to make predictions. The challenge was that different AI platforms were devoted to monitoring something specific, such as water consumption, financial transactions, or epidemiological data. The

Global AI system fostered interactions between platforms to create predictive scenarios that could guide local decisions and balance global needs. This was not a simple task, technically or politically, but as the benefits of balancing local and global perspectives became clear, the new AI system saw greater adoption.

"Exactly," Katya continued, "and what emerged was an equitable, large-scale political system capable of balancing the local needs in a city and state, with corresponding needs on the other side of the planet. Not by a direct link but through the multiscale architecture.

"The Global Council is more a coordinating committee rather than a governing body. They do make decisions, of course, but they are most effective when they work to coordinate interactions between jurisdictions and entities."

"But they still have to make decisions, Katya," Logan added, "or else they would not have asked us to come here."

"This is true, Logan," Katya continued. "I don't want to give the impression that they do not. The analogy is not perfect, but it captures the idea that complexity is a thing to aspire to because it led to the emergence of the Global Council. I emphasize 'emergence' because the actual function of the Council differs from what was initially intended.

"This is where the analogy gets difficult. The organizational chart for the Global Council looks very traditional top-down. But, if you sketch out the connecting parts below it, you quickly see the network properties that convert the structure into a dynamic function."

"Your breakfasts." The staff brought the food to Terry and Logan. "Did you order anything?" one of them asked Katya as they placed the plate in front of Terry.

"No, no. I had breakfast earlier. I am happy with the cappuccino for now." Katya held up her cup.

The staff walked away, and Terry poked at his poached eggs, hoping to let the yolks run out. "Ah, damn. They over-cooked the eggs, and the yolks are hard," he sighed. "I guess ketchup and hot sauce to the rescue." He reached across the table to grab two bottles and decorated his plate with red sauces.

"Your tastes are sometimes questionable." Logan frowned.

"Wanna try?" Terry said, as he cut the first piece of egg, salmon, and bread.

"Uh, no." Logan wrinkled his nose. "Sorry, Katya, please continue." He cut into his breakfast steak.

Katya smiled. "I think I've made my point. The question is whether this description of the Global Council's emergence as a movement from disorganized to organized complexity will be helpful."

Logan finished chewing a piece of steak and sat back. "To be honest, it does make an excellent illustration for emergence, but you already have this in your presentation. I think additional vignettes may make things more confusing."

Terry added, "Actually, there is another thing we should consider. This is only the second cycle for the Global Council, and there may be sensitivities to some of the history that could get triggered. It's only been eight years since this all came to be."

Terry's comment referred to the first proposals for a Global Council. The turmoil that came out of the isolationism of the USA and the withdrawal of the UK from the European Union had a broad divisive effect on the planet. Old alliances fell, replaced by fair weather agreements that seldom lasted beyond a few months. The European Union kept a core engaged, but internal politics left many of the country's leaders unable to make decisions, having to balance their own country's needs against the union. Mistrust of intentions became rampant between the European Union leaders. Canada, Mexico and a few Central and South American countries changed their focus on rapid information exchanges to address economic needs because the USA was no longer a willing partner in trade.

The mistrust spiralled out of control until the US and Russia made a declaration that all nations would renegotiate trade agreements to "better equalize" the economies. Multinational corporations drove this decree, which secured political backing in both countries. An ensuing emergency meeting of the United Nations to discuss "aggressive nature of the decree" was a disaster. The US and Russia blocked any proposals, and continued to insist on compliance with theirs. Canada and France expressed suspicion that business prospects drove the US/Russian agenda rather than altruism. The meeting with a threat of military action from the US and Russia if members did not agree to the terms.

Actions from within the US set the stage for a change. Internal investigations pointed to the influence of large corporations at the cost to local economies. The corporation transferred much of the locally generated wealth out of the country, essentially putting the local jurisdictions into a spiralling deficit. The federal government placed the blame on local mismanagement, and it wasn't long before political bickering escalated to animosity, placing the US on the verge of a civil crisis.

During an emergency meeting of the UN, the proposal for a Global Council was brought forward, with the mandate to inform and advise council members, ensuring that economic interactions were mutually beneficial. Soon the exchanges extended outside political boundaries, causing immediate tension from the US/Russia alliance, which saw this as a backdoor strategy to avoid their decree. It was only through the actions of politicians within the US that a full-out war was avoided. A smaller scale but similar outcome occurred in Russia.

From this, the Global Council's efforts received backing across most of the planet. There remained factions who refused to come along, seeing the Global Council proposal as removing their autonomy and stealing their resources. The tension that preceded this event, the threat of planetary war and the perceived loss of wealth and independence, continued to be a sore spot in the history.

"This is a valid concern, Terry. I don't want to revisit these old tensions," Katya acknowledged. "I just wanted to make sure I grabbed their attention early in the presentation."

"Maybe you already have this in the presentation. We can reframe it to make it clear that the functions of the Global Council emerged from the new networks. You have some visuals that show this, right?" Terry encouraged.

Katya looked up toward the ceiling. "Ah, yes! I have one that shows a series of small local networks that are densely connected merging into larger networks with less dense inter-connections. I can use this to illustrate how that structure emerged through mutual reinforcement rather than deliberate construction, and established the conditions for the Global Council." Katya made a note to this effect on her napkin.

Logan added, "I like this. It puts a more positive perspective on the historical achievements and primes them for our proposal. Once they understand 'emergence', our proposal to facilitate it through the intersection of BrainMaze and the Global AI system will be more convincing."

Katya continued. "I think I can illustrate this nicely by drawing the interacting economies as network nodes. For example, some local economies that came about were responses to the lack of clarity from national governments. There establish a sort of 'barter and trade' systems where the local farmer would only sell to local businesses because they knew the income would go back to keeping their farm going. This scenario played out elsewhere, and then these local systems started interacting with other local systems to exchange resources. The farmer needed fuel and equipment from neighbouring systems, which set up a link between them. With the digital communication systems we have nowadays, such links are easily established, and if there were ineffective, they were removed. The cool thing is that this cycle of testing connections played out across multiple spatial scales, leading to what we have now that sits under Global Council oversight." Katya paused. She realized that her accompanying illustration spilled over from the napkin to the tablecloth. "Oops."

Terry laughed. "I wonder if we can bring the tablecloth to the presentation."

"Anyway, I have the idea in my head." Katya took a snapshot of her sketch with her Motif handheld device. The trio agreed on the name "Motif" as it represented a feature of complex systems where rudimentary building blocks, or motifs, could be used to test new adaptations. Each of them had a Motif that gave them the flexibility to interact with BrainMaze remotely, coming up with solutions for a problem through their joint operations. And the Motif acted as a smartphone.

"I will try to modify one of my videos to reinforce this. It will take about 15 minutes, and I would like to clean up a little before we go. Could we meet in the lobby in about 30 minutes?"

"That should be good." Terry looked at Logan's plate. "I think we are almost finished, so you can go work on the video, and we'll take care of the bill."

Katya smiled and rose, took one last sip of her cappuccino, and walked out as Terry and Logan watched.

"I have a good feeling about this, Logan." Terry cut a piece of egg. "This could be huge for BrainMaze and our collaboration.

"Don't get me wrong. I think we have amazing success in the brain modelling platform, but this is exactly the kind of opportunity we envisioned when we first sketched BrainMaze out on a very similar napkin as we have here." Terry held up a red-stained napkin.

"Except that was beers in a pub, not your nasty ketchup and eggs in a restaurant." Logan smiled. "There is one thing we did not expect in that conversation. Remember that we focused on trying to set up a platform that used real data to create models of a person's brain. This led BrainMaze applications in clinics, by creating a virtual version of a patient's brain where the clinicians simulate interventions, to help select the more effective therapy. I don't think we expected that the simulation system in BrainMaze would have the potential for applications outside of neuroscience."

Terry thought for a moment. "That's probably true. That extension only became obvious once Katya joined the team. Her engineering background opened the door to the new possibilities for brain-computer interfaces. That's something neither of us considered."

"Exactly." Logan held up his fork. "But here is a nice connection. Consider the skills you and I brought. You have the background in data analytics and cognitive neuroscience, and I have the background in dynamical systems theory and movement science. Katya brings in engineering and medicine. With the combination of the three competencies, what 'emerged' was a platform that was more than simply the sum of our expertise." He shook his fork to make the point.

"BrainMaze is an emergent feature of our collaboration?" Terry looked nervously at the food-crusted fork that Logan was waving at him.

Logan noticed Terry's fixation on the fork and smiled. "One could say that. But more accurately it would be a multiplicative aggregate property of our work."

Terry laughed. "I think 'emergence' is easier to understand than 'multiplicative aggregate.' At least, it's easier to say."

"Whatever." Logan rolled his eyes in jest and sat back. "Are we finished here? We need to get our cute little butts moving."

"Yep." Terry rose and looked for one of the waitstaff.

Logan stepped back from the table and began walking. "Your turn to take care of the bill. I will see you in the lobby."

As Terry tried to remember whether it was, in fact, his turn, Logan exited, and one of the waitstaff approached him. "Shall I charge the breakfasts to your room, sir?"

"I, uh, yeah, sure," Terry replied. He glanced out the window to see the morning sun coming over the courtyard outside, reminding him of the garden back at his home. "Maybe when we get back from the meeting, we can relax out there." He made a mental note for himself.

Trip to Headquarters

Thirty minutes later, the trio was in the hotel lobby.

"You boys clean up well." Katya admired their change in attire compared to an hour ago.

"All for you, my dear, all for you." Logan bowed. His trimmed beard was an excellent complement to his lightweight blue suit, giving him the appearance of a C-suite executive rather than the stereotypical scientist.

"Okay, okay, let's get going," Terry said, smiling and moving to the door. His khaki trousers and blue sport coat jacket fit the scientist stereotype well.

As they exited, their vehicle moved up in front of them. It stopped, and the rear doors slid open.

"Age before beauty," Logan said, looking at Terry.

Terry smirked and entered the vehicle, followed by Katya. Logan entered and pressed the "CLOSE" button next to the door.

"Good morning, Professors. I understand we are going to the Global Council Headquarters today?" a voice from the vehicle inquired.

"That is correct," replied Terry. "Do you need directions?" He realized that was an unnecessary question but had gotten into the habit of asking anyway.

"That won't be necessary. I have the coordinates already," the vehicle responded. "Please be comfortable. With current traffic, we should be at the Headquarters in 20 minutes."

"This is so cool," Katya said, pointing to the vehicle's console. "I will definitely consider getting one of these for my next vehicle."

Logan nodded, as he did not feel comfortable with the idea of autonomous vehicles negotiating the heavy traffic in a major city.

"Let's focus for a moment," he said.

"Katya, we are happy that you are taking the lead on this, and I repeat that of the three of us, you are the best to make the pitch.

"Number one, remember that the audience is very diverse. Although the Council has been briefed, they won't have the details that their staff will have. Be ready for interruptions, as some members have short attention spans and may feel the need to speak up.

"Number two, I took the opportunity this morning to look at the visuals you will be presenting, and they are fantastic. I really must credit your team for such compelling illustrations of such difficult concepts."

Katya smiled, thankful that she had put her presentation on their BrainMaze system so they could all access it.

Terry felt a buzz from his Motif in his pocket and removed it to see the message: "EVERYTHING IS READY FOR YOU HERE. PLEASE ACKNOWLEDGE THIS MESSAGE ONCE YOU ARE ON THE WAY TO HQ - SB "

SB would be Secretary Baren, I guess, Terry thought. He sent an acknowledgement and looked up at Katya.

"I think Logan and I will sit next to you during the presentation, so we can monitor the mood of the Council as you present," Terry added. "If there are opportunities to address any concerns, we will try to flag you."

"Do you think there will be a decision on our proposal today?" Katya asked.

"It's hard to know," Terry replied. "The full Council will be there so that they can vote today. There is some urgency, so hopefully, they will feel this."

Katya breathed a sigh. "Good, these bureaucracies usually take an eternity to decide."

The vehicle arrived in the driveway of the Headquarters. The vehicle paused while it sent the validation information to the gate control. After a few seconds, the gate opened and the vehicle proceeded.

"Welcome, Professors. The Secretary will be at the door to greet you," came a voice from the gate.

"I still can't get used to this. Was that a person or a computer?" Logan asked.

Katya smiled, looking sideways at Logan. She fixed her attention forward as she marvelled at the mixture of technology and old architecture in the design of the Headquarters. "It looks so much more impressive in real life." She stared with admiration at the large columns that bounded the stairs to large wooden doors.

The vehicle stopped 20 metres from the end of the driveway.

"You will need to get out here as the communications field from the building blocks transmissions. If we get any closer, and I will be unable to move," the vehicle said.

"Stranded like a turtle on its back," Logan chuckled. A little emoji smile flashed on the vehicle console as the door slid open.

The trio exited and adjusted their clothes. The door closed, and the vehicle backed down the driveway.

Terry looked ahead to the building and back at his two partners. "Are we good to go here?" he asked as he motioned to move ahead.

"Yep," Katya sighed as she started walking.

Terry looked at Katya. "Don't sound so gloomy."

"I am fine, just a bit tired. Riding in the back of the vehicle sometimes makes me a bit uneasy."

"Yes, I remember that." Terry nodded as he walked.

Logan was looking at his Motif, then noticed his partners had started walking.

"Sorry, there was a message that BrainMaze needing to restart one of the cores." Logan puffed as he caught up, pocketing his Motif.

"What?!" Katya's voice quivered. "This could not happen at a worse time! Will it affect the demo we are planning?"

Terry stopped walking and looked back at Logan.

"We were going to have to do this in local mode anyway. The field around the building will mess up any feeds from the BrainMaze cloud system. We will tether our Motifs inside as we had planned to support the demo. No worries." Logan smiled and winked.

"Sorry, I forgot about that part. I have been so focused on the presentation! I am happy you both took care of the interface challenge," Katya said, relaxing. "This is why we are a great team!"

Chair and TechStaff

As they started walking again, the front doors opened, and the Secretary stepped out to greet the trio.

"Good morning, my dear friends," he said. Despite his heavy accent, there were phrases he could say that erased any sign that he was not a native English speaker. This greeting was one such phrase.

He was the same height as Terry, but slimmer. He wore a light grey, three-piece suit with a dark tie that was an odd choice, given the persistent heat. With a head of thick, grey hair and a beard, it was surprising that he was not sweating.

"I trust your trip to Berlin has been pleasant so far," he continued. "And the apartment-hotel option for your accommodations?"

"Perfect!" Logan smiled as he extended a formal greeting to the Secretary.

"Great to see you again, Secretary Baren." Katya extended her greetings. "Having my friends stay in the same building as my flat was a great idea."

Terry followed. "Thanks to you and your team for arranging this. So far, everything has been perfect."

"So far." The Secretary smiled slyly as he greeted Terry.

The trio entered the building, and the door closed behind them.

The Secretary turned to face them. "I know that you, Logan, have been here before, but for the benefit of your colleagues, I will remind you of the protocol.

"At this moment, you are being scanned and digitally tagged, so your visit is logged. The tag only applies within the walls of this building."

At least, that's what they tell you, Katya thought. She was uneasy with the possibility that they could monitor her every movement without her knowledge.

Terry studied the massive entry hall as they started walking. Like the outside, the interior had a charming mixture of old architecture with a reminder of the technical advances that made this global alliance possible. Subtle reflections of pin-hole cameras were apparent but blended to look like artistic highlights.

"You may recall that the field around the building limits communication. If you are expecting any feeds from outside, we can establish a secure bridge to allow the communication, but Logan told me earlier that he did not think it necessary," the Secretary continued.

Katya spoke up. "Could we set up such a bridge to the BrainMaze system just in case we need it for the demo?"

Logan glared at Katya with a look that said, "I thought we discussed this already?"

Katya noticed this, but continued. "I know we said we didn't need it, but it might be a good safeguard, just in case. It would be a pity if the demo failed because we may not have another chance with this group."

The Secretary nodded. "Let's see what we can do when we get to the main hall. We have 30 minutes before the Council shows up, so we can work with our technical team to establish the bridge."

Katya leaned over to Logan as they continued walking and whispered, "I'm sorry. I know we don't need it. I will be more comfortable if I know it is there, just in case."

Logan nodded, but did not speak.

Terry had fallen behind as he looked at his Motif. *This is weird. It looks like we're still able to connect with the BrainMaze system from inside here,* he thought. *The indicators suggest a slightly weaker signal, but the connection is more than adequate for feeds to and from BrainMaze.*

As the group approached the main hall, Logan spotted another entourage approaching from the left. He recognized the Chair and several of the other Council members.

"Ah!" Logan exclaimed as he stopped to face the entourage

with a smile. "Good morning," he followed with a slight bow.

Terry, Katya and the Secretary stopped as well.

Chair Meyer smiled and continued to walk toward the group, extending her hand. "Good morning, Professors. We are delighted you could make it." She greeted Katya first, and then Logan.

"Your request honours us," Katya replied.

Katya and Logan observed the Chair's definitive commanding presence, an air of confidence that made it clear she was the leader of the group. Her manner of speaking, however, gave a sense of comfort and ease.

"And good morning to you, Secretary Baren." The Chair nodded in his direction. He nodded in response.

Terry fumbled while pocketing his Motif. "Greetings, Chair Meyer. We are looking forward to some good discussion today." The Chair and Terry greeted each other, and as they turned, the Chair gestured, "This is the main entrance to the hall, but I think it would be better if we came in through the side entrance so you can meet with the technical staff right away. I gather that there may be some problems with your BrainMaze feed?"

"Indeed," Katya said cautiously. *I guess she heard us on the video monitors as we came into the building,* she thought.

"Good idea." The Secretary continued to guide the group. They rounded a corner and saw a door with a dimmed light with 'IN SESSION' printed on it.

"Please enter here," he said, opening the door.

The Chair and her entourage entered first and continued down the corridor to another door.

"Can you please help our guests?" she said as she passed someone with 'TechStaff' on her lapel. Her small stature and youth belied her status as the primary person overseeing the technology for the Global Council.

"Absolutely," TechStaff responded and, looking at the trio, she said, "Professors, please come with me into the control booth." TechStaff bounded up a small staircase and opened a heavy door. Katya followed behind, and then Logan. Terry was watching the Chair and Secretary disappear through the door at the end of the corridor. He gazed at his Motif and saw the signal from the BrainMaze system was still strong.

"That won't work in here, Professor," TechStaff commented. "Please come up. I want to get you hooked up so there is time to test the audio and video."

Terry glanced up at her.

"Sorry, it's a bad habit," he mumbled, and he ran up the staircase.

Katya was talking with the crew in the control room.

"We don't want to burden you with having to check our feed constantly, so we have set up a local tether that allows our devices to support the BrainMaze demonstration," she explained to the crew.

"Okay, Professor. Can we link up your device to test?" one of the crew asked Katya.

"Sure, but one more thing. I do not believe it will be necessary, but I prefer to be prepared just in case our three-node network is not enough to support the demonstration. Can you set up a temporary bridge between one of our devices and the BrainMaze system if we need the extra computation for the demo?" Katya continued.

Terry peeked at his Motif and saw it was still linked to BrainMaze. As he sighed, Logan glanced back at him with an inquisitive look.

"Nothing, Logan. It's nothing," Terry whispered and shifted his attention to Katya.

The crew paused at Katya's request, and TechStaff said, "That should be no problem, Professor. We can give one of you a secure channel on standby. I need to mention that we will monitor the feed for security if you use it."

"That is fine," Katya responded, turning to Logan and Terry.

"Terry, shall we use your Motif as the link?"

Terry grimaced, looking at his Motif. "Mine's been flaky this morning. Maybe we can use Logan's, okay?"

Katya frowned and said, "Okay. Good thing we have this option!"

One of the crew approached Logan, and the other approached Katya to test her audio and video connection. A few minutes later, the two thumbs-up signal came, and TechStaff motioned to the trio to follow her to a door on the opposite end of the control room.

"This will take us into the meeting hall. We'll finish setting you up there."

The hall had a modern look compared to the rest of the building. The centre had a massive, black stone boardroom-style table with large leather chairs. Each chair had a coloured headrest, which helped to break up the blackness. The walls were pale yellow with darker yellow acoustic tiles at regular intervals along the wall. There were smaller chairs placed around the edge of the room.

"Believe me, they did not consult me on the decorations for this room," TechStaff said with a smile.

Katya noticed her steps were muffled on the floor as she

walked to the table. The floor looked like dark wood at first glance.

"Cork panels," TechStaff said, noticing Katya's downward glance. "There's a ton of infrastructure that runs underneath the floor, so these panels give access without having to rip the floor up every time we make an upgrade. The cork is rather nice to walk on."

"We did a similar thing in my lab," Katya commented.

TechStaff stopped at the head of the table.

"Once everyone is seated and ready, the Chair will ask you to come up here. We've asked everyone to hold questions until the end, but this is an excitable group, and they may interrupt. Fortunately, we've trained them to be polite and indicate that they have a question, so if you see a light on the table in front of someone, or above one of the video screens, that's someone with a question.

"This is the remote control to activate and deactivate your video feed." She handed Katya a black oblong controller that had two buttons on it, one blue and one red. "The blue button is the video."

"Is the red a panic button?" Katya asked with a slight chuckle.

TechStaff gave Katya a puzzled look and said, "Of course not. Why would you panic?"

Before Katya could respond, TechStaff turned to Logan and Terry. "Perhaps you two could sit just off to the side on those chairs while your colleague presents?" She gestured toward the wall.

"I will go with them," Katya said, partly as a question.

TechStaff nodded as she turned and pressed a switch on the table that opened wall panels around the room, revealing video monitors. All the monitors had the word 'STANDBY' on a blue screen.

"I forgot to mention that we will broadcast your demonstration to other jurisdictions for Council members who couldn't be here today," TechStaff said to Katya.

Katya smiled. "No problem."

She felt an increase in tension when the Council members entering the room. By her estimate, there were about 50 people. The 10 Council members sat at the large table, and the rest of the people, whom she assumed were the Council's staff, went to chairs at the edge of the room.

She walked over to Terry and Logan.

Katya held the controller out. "What does the red button do?" she whispered to Logan.

Logan glanced at the controller and said, "I don't know. Let's find out." And before she could say anything, Logan pressed the red button.

A little black cover popped off followed by the battery that powered it.

Katya's eyes widened as she watched the cover and battery fall to the floor, almost in slow motion. Fortunately, Logan was fast enough to grab both before they hit the floor. He took the controller from Katya's outstretched hand and turned his back to the room as he replaced the battery and cover.

He handed it back to Katya, who was flushed.

"Sorry about that," Logan whispered.

"Everything okay, Professors?" TechStaff asked.

Katya and Logan nodded vigorously. Terry was having a hard time containing his laughter.

Chair Meyer was the last to enter the room, walking as she

continued talking with Secretary Baren. When she approached the head of the table, the Secretary moved off and walked over to where the trio was waiting.

"Welcome, everyone," the Chair began. "We have our special guests here with us today to give a demonstration of their solution for the problem we're facing," she nodded toward the trio.

"You are all aware of the seriousness of the issue, and I cannot emphasize how important it is that we decide on this today, so I would ask that you carefully consider the Professors' proposition. The decision we make here today will have critical implications for our planet."

With that, the Chair turned to Katya. "We are ready for you."

The speech

Katya nodded, looked over to Logan and Terry, and walked to the table.

"Are the video links operational?" the Chair asked, turning toward the control booth behind her.

A voice came on overhead, "All active but muted for now."

"Excellent," the Chair stated as the video monitors changed to show scenes from different places across the globe. "Welcome to all my colleagues who couldn't join us in person today."

Katya recognized most of them. Councillor Xi (monitor #1), Councillor McLaren (monitor #2) and Representative Zaren (monitor #3), but monitor #4 showed a group of people she did not know.

"Who is on monitor #4?" she asked.

"Oh, that's our technical team over in another facility. If we get the approval today, they will be the ones to implement it. I thought it would be good to have them see your presentation to give them a head-start," the Chair said, pointing to the eager group on the monitor.

Katya smiled. "I see."

The Chair stepped back from Katya.

"Shall we get started? Please, everyone, give the Professor your undivided attention," the Chair said, walking to her seat.

Katya began. "Thank you, Chair Meyer, and thank you Council members for agreeing to meet with us today. It is a great honour for my two colleagues and me to have this opportunity." She acknowledged Logan and Terry sitting to her right and turned to face the large screen behind her as she pushed the blue button — "Not red!" — to start the video feed.

"Our civilization is at an amazing phase in its development."

The video feed showed a cartoon of the Earth. Small lights flashed from the continents as the planet slowly rotated.

"We have seen big changes over the past decade as the political structures collapsed. The political and economic turmoil from North America and Europe was too great a risk for the planet, and hence this Council evolved to unify the globe in a manner that has not seen been before."

Connections formed between the small lights within each continent, with the title: "Global Council" hovering above the globe.

"The formation of the Global Council gave us, for the first time, a coordinated effort to ensure equitable distribution of resources. Basic sustenance is now less of a problem, and poverty is being eradicated. The literacy level and global health continue to rise.

"This did not come about because of a top-down solution,

where a few powerful countries imposed their solutions. The solutions resulted from the adaptive configuration of the new system. This was possible only because the AI system you put in place shared data, which enabled solutions that addressed local and global needs."

On the globe, each connection formed local clusters that became connected at longer distances to other clusters.

"I will introduce the term 'multiscale' architecture to you now. Keep this tucked away because you will see what this means later, and more importantly, what it implies.

"The Council linked smaller local groups to regional groups to countries and then trans-continentally. If you look at the screen behind me, you will see a pattern forming. The connections concentrate around local hubs, much like for airports, and the hubs interact regionally to form other hubs, and so on, until you have the long-distance hubs linked too."

The cartoon image behind Katya zoomed out, showing the progressive formation of hubs and their connections.

"The connections you see here are not physical but rather show the lines of communication most often used. Hence, you see far more communication among the local clusters than clusters that are farther apart."

The connections on the globe changed colours to simulate their actual communication activity, presenting an effective illustration of Katya's point.

"An important advantage of this architecture is that coordination of activity at each scale is more facile. Strategies used in one cluster can be shared quickly, tested in another, and modified to accommodate local conditions. This same architecture can be replicated across larger scales, which ensures effective strategies are kept, and ineffective ones are not. In other words, the architecture is adaptive.

"This works because the 'command structure' is more distributed than it was in the past, working through consensus and focused on evidence of efficacy. The Global AI system was crucial for this. It provided decision support to help consider several solutions, all with slightly different outcomes. This empowered the Council members with informed guidance for recommendations."

Katya scanned the room and video monitors. Most of the Councillors. The group on monitor #4 was nodding excitedly.

Terry looked around the room and noticed one of the Council members staring at him. *Wow, this guy needs to get some sun!* he thought, seeing the pale complexion of the Councillor.

The stare was not broken, with Terry returning the gaze. Terry looked at Logan, who appeared to notice the same thing.

"What's up with the Councillor?" Terry whispered as he leaned over to Logan.

Logan snapped around to face Terry. "Sorry, what?"

"What's with the stare down?" Terry repeated.

Blinking, Logan said, "I don't know what you are talking about." He turned his gaze to Katya.

Terry furrowed his brow and looked back at the table. The space where the Councillor sat was empty.

Katya's presentation continued. "The features I am talking about are characteristics of Complex Adaptive Systems, or CAS, for short. Adaptive systems do well because they take advantage of the multiscale architecture to test many solutions in many environments. These solutions are not imposed by some central coordinator but rather emerge essentially through trial and error.

"Trial and error does not mean the solutions are random. This is key to the adaptation. The system builds from a foundation that has proven to be successful, and hence new solutions stem from this foundation. You can consider a CAS as a system that builds on its successes."

On the screen behind her, the image turned to a brain schematic.

"The brain is a splendid example of an adaptive system. Our brain is in a constant state of exploration." Behind her, the image zoomed in to show brain circuit activity as lights speeding along connections.

"This activity reflects an attempt to predict was is happening and select the best response. Although we have good capacity to take information in through our senses, it's not possible to take it all in. That would be far too ineffective and probably maladaptive. By the time we got everything integrated, it would be too late. In our early existence, for example, it would have been disastrous to take the time to be absolutely certain that the movement we heard in a bush was not a predator. It was far more effective to predict from the minimal information that there was a predator close and escape.

"We used to think this prediction and updating was a deliberate process. From the perspective of CAS, however, this prediction is always going on.

"Brain circuits are built to predict what they should do. Neurons are naturally curious and are always testing whether other responses to inputs yield better outcomes."

The image zoomed out, showing multiple circuits with a few connections between them. The animation showed a cascade of impulses passing the circuits, changing colour each time one circuit passed the impulses to the next circuit.

"Most of the circuits are reciprocally connected, which sets up feedback to update the predictions earlier in the chain. The feedback reinforces positive outcomes, while eliminating negative ones.

"This same scenario takes place across the entire brain. The local processes of testing and updating are repeated across the entire system, enabling a cascade effect where only the most adaptive strategies are reinforced.

"The important feature of adaptive systems is the interactions. They make the system more resilient to attack, which also allows adaptability. The system will fail if the interactions are compromised. This can happen in disease, where some key circuits or hubs are removed breaking the reinforcement chains."

The video shifted back to an image of the planet with the communication network overlaid.

"The Council has been successful in setting up a political and economic system that shows some properties of a Complex Adaptive System." She paused again to let the point settle. "But consider this. What if we started explicitly trying to link the interaction of different CASs? What if we extended that to environmental control or if we did this with biology and engineering? Imagine if we built human-machine interfaces based on CAS principles.

"This is intriguing because the interactions between CAS's will by design result in another Complex Adaptive System, giving a structure that is maximally adaptive and resilient, keeping the best features of the systems that were brought together to form the new one."

Katya stopped talking to take a sip of water.

"While the Global system has had many successes, the one area where it's failed is in climate. We are healthy, wealthy, and wise, but the volatile weather patterns are becoming a serious threat." She turned to the video screen behind her, which displayed a rapid series of clips from severe, extended droughts on the Pacific Coast of North America and Southern Africa to horrific winter storms through Southern Europe. The stills of the clips then appeared as a montage of the planet, showing severe, atypical weather patterns.

"People clearing snow in Florida. Indigenous communities in Greenland and Northern Canada are suffering from the heat. The weather patterns are shifting so dramatically that we can no longer predict how best to avoid an even more urgent scenario."

Scenes of coastal erosion and buildings collapsing into the ocean flashed behind her, followed by dust storms blasting homes. The scene then pulled back to show the network that she showed earlier in her presentation, but with the locations of the climate disasters overlaid.

"The Global Council has recognized that we can improve our resilience to the climate extremes if we could better manage our resources, such as water distribution. This would help to counter drought effects and prevent humanitarian and economic impacts.

"In water-rich nations, it's hard to imagine how vital water is to our lives, until you no longer have it. The West Coast of North America faced this and continues to struggle. The problem grows: South Africa, the Middle East, Australia and Southern Asia. We are at the stage where there are more people facing a water crisis than ever. It is not possible to ship the water from the

Great Lakes of North America to the southernmost tip of Australia. But."

She stopped to allow the video to dim. She loved the drama of this moment.

The video of the Earth came back into focus with the communication network overlaid. Blue lines appeared that connected vital continental hubs.

"A solution to the water problem is to manage its distribution more intelligently, relying on CAS principles. What if we could more delicately adjust the water distribution to keep it constant? Rather than being retroactive, we could be proactive and minimize the drought."

A light in front of one Councillor illuminated.

Katya gestured toward the Councillor. "I see you have a question, Councillor Evans. Please go ahead." She pressed the blue button to pause the video feed.

Evans sat forward and put his arms on the table. His square jaw and thin hair highlighted the sharp facial features that showcased a few rough years in his youth.

"First of all, amazing graphics! That with your speech makes for a very compelling presentation," he started.

Katya smiled, knowing the word 'but' was next.

"But I feel like we've been down this road before. We have invested billions in artificial intelligence systems across the planet that do the kind of water management you are describing. These AI systems have almost the same intelligence we have. I mean, look at the autonomous vehicles zipping around the city. If I closed my eyes, I would swear there was a human driving my car this morning, not just because we got here fast but also because the driver could carry on a great conversation."

Katya acknowledged the comment and said: "That is a valid observation and, if I may say, a perfect segue to my next point." She pressed the blue button.

The video continued with another network forming in yellow lines similar to the communication network, but it had different connections linking continental hubs.

"This is the BrainMaze system. It is the interface between humans and machines. It will link to the Global AI systems to make subtle adjustments to the water system to account for and anticipate future needs."

The same light illuminated on the table. Katya pressed the blue button on the controller.

Katya smiled and gestured, "Please."

"Look, I appreciate the idea, but the AI system we have already does this. What makes you think you can replace it with 'BrainMaze?' How do you know it can do better?" The Councillor sat back with his arms crossed.

"We are not suggesting that we will replace AI. That would be unhelpful. But your current AI systems do not interact link well. Our goal is to use BrainMaze to forge the link.

"Our brain has been evolving over millions of years and, depending on whose theory you ascribe to, has developed capacities that are unique. AI, too, has evolved, but in a manner different from our brains. However, it is still intelligent. It makes no sense to replace it. It makes far more sense to link with it. This is what we are proposing."

The same light illuminated on the table.

Chair Meyer interrupted, "Let's hold off a bit on the questions and let the Professor continue. I think you have a demonstration in mind, correct?"

Katya was thankful for the intervention. "Indeed, we do." She turned to Terry and Logan, who nodded they were ready.

"The system we propose will act as a bridge between the complexity of our brains and the complexity of the AI systems you have installed across the globe. We believe that the interaction of these platforms will bring new synergy that will ease the climate crisis."

Katya looked around the table.

"The statement 'the whole is greater than the sum of its part' is precisely what we hope to achieve with the interaction of these systems." She put the video controller on the table and pulled out her Motif and goggles.

"These are the interfaces for the BrainMaze system. The device, which we call Motif, allows you to select different operations and to do rudimentary computations. The goggles, or really glasses, give a biometric interface to measure the user's physiology and feed it into BrainMaze.

"The three of us have avatars in BrainMaze that were constructed using data from our brains. The biometric data drives our avatar's behaviour in BrainMaze so that we can interact with each other in the virtual environment."

Katya put her goggles on and glanced at her partners to see that they had done the same.

"Could you please switch the feed from my video to our devices?" she looked towards the control room. TechStaff signalled the control room. The screen behind Katya showed a sort of video game with avatars of her, Terry and Logan, displayed in a computer-generated scene of a complicated network of pipes and control consoles.

"What we have here is a simulated control room for a water

control system. Our three avatars are there to interact with the system. Our actions will affect aspects of the control system's function, and we will see the cascade effect on the water distribution. What we are doing is simulating different interventions that we can do, which will help us select the best interventions."

"The advantage of the simulation is that the spatial scales are easily evaluated. We have access to the water control systems for an entire country so that if I make a change, Logan and Terry can make complementary changes on their console to balance the flows. We can change the scale to capture continental systems. We can also change the time steps to predict the immediate effects and those several days, months or even years ahead."

With that cue, Terry's avatar made a change on his console that reduced the water intake in his part of the system. Katya and Logan's avatars immediately altered their local flows to reduce the exchange to Terry, so as not to create a local flood risk. Terry increased the local intake, and Katya and Logan responded in-kind.

"This is a simple example, but let's make it more complicated."

An indicator next to Terry's avatar signalled red, which the Council took to signal drought conditions, or at least that something was wrong.

"The usual response in our current system is to move excess water to accommodate the flow reduction in Terry's area. This may work in the short-term, but we don't know the long-term effects. We need more information. For instance, what is the long-term weather forecast? Can we establish some certainty around precipitation for Terry's area over the coming months?

"Another issue is the economic impact of the drought and the responses. This is where the system interactions become essential. Through BrainMaze, Terry can feed in the economic activity of his area to predict the impact of the water shortage. The local economy may be less affected than the daily water needs of the population. Or maybe the agricultural activities are decimated because it is starting from a precarious position, and the drought conditions would be a tipping point to failure. We could gather the same information from the other sites to see if there are multiplicative effects that are not obvious."

She focused on moving her avatar. Logan's avatar had already made adjustments at his console. Katya's avatar made a slight adjustment at her console. The red indicator light at Terry's sector turned yellow.

"Each move our avatars make sets up a simulation. Depending on the settings, we can launch several of these and select the best scenarios. We have visualized only one, but we set the system up to consider a multitude of scenarios and outcomes."

On the video screen, pop-up windows showed the outcomes of other simulations. In one, the drought response decimates Terry's territory, while in another, the response solves the drought in Terry's territory but sets a cascade that damages Katya and Logan's financial systems. "We can launch thousands to millions of these simulations, and using our full system, the simulation outcomes are instantaneous, giving you the capacity to act immediately.

"I should mention that like any CAS, these outcomes are probabilities, not black or white. We get a rank order of the outcomes based on probabilities, which sets up a filter for us."

Terry's Motif had a blip. His avatar faded as the Motif switched to an external link to BrainMaze and back to the local tethering. Terry wasn't sure if he should ask TechStaff to switch to the secure bridge, but within a couple of seconds, his connection was stable again.

Katya checked the local tethering status and asked, "Everything okay, Terry?"

"Yes, yes. All good. My avatar needed a bathroom break because he had too much coffee," Terry joked, happy to hear a few of the Councillors laugh.

Katya continued, "So, to summarize, we have developed an interface, BrainMaze, which is based on CAS principles and can interact with other adaptive systems. The advantage of BrainMaze is, first, because of the link to the user, the user can bring other information. The control of a water system may depend on the economy as much as the weather, so using information from both will help the prediction. Second, we can simulate scenarios of how the systems co-evolve with a change in parameters. From these simulations, we can find the best outcomes before we enact them in reality. And third, we can design a very cool avatar for each one of you." She ended with a broad, welcoming smile.

The lights above monitors #2 and #4 were flashing, followed by three more around the table. Chair Meyer stood and came around to stand next to Katya.

"Thank you, Professor. I know we have all been briefed and have read the material you sent in advance. The presentation brought this all together very well.

"So, to save time, we will have a few questions as I want to make sure that we," she gestured to the Council members, "have time to discuss this fully among ourselves. As I said earlier, we need to decide today, so I would ask that you keep your questions focused to help our discussion." She finished by looking at Councillor Evans, who frowned and then deactivated his light.

"Monitor #2, Councillor McLaren. You have a question?" the Chair asked.

"Yes, thank you, Chair Meyer and thanks to you Professors for a very engaging demonstration. I do believe this holds promise for us, but I want to understand better why we need human interaction. From the demonstration, I got the impression that the human involvement beyond starting the simulations was minimal," Councillor McLaren stated in a warm but stern tone.

"Excellent question, Councillor," Katya commented. "I have been doing most of the talking today, so perhaps I can ask one of my colleagues to answer this one?" She gestured to Logan and Terry.

Terry and Logan looked at each other, and Terry stood.

"That is an excellent point. The system we are proposing could work without human interaction. But the key innovation is to establish a platform that allows CAS's to interact with each other. As my colleague emphasized earlier, artificial intelligence has come a long way to where it almost counts as an organism. The gap remains in how we interact with AI. Rather than forcing an 'artificial' solution to this, we established an adaptive framework where we combine the best features of each system to get novel solutions. AI is fantastic at rapid evaluations and can devise new solutions, but it still is limited by the available data. Humans are great at coming up with new ideas that may lead down different paths but yield genuinely novel solutions. We sometimes call this 'fluid intelligence.' By allowing humans and AI to interact directly, you not only get the best of both worlds but probably even more." Terry looked at Katya and Logan to see if they wanted to add anything.

"Thank you, I think I understand," Councillor McLaren responded.

"Okay, let's go to the table. Councillor DeValois?" Chair Meyer pointed.

"Thanks, Chair Meyer. Since you've introduced a new interface between the AI systems and us, how do you guard against someone hacking into your BrainMaze platform and inserting themselves?" Councillor DeValois commented rather directly.

"Perhaps I can answer this one." Logan stood.

"The interface we have developed is based on CAS principles. This also means the security measure rely on CAS. Some hackers may not be well-versed in CAS principles, so even if they do hack into the system, they will not have an appreciable impact. CAS systems are in a state of constant exploration and updating, so if a hacker introduces something that is not adaptive, BrainMaze will quickly eliminate it. This is the beauty of running simulations to test solutions. It will be apparent from the simulations that the hacker's interventions are maladaptive, and so it will be discarded.

"Now, before you ask, what if the hacker understands the principles of CAS, like my colleagues and me? Ah, here is the beauty of CAS. Many things are possible, but not everything is equally probable." Logan ended with this, unintentionally leaving an air of uncertainty.

Chair Meyer interjected, "So if I understand, the system has safeguards built in that would neutralize a naïve hacker. On the other hand, if you have a more sophisticated hacker, the probability of adopting a maladaptive solution is small."

Logan smiled at the paraphrasing and said, "Exactly."

"Good! Okay, the last question we will take from monitor #4," the Chair said as she raised her head toward them.

There was an uncomfortable silence from monitor #4 as they decided who was going to ask the question.

"Okay, sorry. Okay, wow! This is amazing, Professors," spoke the youngest member of the group. "My question is about the technical challenges. I can see how it would work for a system in a city or maybe even a country, but how would you scale what you have now to make it global?"

Katya answered. "This will be a challenge, no question. But this is why we are here today. I am confident that the foundation we have built is scalable because we are using the principle architecture of CAS, with multiscale organization and replication of patterns. This allows a rather simple scaling by clustering and connections in the same way that I showed early in my video for how the Global Council evolved.

"In fact," she continued, "I am happy to welcome you to my lab, where we have a prototype of this operating, which we established for our three labs to interact with other collaborators worldwide."

The speaker on monitor #4 was wide-eyed. "So cool! Okay, I'm good with that. When can I come to your lab? Or sorry, when can 'we' come to your lab?"

"Whenever you wish. We keep an open policy so that everyone can benefit from our work." Katya smiled as she replied.

"I think we will stop here and allow the Professors to get back to their hotel while we discuss their proposal," the Chair said abruptly, turning toward the trio. "Thank you again. You have given us much to ponder. I will have Secretary Baren escort you to your car, and you can expect to hear from us before the end of the day."

Before any of the trio could reply, Secretary Baren rushed them to the door.

"What just happened?" Terry asked, turning to Logan.

Chapter Three:
Trip back to the hotel

Detour

Baren exited and turned to allow the trio to go through the door before closing it. They walked past the control room entrance and past the illuminates "IN SESSION" sign.

"Secretary Baren?" Katya called. "Excuse me, but was there something that was said that offended the Council? Our exit seemed rather hasty."

Baren turned to Katya. "Not at all. This is very common with our new Chair. The Council sometimes over-discusses things, particularly if there are guests. Some Councillors love to debate, which you saw.

"The Chair prefers to move things along. While this increases our efficiency, I think it stifles debate, but that's only my opinion."

Katya wasn't sure if he was being facetious or critical.

"I will accompany you back to the hotel, if you don't mind," Baren commented as the main doors for the building opened.

The sun was extremely bright. Katya grabbed her sunglasses, as did Logan. Terry squinted to shield the light, grumbling to himself for forgetting to bring his own.

"What lovely light we have today," Baren commented as he put on a fedora to shield the blazing sun.

Terry squinted down the driveway to see a vehicle approaching. The design and deep blue colour suggested an official vehicle, and the Global Council insignia on the side confirmed this.

The vehicle door slid open, and the trio entered, followed by Baren. He looked back at the building to see TechStaff. He waved to her as the vehicle door closed. There was a brief moment where he stared forward toward the vehicle console and returned his gaze to the trio.

"Our vehicles work on face recognition and have the destinations for the day pre-programmed."

"I think I prefer a more talkative vehicle," Terry said, as he scanned the interior. Save for the darker colour scheme and more comfortable seats, there wasn't any appreciable difference from the vehicle they used earlier that day.

Baren told them how the decision process would likely play out as the vehicle moved to the road. He expressed concern that some on the Council were skeptical of the new technological solution, having already put a lot of faith in AI. However, he believed a decision would be possible today, but it would take several hours as the Council members would want to consult their advisors. Baren also noted the Chair often expressed fatigue with this decision paralysis.

"These Council members are appointed because they are the most qualified in their district, yet they sometimes act as if they just heard about an issue for the first time!" The Secretary mimicked the Chair's speaking style in stating this. "I honestly think a bit more debate is healthy." He had a hint of disappointment in his voice, suggesting his early comment was not facetious.

Global Council members are selected based on qualifications and on consensus by cascading votes. At the district level, Councillors were appointed for five-year terms. The Councillors then voted for the Council Chair. The Chair's term was five years with an option for a second term if the Council and Chair agreed.

"I am sure the group is difficult to manage. It seems the new Chair has done a great job of getting new initiatives moving," Katya spoke, feeling the need to defend the Chair.

"I suppose you are right," Baren sighed, looking ahead out the vehicle. "Some would say this progress has come at a cost, however."

As the vehicle approached the hotel, Terry noticed it had not made en route adjustments to prepare for the exit off the road. He glanced at Baren, whose gaze was focused out the front window.

The vehicle passed the hotel.

Baren spoke, "Vee, Phantom Mode," and the tinting on the windows became darker with a glass panel appearing between the rear compartment and the console in the vehicle's front. The emblem on the outside also faded into the dark blue colour of the vehicle.

"Uh, we just passed our hotel, and what's with the cliché glass barrier thing?" Terry exclaimed, as he looked over to his colleagues.

"Baren, this was not in our itinerary. Please explain." Logan straightened up in his seat.

"Be calm, my friends, please. There is no reason for alarm. We will get you to your hotel soon, but first, we must discuss the real reason we brought you here," Baren spoke calmly as the vehicle turned on to a service road that ran next to the river.

Hidden conversation

"Okay, you obviously have our attention." Logan relaxed.

"I apologize for the drama, but this is the only opportunity to have this discussion." Baren turned his full attention to the trio.

"The Phantom Mode for the vehicle means we are no longer being tracked at Headquarters. The shield between us and the console is a deflector that masks the view of cameras on the road. All communications are further encrypted, so we cannot be traced." Baren reached into his pocket. "Headquarters will see the vehicle stopped near the hotel, so they will not be alarmed, I hope." He pulled out his device and glanced at it before continuing.

"Your early comment, Katya, oh, may I call you Katya since we are away from the formal session now?" Baren inquired. Katya nodded once, maintaining a stern gaze at him.

He continued, "Your earlier comment regarding the progress the Global Council has made is most accurate. We are pleased with the success of the AI's efficacy, so far. But, we have noticed a worrying trend over the past several months.

"At first, we thought it might be a bug in the system. Many corrections to the system were unsuccessful. We then started seeing this happen more often at local and national systems. Modifications were made, but the AI system rejected them.

"Some on the Council suspected that this was intentionally, done to undermine our credibility. As you know, the support for the Global Council is not unanimous." Baren paused.

"So you have dissension in the Council, or is this someone from outside?" Terry asked.

"I can't be sure. There has not been a formal investigation. It's a very sensitive topic. There is a real possibility that problem is indeed within the Council. This is why we are having this conversation. Some of us have taken it upon ourselves to investigate this more fully," the Secretary explained.

"So, you've gone rogue?" Terry said with a small smile, "and kidnapped a bunch of scientists."

Baren laughed. "Exactly! An effective strategy, don't you think?

The trio found no comfort in his response.

Baren continued. "In all seriousness, as you have said, the climate crisis is growing despite our efforts to contain it. We thought the strategy to focus on water distribution was suitable response to counter the pervasive droughts while we designed a better response. But every time we try something new, we are pushed back to the start."

"We understand, Secretary Baren, but how can we help?" Katya spoke the question that each of the trio had in their minds.

"Please call me Sebastian," he continued. "You have already started just by being here. You see, we were not sure how we would detect the infiltration in our AI system, so we needed an outside source to help.

"Terry, you may recall getting a message from me early this morning?"

Terry acknowledged.

"By responding, we could introduce a small, shall we say, 'patch' to BrainMaze that linked the AI system at Headquarters so we could feed you the communications flow. This is why your connection to the BrainMaze system was active within the walls of Headquarters.

"We hope you could analyze the communication flow to determine if there was another source present that was monitoring or biasing our flows." He paused again.

This intrigued Logan. "Of course, we can consider the stream that you fed to BrainMaze as any other set of data that we would use to simulate a complex system. But — careful — if what we are talking about is truly a nonlinear system, a single data feed will not be sufficient to characterize how your system is working."

"Yes, of course, Logan. You have been working on these things for your entire career."

"May I interrupt for a moment?" Terry said. "I am still having difficulty getting past the part where you introduced a Trojan Horse into BrainMaze!

"Do you know what trouble that could have caused? We already had a node failure, and if another node was compromised, the entire BrainMaze platform could have been in jeopardy." Terry leaned toward Baren.

Logan interjected. "Well, not really in jeopardy, but it could have messed up the demonstration. Remember that BrainMaze has internal consistency checks to prevent such takedowns by a computer virus."

"Exactly, Logan," Baren said. "Besides, we did not intend to use your platform for some nefarious deed but simply to give you the data you would need to run the simulations."

Terry frowned. "But how did you get into our system? I know our platform is open source, but there aren't many people around who know the system well enough to do such a thing."

Baren smiled and looked at Logan. "You recall the student you co-supervised five years ago with your colleagues in Barcelona? Did you pay attention to monitor #4?"

Katya spoke, "Really? Monitor #4 was the student from Barcelona? You mean Yvette? She looks so different now!"

Logan showed a faint glimmer of recognition. "I think she used to wear glasses."

"Right again. She was eager to work with the Global Council

when she completed her work with you. She was a perfect candidate to help with the AI system. When we asked her to write the little patch to link with BrainMaze, she was delighted to work with you three again," Baren said with a slight smile. "Of course, we assured her you would understand the need for us to set up the link without telling you.

"It was fortunate that you asked for a dedicated connection at Headquarters. We used that to send a dummy feed to make sure the data we sent you was secure. Whoever is tapping into our AI system is very clever," Baren finished.

"Seems your team is equally clever," Katya commented.

"Ah, thank you, Katya. I am not merely a politician. I do know a thing or two about CAS and AI," Baren said with pride.

The vehicle continued along the service road and back to the main road. The direction of travel suggested they were going back to the hotel.

"Logan, the information in the feed should be enough to give you a start at modelling the communications streams. Hopefully, it will provide a decent foundation. If you would be so kind as to start the simulations when we drop you at the hotel, we could look at the outcomes together later today. I will return to convey the Council's decision back to you in person," Baren said as he spotted the hotel ahead.

Logan looked at his two partners and back at Baren. "We will do our best. What time do you expect to return?"

"Probably close to dinnertime," Baren said. "In fact, it would be my honour to invite you all to dinner. I can guarantee it will be more pleasant than this ride."

"Perfect," Logan said, looking back at his colleagues.

"Vee, Phantom Mode off," Baren commanded, and the

window tint lightened, and the glass panel receded. The vehicle turned into the hotel driveway. The door opened and the trio exited.

"Shall we say 19 hundred for dinner tonight?" Baren asked.

"That would be perfect, Sebastian," Katya said, trying to hide her growing discomfort.

As the trio entered the lobby, Katya paused. "Logan, perhaps you can start the simulations he suggested, and then we can go for a run? I think we can talk more freely out on a run."

"And besides," she added, "the way you two have been eating lately, a second run will be good for you."

GC deliberations

Back at the Global Council Headquarters, TechStaff walked up to Chair Meyer as the Council continued to discuss the trio's proposal. "I just called the hotel and The Profs have not yet arrived," she whispered.

The Chair considered the comment and said, "Perhaps they are taking a little tour of the city. Let's check back with them later, okay?"

The Chair sighed as she returned her attention to the Council. She chastised herself for her impatience with the debates, but realized this was necessary to make sure she kept the support of the Council. As only the second Global Council Chair, it would be easy to have any procedural anomaly used to discredit a decision. While the majority supported the Council structure, a small but vocal group felt the Council removed too much autonomy from the countries and prevented economic development. The Council operated by considering local and global needs using the AI system to evaluate the consequences.

Some local groups felt they were being ignored, or worse, said they didn't care about global issues, put their needs first.

Sara knew these arguments well. Her extensive scientific background gave her a formidable foundation to counter these criticisms on factual grounds. But one of her most useful skills as Chair was in building consensus. Rather than counter-arguments with "Yes, but…" she would often use "Yes, and…" which gave the impression that the dueling perspectives could find a middle ground.

This sort of diplomacy was vital now because the number of extreme climate events was increasing across the Earth, and many local jurisdictions were skeptical that a single global political body was facile enough to address their individual needs.

"We have to remember that these events are connected," she emphasized to the Council a month ago when they made the decision to speak with the trio. "The severe frigid temperatures that we saw in equatorial regions occurred at the same time as uncommonly high temperatures at the more extreme latitudes. I appreciate that such local events have consequences that need immediate action, and we continue to do that. In addition, we need to consider a more effective system-wide solution."

She had to prevent herself from taking it too personal. Spring floods five years ago had a devastating impact on her family. The volatile seasonal changes led to a rapid thawing, which dumped melted water faster than the system could handle. The late winter rain made the situation worse. She was in a Council meeting when she received a call that a flash flood wiped out her family's farm. Her parents survived, but they did not find her younger brother. She choked back rage and tears whenever she heard someone assert that she had no real insight into the local's difficulties. "You never really know the challenges someone has," she would often counter, "so before you make such assertions, keep in mind the reason I am the Chair is not only because of my skills but also that I have intimate knowledge of the challenges we all face."

The Global Council's AI system became an invaluable tool to predict extreme events. The predictions enable the Council to enact preventive measures, but many of the measures were not completely effective. The drought response on the Pacific Coast was rapid but dealt only with the immediate need and had little lasting effect. As the Professor noted in her presentation, the cascade effects of poor decisions are hard to appreciate if you do not consider the connection between systems. The strategy to handle the drought had local economic consequences. Other jurisdictions redirected some funds to help, but this left them with severely weakened purchasing power.

"The Professors have developed the BrainMaze system, which can interface with our own AI system, to provide the new capacity that we can't achieve with our current architecture. We can make more effective use of the AI system that we have invested so much time and effort in, and use BrainMaze to make sure the predictions and solution we enact have the best consequences for local constituents and larger entities, from state to country to our planet." Sara's authoritative tone made it difficult to offer a strong counter-argument without appearing petty.

Her mind snapped to the present task, and she returned to the table and joined the Council, who were engaged in several small parallel debates. "My colleagues, shall we return to our group discussion? Remember, we committed to making a decision today."

She gave a glance at the time and spoke, "Let's pick up where we left off. Councillor Evans, I believe you had the floor."

Consider this

The trio proceeded through the hotel lobby, and Terry turned to his partners and suggested they pause.

"I'll state the obvious — that was crazy!" Terry tried to keep his voice down. "Do you two actually believe what he is saying? How do we know we can trust him?"

Logan sighed. "I've known Sebastian for a long time. I haven't kept in touch since he took the Secretary position, but I have never known him to be dishonest. Despite his political leanings, you can believe what he says. Now, whether his perception is accurate is a completely different matter."

"That doesn't make me less suspicious," Terry replied with a frown.

Katya moved things ahead. "At the moment, we have no reason to be concerned. Well, except for the minor glitch in Terry's Motif that allowed them to hack in.

"Let's do the simulations as Sebastian suggested, but before that, do some integrity checks on BrainMaze to confirm his actual intentions."

"Aye, Katya!" Logan grinned. "I will set these up, and we can meet back here in, shall we say, 20 minutes for a run?" Katya and Terry nodded in agreement, and the trio was off to their respective rooms.

Katya felt uneasy as she entered her apartment. The preparations for the presentation had taken much mental effort, but this revelation from Baren injected an odd adrenaline rush into her tired body. The run would help clear her head and review the events to make sure her impressions were like her partners'. She always felt connected to her colleagues, but much less so today. Katya changed out of her suit and into her running gear. Then the indicator on her Motif was flashing.

Terry was as impressed as he was annoyed that he was the target for the hack into BrainMaze. *I really need to spend more time learning the guts of this thing,* he thought, knowing that likely it would not have made a difference. He remembered Yvette as a brilliant programmer with an intuition that made her a pleasure to work with. Terry and Logan tried to keep her on the team, but she disappeared shortly after finishing her degree. He glanced down at his Motif to see its indicator flashing.

Like Terry, Logan was reflecting on his past work with Yvette. She was a brilliant student and learned the core principles for BrainMaze within a year after starting. Yvette benefited from the collaborations with Katya and Terry, making frequent contact with each of them and even travelling to their labs to become immersed in their research programs. Logan proposed to Katya and Terry that Yvette could become a project manager for BrainMaze since she had the knowledge to bridge between their labs and could better integrate the work. When he presented the offer to Yvette, she was surprisingly neutral. Shortly after that, Yvette withdrew from the program and disappeared. Katya suggested Yvette may have been overwhelmed by the responsibility of the position, but Logan was unsure. To him, it was more than Yvette wanted something else that he couldn't quite grasp.

Logan docked his Motif and put on the navigator gloves,

allowing for a more facile interaction with BrainMaze. As he checked the activity log he chuckled that Yvette would work with Baren on a hack into the very system that Baren had criticized in its early days.

Logan gestured to start the BrainMaze system check. It took a few seconds for the "SYSTEMS NORMAL" message to flash on the display. Logan checked the data stream that came through Terry's Motif to see what information was there.

It looks like a regular communications stream, he thought as he passed the data stream through a nonlinear filter to identify the underlying structure. The added information from Sebastian provided a more robust framework to run the nonlinear filter.

This appears to be several month's worth of data, he noted as he watched the BrainMaze analytics construct a multidimensional surface that defined the space that contained the communications in and out of Headquarters.

My, what a lovely manifold you have. Logan defined the parameter ranges for the simulations. The simulations would define all communication flows for Headquarters, even those were possible but seldom used.

"Okay, I will let that run, and I will run too," as he turned to get his gear from the bathroom.

There was a knock on his door. "Logan, may we enter?" Terry asked.

Logan was shirtless but opened the door for his friends. "Hello, cuties," he said, striking a he-man pose.

"Hello, yourself," said TechStaff, who was with Terry and Katya.

"Oop, you guys! You could have warned me!" Logan said, walking into the bathroom to grab his running shirt.

Terry began, "She has been trying to contact us through our Motifs, and we only now saw her message. Logan, is it on yours now?"

Logan glanced over and, seeing no sign of a new message, shook his head no.

"Anyway, she wants to talk with us about the Council deliberations." Terry turned to TechStaff.

"Thank you, Professor. Umm, I'm sorry to barge in on you all like this, but Chair Meyer thought you might want the heads-up on the deliberations."

"Please call me Logan. No need to be formal anymore." Logan pulled his shirt over his head.

"Okay, thanks. My name is Kim, by the way." She continued, "The Chair knows this violates protocol, but it may change how things progress over the next few days."

She gathered her breath and said, "The Council will approve your proposal but with very tight constraints."

The trio was used to this kind of feedback on their platform, at least in scientific and technological proposals.

"Please continue," Katya commented, trying to make TechStaff comfortable.

"There were a lot of positive comments on your platform. The issue, which came mostly from Councillor Evans, was that they didn't believe that a global mobilization of your platform made sense, given the risks involved. Someone commented that the little glitch in your demo made them concerned about what would happen if an avatar took a bathroom break in the middle of a flooding crisis," TechStaff said, looking at Terry.

"Great. One person with no sense of humour, and we're sunk," Terry mumbled.

TechStaff squinted at Terry and continued, "So the decision was to test it in a smaller jurisdiction. I don't know where that is yet, but the idea is to show the effectiveness of BrainMaze in working with the local AI system to improve the water management of the area."

Katya spoke. "We appreciate the information. Let me see if I understand. Basically, they like the idea but want to be sure it's safe, so they want us to do a smaller-scale project. If that works, then we can scale up?"

"Yes. That's my understanding. Do you think that will be a problem?" TechStaff asked.

The trio thought for a moment, looking at each other.

Logan spoke first: "I don't foresee any problems at the moment. We will need to deal with the lack of data on the interactions of the local AI node with the global system. It's unlikely that the functionality we see in a local system will be the same when we scale up to interface with the entire system. The impact of local dynamics depends very much on the status of the other parts of the network. It's like setting a context. If we can't sufficiently model the global context, the proof of principle may be useless."

"I don't think you should be so pessimistic," Katya replied. "The AI architecture is very similar across the globe, so we include that information as an assumption and see how BrainMaze handles it."

"It's not a trivial matter, Katya."

"I didn't say it was."

TechStaff looked at Logan. "I see you all might need time to think about it. I should get back to Headquarters anyway, as I have a lot of stuff to do before the evening begins. I think you can expect Chair Meyer to join you and Secretary Baren tonight." With that, she turned and left.

Terry closed the door. "So," he looked at Logan as he considered TechStaff's comments in silence, "you take forever to get changed for a simple run! Can you move that butt of yours, please?"

Katya said, "Shall we discuss the implication of the Council's decision now?"

Logan shook his head and put a finger to his lips. "Let's go for a run."

Terry and Katya nodded as Logan disappeared back into the bathroom to finish changing.

"So, how about those Canucks?" was Terry's attempt at small talk.

Katya looked at Terry. "I think Canadians are fine people."

"No, no, the hockey team," Terry said. "Never mind."

Run and think

A few moments later, Logan came out of the bathroom in his running gear. He noticed the odd expressions on his colleague's faces. "What did I miss?" he asked.

"How about those Canucks?" Terry tested again.

"I usually find them quite pleasant, though sometimes they can be, shall we say, obtuse?" Logan said with a grin.

"Ack! You two are impossible. You'd figure that being from Northern Europe, you'd know a little about hockey," Terry said, throwing his hands in the air. "Vancouver Canucks! They're an NHL hockey team and are kicking it this season!"

Katya and Logan feigned surprise. "These Canucks are darling, don't you think, Katya?" The two chuckled.

"Let's go. We should have about 30 minutes before the simulation finishes. We can continue this conversation during our run," Logan stated as he walked to his desk. "Shall I take my goggles?"

"Probably too distracting. Katya and I have our Motifs if there is anything we need to check," Terry commented as he pulled his Motif from his running pouch. "It will log your run so that we can sync your data later."

"Okay, but we should try these goggles out on a run sometime," Logan said as he started toward the door. He grabbed the "DO NOT DISTURB" sign and hung it on the door handle so the cleaning staff would not enter the room and interrupt the simulations.

The trio left Logan's room, proceeded to the stairway, and descended to the main floor. When they entered the lobby, Terry saw the same pale Council member standing by the reception desk, watching them.

Terry turned to his colleagues and said, "I think we are being followed." He cocked his head in the Councillor's direction. Logan and Katya glanced in the direction Terry showed. "What makes you say that?" Katya asked.

"The Council member by the counter." Terry checked to see that the Councillor had gone. "Let's just go," he said with frustration, and quickened his pace to the lobby entrance.

The air outside was much hotter than it was only an hour ago. "I know this temperature is hard on you Canucks, Terry, but it's good for you." Katya smiled.

"Yeah, I'll remember that as I pass out from heatstroke," Terry said as he started jogging.

The trio headed out to the main road and then to a by-pass to the river. The shade of the trees along the river path helped temper the effects of the heat.

Terry adjusted the pace to keep the three of them in stride. He looked over to his colleagues, who were focused ahead. Terry shared the silence for a few more moments. Despite the imperative to "talk about what just happened," they needed time to "think about what just happened."

Katya scanned the path ahead of her. She appreciated the heat, given that her vigorous exercise routine left her with little body fat for insulation. Still, she felt the temperature, 35 degrees Celsius without factoring in humidity, was getting too hot even for her. She thought the heat was appropriate since they seemed to be getting into a situation that could be "too hot for them to handle." Why should they be asked to help the Global Council, when there were obvious internal problems that the Council show fix on their own? What most concerned her was she did not know whom she could trust. Baren's actions appeared honourable. But if there is a traitor on the Council, what's to say that it was not him?

Logan's legs felt tight from the morning run with Terry. He tried to adjust his stride to work out the kinks. He glanced over to Katya, who appeared to be involved in an internal debate. Logan then recalled the conversations he had with Baren years ago about the BrainMaze prototype and his team's aspiration to take it out of the lab and into the real world. Baren felt that moving BrainMaze to the real world would turn it into nothing more than a new gaming platform. Logan replied that BrainMaze would be a personal monitoring platform where you could feed in your brain and body data. With enough data, BrainMaze could create an exact characterization of your personal manifold — a formula that predicts brain states for particular situations.

If BrainMaze were to become adopted widely, they could combine personal manifolds to create distributions of features in the population. Logan felt this would have tremendous clinical utility, where a population of manifolds would provide a more exact index of risk. The landscape of your personal manifold relative to the population could show if there were configurations of your brain and body that could compromise your health.

Baren felt this was nonsense. There could never be enough data to do such a mapping with any certainty. Logan regretted not explaining that data were less important at some stage than the understanding of general rules that constrained the structure of one's manifold. Looking over toward Terry, he remembered when they first articulated this principle: *The goal is to define the system parameters that govern how behaviour coordination. By knowing these rules, you can recreate all realizations, including those that may not yet have happened.*

After a few more minutes into their run, Terry was the first to speak aloud. "So, Logan. What do you think about the Council's decision?"

"To be honest, it is reasonable. They do not know us beyond what they have heard, and I doubt any of them beyond Sebastian have read our scientific papers," Logan replied.

Katya interjected, looking past Terry. "Really, Logan? I think the Chair at least would have read our work. She has the background, and it would be her responsibility to understand our system before she allowed us to present."

Logan nodded. "You may be right. I do not know. I think there's more to the Chair than meets the eye. I can't say I completely trust her at the moment, but given what we've just experienced since breakfast, I am not sure I know whom to trust. You see what I mean?" He frowned.

Terry interjected. "I hear you. I am suspicious, too. There's a lot of weird stuff going on today, and we don't know enough to decide where to go or what to do next."

The river trail narrowed to wind through a small forest, requiring the trio to run in single file — Logan, Katya, and then Terry. The pace immediately increased, putting some distance between Logan and Katya and Terry. "I hate when they do this," Terry grumbled. He heard parts of the conversation between Logan and Katya, but couldn't quite hear. "Pace, guys — pace!" he called out ahead of him.

The pale Councillor appeared suddenly in front of Terry. Terry stumbled and fell, trying to avoid a collision. He looked up at the Councillor, who merely looked down at him.

"What are you doing?!" Terry exclaimed. "I could have knocked you on your ass!" Terry looked ahead to see if his colleagues noticed.

The Councillor extended his hand and helped Terry to stand. The hand felt cold, despite the heat of the day. "Apologies. Things will move very quickly now. We are approaching a critical point in the system. There could be many unpredictable changes," the Councillor said, or at least that's what Terry heard. It wasn't clear that the Councillor was actually speaking.

Terry stared at the Councillor, whose face appeared to be like a mask. There was no discernible expression.

"It would be beneficial for us to work together." The Councillor turned attention to a sound behind Terry.

"Terry, are you okay?" Katya called, as she ran toward him.

Terry said, "Yeah, just talking with the Councillor here." When Terry turned around, he was only slightly surprised to see the Councillor was gone.

"Talking to who? There is no one there, Terry," Katya said with some concern.

"Must be the heat," Terry said, brushing the dirt from himself. "I'm okay. Let's go."

Katya and Terry caught up with Logan, who was watching the water flow around the rocks that scattered across the riverbed.

"Is everything alright?" Logan asked.

"All good. I just ran into a ghost and fell," Terry joked.

"I think the heat is getting to you, buddy," Logan said as he started running.

"Before we lost you, Katya and I agreed that, for the time being, we can put our trust in Sebastian, given our history, and that he appears genuine in his desire to work with us. There was nothing in the data he fed into BrainMaze that suggests anything of concern, else we would have detected it already." Logan spoke with more confidence.

Terry added, "I am okay with this, but let's not dismiss the Chair. She did send TechStaff to help prepare us for the Council's decision."

Katya added, "I don't think these are incompatible, but first, we should see what the data Sebastian gave us reveals about the AI system. We cannot do anything more with the Council's decisions until we have more specifics."

Terry looked down at his Motif to check the map feed. "We should cross the bridge here, and we can loop back to the hotel." He thought about the Councillor's comment about rapid changes and being close to a critical point.

The crossing was a suspension bridge with steel cables affixed to large posts on either side of the river. Although the bridge looked stable, the trio opted to walk across to minimize the resonance effect from running.

As they crossed the footbridge, Katya pointed. "Does it seem to you the water levels have just risen?"

Logan looked back at the bank where he had just been, noticing the rocks he had seen were now underwater. Terry felt a warning buzz on his Motif and saw a flashing red mark on the map several hundred metres upstream.

"Off the bridge, NOW!" Terry yelled, pushing his friends forward.

As they sprinted, they saw an immense wall of water coming down the river.

"Keep moving. It's going to flow over the banks!" Terry instructed.

Once the trio crossed the bridge, they ran uphill away from the bank and turned to watch the wave crash over the bridge, spinning it around like a thread. The water spilled over the banks where the trio had just stood.

"Did someone open the floodgates?" Katya yelled. "I heard no sirens!"

"I don't know. I got a warning notice just a few moments before the wave hit. This appears to be a local phenomenon. Look, the water is subsiding now that the wave has passed," Terry gestured to the shore.

"Are you still linked with the Global AI system, Terry? I don't see how BrainMaze could monitor the water in the river without accessing it." Logan walked over to Terry.

Terry looked more closely at his Motif and checked the connections. He could see Katya's Motif and his connection with BrainMaze but nothing more. His connection log showed the link to the Global AI system was severed hours ago.

"Seems not," Terry replied. "Could it be a residual effect from the initial feed? Perhaps BrainMaze integrated this into its prediction algorithm and expanded the scope?"

As Logan considered this, Katya spoke. "I suggest we get back to the hotel immediately. We have more resources there to check BrainMaze, and hopefully, the simulations are done." She added, "We may also be too vulnerable out here in the open."

Terry was about to reply, then held back, thinking of the pale Councillor who appeared on the trail and watching the footbridge continuing to flail. "Let's go up to the road. We get to a larger bridge, just in case there are more surprises around the corner."

With that, Terry ran up from the path to the road that paralleled the river. Once they got there, they saw an emergency vehicle pulling up. "Are you okay?" one of the emergency officers called out. "We got a notification of a water surge and weren't sure if anyone was in the area."

"Thanks, we are fine. We were on the banks when the wave came," Terry replied. "Do you know what caused it? We heard no warning."

"Can't say for sure. With the updated water distribution system, there are several new artificial tributaries that can release tons of water into the river quickly. I've heard that these things are a bit temperamental," the emergency officer said. "Do you need a ride anywhere? I will be going back, while the others check the area."

Katya said, "We appreciate the offer, but I think we will jog back. It will help diffuse the stress of the situation."

"Okay," the officer said. "Where are you staying? I may need to speak to you later to get some details of what you saw, for the record, of course."

"We are at the Hotel Obelisk," Katya said, pointing across the river. "Here is the contact information." She transferred her name and access number to the officer. "Are we free to go?"

"Of course!" the officer said with a somewhat puzzled look.

The trio started running again. Once they were away from the emergency crew, Katya spoke. "How did they know we were visiting?"

Terry replied, "He didn't say that exactly. But it's a million degrees out here, and we are out running. Most of the locals would be at work or school, it's likely that we are visiting. And then there is the matter of our attire," Terry said, pointing to Katya and Logan. "You are definitely not from around here." Katya's bright orange running shorts and silver tank top were a perfect complement for Logan's outfit.

Katya laughed and gave Terry a kick. "What about you?" She pointed at his plaid running shorts.

"Anyway, let's keep moving. I grow more concerned that we are being watched." With that, she continued running, with her two companions close behind.

Her fast pace made conversation difficult. The trio approached a bridge. Katya paused midway through, looking back toward the suspension bridge. The area downstream of the bridge had signs of a recent flood, but the upstream area was untouched. She glanced down from the bridge, seeing tributary outlets on the columns of the bridge. "So that's where the water came from," she said as she pointed below. Her two companions were too winded to reply, and simply nodded. "I forgot you had already run today. Sorry about my pace!" Katya said as she continued at a more moderate pace.

When they arrived at the hotel a few moments later, they saw the emergency vehicle parked in front. It was unoccupied.

"Is there another entrance?" Logan asked.

"We can go through the side door using our room keys." Katya gestured to the left.

The trio hurried around the side of the building, card-swiped the lock, and entered. The corridor inside led to the lobby elevators where an emergency officer was walking around.

"Let's take the stairs," Terry whispered.

Arriving at their floor, Terry peaked around the door into the hall. He stepped out and motioned for his companions to follow. Katya's apartment was first, so the trio went inside.

"There is a message for you, Katya." Terry pointed at the video monitor.

Katya pressed the button on the video screen, and the voice of the emergency officer she saw earlier played, "HELLO PROFESSOR. IF YOU ARE ALREADY BACK AT THE HOTEL, I WAS HOPING WE COULD SPEAK ABOUT THE INCIDENT. IT WON'T TAKE BUT A FEW MOMENTS. WE WILL BE IN THE LOBBY WHEN YOU ARE READY."

"Horrible timing!" Katya exclaimed.

"Terry, may I see your Motif, please? I want to see how the simulations are progressing," Logan asked. He checked the progress meter. "There are still about 20 minutes before the simulations are complete, so we have time. Perhaps I can go to my room and start compiling the simulation outcomes, and you and Terry can go talk with the officer?"

"Sure," Katya replied. "I'd like to change, though. Terry, do you want to change out of your running clothes first?"

"Yeah, sure. We can shower later," Terry said, as he walked to Katya's door. He opened it and scanned the hall again. Seeing it clear, he motioned to Logan, and the two of them left Katya's room.

Katya went into the bathroom and filled a glass with water. As she drank it, she saw the sweat on her face and forehead in the mirror. She didn't feel like she exercised that hard. *It must be the stress of the situation*, she thought. She removed her top and grabbed a towel to pat herself dry. She glanced down at her Motif to see that the simulation count was nearing completion.

There was also a message from her daughter: "Grandma will take us to the lake today. Can you come, too?"

Katya felt the pain of separation from her family while she worked. She was thankful that her mother could take care of her daughter, Ileana, but regretted this would be another event she could not share with them.

She left her running shorts on and put on a dry shirt.

Terry let out a long exhale when he entered his room. He opened the refrigerator, grabbed a bottle of water, and gulped half of it down. The heat, the run and the excitement left him parched. He scanned his room to see if there was something he could change into and pulled out a t-shirt that he usually used for sleeping with the word "COFFEE" emblazoned on the front. He took off his running shirt and went to the bathroom to rinse his face and towel off. As he wiped his face, a brief flash in his mind occurred where he had expected to see the pale Councillor standing behind him in the mirror. He looked up and saw only the shower stall behind him. *I'm getting too jumpy*, he thought. He pulled on the t-shirt, walked out of the bathroom, and looked at his Motif on the desk. He checked his messages, seeing only an older message from his wife saying she was glad he arrived safely. Then, like Katya, he saw the simulation counter was almost done. He pocketed the Motif and turned to the door. As he opened it, Katya was standing there about to knock. "You are very slow," Katya joked.

Katya and Terry took the elevator to the lobby. As the doors opened, they saw the emergency officer and his colleagues sitting in the lobby chairs. The officer rose once he saw Katya approaching.

"Ah, hello, Professors. I am glad you received my message. You must have arrived just as I sent it," he said, bowing slightly. "This won't take long. I just wondered if you could tell me what you saw on the river before the wave came."

Katya stepped forward. "Sure. We were running along the river trail on the south bank, heading east."

"West," Terry said.

Katya looked over at Terry. "West, right. We came to the pedestrian suspension bridge and crossed there to make our run a loop. Terry saw the wave first, so perhaps he could fill in from here."

Terry smiled and said, "We noticed the water levels changing quickly, which usually means a change in water distribution, which is obvious, I guess.

"Then I saw the wave coming downstream from us, and we ran across to get to the hill above the bank to avoid getting swept away by the water," he concluded, leaving out the fact that he received the warning signal on his Motif.

"You heard no sirens or any other warnings?" the officer asked.

"None," Terry replied.

"I see." The officer paused and looked at his device. "Did you see anyone else on the trail?"

"No," Katya spoke before Terry could respond. "We were the only crazy people out in this heat." She ended with a broad smile.

"Okay. Well, that's all for now. If there is anything else you can think of, could you please call me? We were lucky this time, but these things are happening more frequently. Someone will eventually get hurt if we can predict these floods." the officer continued. "I thank you for your time. Enjoy the rest of your evening."

"Thank you, Officer. We shall," Katya replied as she and Terry turned toward the elevators.

As the emergency team left the hotel, one turned to the other. "They're lying, you know. That wave was moving way too fast for them not to have gotten a warning before they saw it."

The officer nodded and continued walking to their vehicle. "I know, but the lobby is not the place to interrogate them. We may have another chance soon enough."

Simulation outcome

Logan arrived at his door to see the "Do Not Disturb" sign had fallen to the hallway floor. He looked down the hall to see the cleaning cart several doors ahead.

"Have you done my room already?" Logan called out.

"No, sir, I should be there in about 30 minutes. Do you want me to come back later?" the cleaning person asked.

"There actually isn't a need to clean it. I'm a tidy person,"

Logan said with a smile and card-swiped the door lock.

Once inside, Logan confirmed that no one had been in his room. *If there had been, they were very careful,* he thought as he removed his running shirt and grabbed a towel from the bathroom. He grabbed a bottle of water on the counter as he approached his dock station. He opened the bottle and took a large gulp. *Ugh, I should have put this in the fridge,* he thought as too warm water passed his throat.

Logan removed his Motif from the docking station and saw the video message.

"Hey, Papa!" The image of his two sons filled the screen. Logan could make out the partial image of his wife in the background. "Mama says it's too hot to go outside for football. Can you fix it?"

Logan laughed aloud, knowing his boys assumed that his meeting with the Global Council was to fix the weather immediately.

He recorded a quick response. "Hello, my loves. Sorry about the heat. I promise we are working on it here. In the meantime, why don't you practise your ping-pong skills so we can have a tournament when I get back?"

Logan had set up a large recreation room in the basement of their home to accommodate the heat, with temperatures becoming dangerously high for several months in a row.

Logan sent the message and switched to the simulation cockpit program, which was projected in front of him. The simulations would finish soon. He also saw that 25% had failed, which Logan felt was too high. He checked the summary of the simulations and saw nothing out of the ordinary in the overall statistics. I should let this finish, he thought as he scanned the rest of the display.

In parallel, BrainMaze was analyzing the data from the trio's run, which had become a useful additional feature of their platform not just for fitness tracking but also to help interface a proposed running route with other information to guide them to the best route. The prediction was based on their current physical exertion, their desired run duration and the estimated fitness level. This was sometimes useful in new environments. Logan recalled a recent run where BrainMaze took them up an apparently endless hill, when it would have been faster to go around it. "Maybe BrainMaze knows about the extravagant dinner we've planned and thought we should burn a few more calories," he chuckled, remembering Terry's comment.

Logan scanned the recording of their run, looking at the path they took. The three were running abreast for the first several kilometres until they reached the forest. Then their paths intertwined. Terry's path was missing in the middle of the forest. Not too much, only 50 metres, but it was as if Terry had jumped off the planet for a moment and landed 50 metres ahead. "This he would do," Logan smiled, attributing the missing data to a glitch in tracking the run.

Continuing, he came to the part just before crossing the footbridge. Logan paused the replay and scanned the data feeds BrainMaze was accessing at that moment. "NEW CONNECTION FORMED" displayed on the screen, and the water flow system appeared on the running map.

"This is getting interesting!" Logan commented, taking another sip of water.

The water system showed normal flow for a few moments and then a large surge of activity in four tributaries upstream from the bridge. The volume of each tributary alone was not above a critical value. Still, a quick calculation in BrainMaze showed the convergence of the four would have a disastrous multiplicative effect, similar to constructive interference that is thought to cause rogue waves in the ocean. By that time, the trio had began crossing the bridge, and BrainMaze sent the warning to Terry's Motif.

Logan paused the replay and sat down on the bed. He was unsure what to make of the record.

He heard a knock at his door. "Yes?" he called out.

"We need beer!" He heard Terry's voice.

Logan stood up, laughing, and grabbed a fresh t-shirt. "I have only warm water, but we can call for room service."

He opened the door and let Katya and Terry enter.

"Please sit, my friends. We have much to discuss," Logan said as he walked over to his desk and put on the data glove. "How did it go with the officers?"

"No problem," Katya said. "I think they were following protocol since we were at the flood scene."

"You may be right. Let's get down to business." Logan turned. "Could you order three beers for us, please, dear Professor?" Logan said, looking at Terry.

"If you want anything done..." Terry trailed off as he placed the order for drinks and returned his attention to his companions.

"I have two things to show you. One is the simulation outcome, and the other is the record of our run. Both are likely to have critical information for us," Logan began. "How much time do we have?"

Terry checked and said, "Probably an hour."

"Let us start with the simulation, Logan," Katya suggested. "I think that has more urgency."

"Okay," Logan projected the results of the simulation. "There was enough information from Sebastian that we could reconstruct a fairly complete data manifold."

The display showed an elaborate, three-dimensional surface with many peaks and valleys. The surface provided a complete characterization of the communication paths the AI system could enact, given its current configuration. In essence, it was the mathematical landscape over which the AI system worked.

"From our calculations, the manifold covers roughly seven dimensions. This is impossible to visualize, of course, but we can navigate this space now that it's virtualized to explore these dimensions." He used his data glove to flip the manifold and reveal different surfaces.

Logan rotated his other hand, and trajectories formed along the manifold. The paths wavered as they traversed the surface, and some ended up moving through different valleys. For others, the paths split across different parts of the terrain.

"What is the parallel stream?" Terry asked, pointing to where the stream split. He was not used to seeing this representation for communication channels.

"This is like what we've seen in the brain," Logan replied. "An impulse comes in through the retina, for example, and it continues for a while along a single path but soon splits along multiple, parallel streams in the brain. This parallel processing is fundamental to brain function and is reproduced in many complex systems.

"We can let the simulation continue, and if we move through the manifold, you will see that these flows all follow a fairly lawful path. There is some fluctuation depending on the initial conditions, but largely, they all end up following the manifold's architecture.

"But let me show you something. If we rotate the manifold again, you see this region here?" Logan gestured to the far end of the surface. "In all the simulations, this area is never visited in the historical record, yet it exists as a potential route. That is until a month ago. Watch."

Several flows came through the surface, and for those that approached the region that Logan emphasized, an additional branch formed immediately, and a flow would traverse this region.

"These trajectories were enabled, and now this region gets touched. But what is intriguing is there is no appreciable loss of information in this splitting of the flow. What I do not know is what happens once we exit this zone."

"Isn't that a natural consequence of how you've defined this manifold?" Katya asked, holding her arms up to express the totality of the structure.

"Normally, yes, but I think we are missing some key information on this part of the space," Logan replied. "Maybe this is why there were so many convergence problems in the simulations. We don't know what happens when a flow goes into that area." He pointed to the 25% failure indicator on the simulation cockpit.

Terry gazed at the manifold. The flows continued, giving an impression of a multi-coloured river that cut through mountains and valleys. "So, could this be how the Global Council's AI system is getting redirected?"

"This is my guess," Logan replied, "though, we do not have enough information to appreciate the consequence. It may be trivial."

"Logan, if you convert the manifold representation to one that shows the actual networks that are contributing to this new activity, can we identify where it comes from?" Katya pointed to these flows as she spoke.

"Network characterization is your specialty, Terry. Would you like to take the helm?" Logan asked as he held out the data glove.

"I accept the challenge," Terry said as he took the glove. "However, I would ask that you answer the door as our beverages are here." He winked as the sound of the knock on the door echoed through the room.

"Well played," Logan said, walking to the door. He checked the door viewer and, confirming it was the delivery staff, opened the door and took the delivery.

"Shall I pour?" Logan asked as he put the beer on a table.

"Yes, please!" Katya replied, and Logan poured the beer into three glasses, handing one to Katya and placing another close to Terry.

"Okay, let's see what we have here," Terry said as he converted the manifold representation to a network graph. The display changed to a sphere representing the Earth, with points placed around it indicating the nodes of the AI system. Several of the nodes appeared to hover above the planet.

"These nodes in orbit around the planet were installed to add redundancy to the system, especially in case the nodes on the ground get knocked out in an extreme event, and to help reduce path length for communication. They are in geosynchronous orbit." Terry talked while the sphere rotated. "We can overlay in the total number of interactions between these nodes over the period the data were collected."

The sphere instantly became covered in lines that linked nodes. It was difficult to understand the pattern, apart from some high-density communications between adjacent nodes and a slight blurring around orbital nodes that reflected the uncertainty of their position.

"This representation of the network is exact but hard to grasp. We have the nodes and connections, or more formally the edges, but it's a bit like looking into a bowl of spaghetti. It helps to get a better picture of the whole if we flatten it, like what we do for brain maps sometimes," he said as he made a cut mark with his finger on the sphere running at the International Date Line. He then expanded his hand, which converted the cut sphere to a flat map.

The flat map made it easier to appreciate an organized pattern of interactions. Terry made a few adjustments and the colours of the nodes and connections changed.

"I weighted the edges by how often information flows through them. The ones in red are the edges that are used most often, and the least used are blue. I've also done a quick analysis of the nodes that receive and send the most information, which is called 'degree,' and changed the size of the node based on degree." He pointed to the high degree nodes in Europe and North America.

"This is a summary of the last several months from the data Sebastian sent us. I don't think it really captures the dynamics of the network flow in the way we saw on the manifolds Logan showed us a few moments ago." Terry pulled off one glove and took a sip of beer. "Oh, that's a good one!" He put the glove on and reoriented the flat map, bringing up an adjacent window to juxtapose the AI system manifold. He slid a few indicators onto the flat map.

"This slider controls the window size for the network dynamics. We can start with a coarse window of, say, 12 hours," he said as the flat map became animated with node degree and edge weights changing with the 12-hour period. On the parallel viewing window, flows began traversing the manifold.

"Hmm, a few things we see. First, across 12-hour periods, there are patterns that repeat. I can set up an analysis that estimates how likely a given pattern will emerge, based on the history of previous patterns. We can see the colours fade when the prediction for a particular configuration is uncertain and become bolder when it is more certain." He took another sip of beer as the animation looped.

"So, what do the periods of high certainty indicate?" Logan asked.

Terry took another sip and responded. "It looks like morning and evening periods, mainly, which you might expect. There is also a high prediction accuracy near the end and beginning of the week.

"I wish we had more data because it would have been nice to do this calculation across different timescales. I could imagine a gorgeous representation where you see how the weekly predictions change by month or season and the seasonal differences between hemispheres. This would give us a good feeling for what happens with extreme climate events, as I suspect this slower timescale dependency across seasons is not something the AI system designers really considered." Terry continued, "But these are the data we have. Okay, let's see how the network analysis links in with simulation outcomes."

The animations continued, with nodes and edges on the flat map highlighted and then dimmed as the flows moved to a different part of the manifold.

"I could watch this all day," Katya's eyes were riveted. "What about flows that come to the new region Logan found?"

"Good question. Let's move this ahead." Terry moved a slider icon ahead in time and rotated the manifold to highlight the new zone. At the moment, the trajectory approached the region, the colours faded, meaning high uncertainty in the global network. "This could be why there were so many failures in the simulation, Logan. There wasn't enough information to predict what happens in that part of the manifold."

"This is what I said," Logan replied.

"I know. I am just reframing it." Terry smiled back at Logan.

"Ah," Terry exclaimed as a few trajectories passed through the new zone. "There is a reconfiguration of the network. You see here? There is a short but influential change in connections that changes the location of the high degree nodes. You can almost see a sort of 'rich club' forming where different high degree nodes interact with each other and then send their output to their local nodes." Terry froze the animation to show the emergence of a handful of highly connected nodes — the rich club.

"Can we get a better idea where these nodes are located?" Katya asked, turning her head to get a different perspective of the flat map.

Terry reconstructed the spherical representation from the flat map and placed a faint outline of the continents to help localize. "I will remove the edges, for now, to make it clearer."

Katya studied the sphere. "So we have hubs in Southeast Asia, the West Coast of North and South America. It seems there are one or two orbital nodes as well. And then two in Europe."

"Terry, I don't understand one part of this. These rich club nodes we see here appear slightly off geographically from the AI system nodes. You see this one in Europe?" Katya pointed to a node that was close to her hometown. "It's appears there are two nodes very close together, with only one of them one part of the rich club."

"You're right, Katya." Terry looked closer at the globe. "It's like another node appeared as the system entered the new zone. I can't tell if this node exists when the system is out of this zone."

"It could be the same node, but with a different function," Logan interjected.

"True," Terry said. "Either way, the way the system operates is decidedly different here, and this is a recent phenomenon. We may have identified where the Global AI network is getting messed up. Hopefully, this information is what Sebastian was asking for," Terry said, finishing his drink.

"Excellent." Katya set her glass down. "This should be enough for Sebastian. Logan, you mentioned you also looked at the data from our run. Could we review that now? We have a bit more time?"

Logan stood and walked over to the display console. He changed the view to a map of their run, with their running paths drawn. The map had three points highlighted: one in the forest where the three paths converged, one just before the bridge and one in the middle of the bridge.

"I haven't looked into this in detail, but at this second point, another connection was established with Terry's Motif." Logan gestured and finished his drink.

"I don't know the source of it yet." Logan reframed the map and displayed the running route in time steps, with a second display showing the BrainMaze network activity, "You see, the new connection appears as we approached this point. I don't know why it goes only to Terry's device. It's not the connection we had earlier with the Global AI system."

Terry studied the first point on the map where their three running paths converged. "This is going to sound crazy, but when I fell back from you in the forest path, I ran into one of the Council members, literally. He — I think it was a he — said, 'We are approaching a critical point in the system so there could be many unpredictable changes.' I took that to mean a critical point in the discussions, but maybe he meant a critical point in terms of system dynamics?"

"A Council member? Which one?" Katya asked.

Terry described the person he had seen three times during the day. The person sat at the boardroom table, which suggested to Terry they were part of the Council. The person also appeared in the lobby and then on the forest trail. In all three encounters, Terry noted the extreme pale visage, to the point of being almost ivory. He wondered aloud whether it was a mask.

Katya looked puzzled. "And each time, the Councillor just vanished?"

"That's right. I know it sounds crazy. I don't usually have hallucinations." Terry tried to hide his discomfort. "I think there's much more here than we realize."

"You should have told us this sooner." Katya tried not to sound like she was scolding him.

"I know — sorry." Terry paused. He often felt like the weakest link of the three and wanted to make sure his friends took him seriously.

Logan was studying the run on a loop, synchronized with the broader activities of BrainMaze.

"This is worth noting, my friends." Logan paused the playback. "At the point where Terry encountered the Councillor, there is a temporary disruption of Terry's feed. It's like his Motif was offline, but if you look closely, it's still sending and receiving but no longer with BrainMaze.

"As we move ahead toward the second point, this link is maintained in parallel with BrainMaze. Here is the intriguing part." He pointed to the BrainMaze network. "This new link came from one of the orbital nodes. Remember we saw this node in the rich club reconfiguration a few moments ago?"

"Well, I am not sure what that means unless there are outer-space beings involved or something. But I am glad the connection was there to feed the info that saved us on that bridge," Terry exclaimed.

"Outer-space indeed," Logan continued. "I cannot tell what information the orbital node was accessing before the link but can assume it had something to do with the water flow systems. There was a connection established that warned of the potential for a flash flood event because of the convergence from several tributaries. This set up a cascade effect set far upstream that came together in the flood. The timing of all this was amazingly coincidental to our arrival on the bridge."

Katya frowned. "Why didn't the local systems warn of the flood? Surely, the flows in the tributaries must have shown this rapid shift before we saw it in the river."

"I don't know. Either the system was malfunctioning, or it is incapable of making the calculations necessary for such a rapid prediction. In both scenarios, the outcome is the same." Logan stopped the playback.

"Or maybe someone did it deliberately?" Terry suggested.

Katya and Logan looked at Terry. "I mean, I don't want to sound paranoid, but with what Sebastian told us on the way back from the Council HQ, it's not out of the realm of possibility that someone may want us gone."

"Sorry. You sound paranoid," Logan replied with a wink. "Just kidding." He tapped Terry's shoulder.

Katya smiled. "Let's not overthink this. It has been a weird day, so let's try to be vigilant and make sure we keep each other informed. We might have time after dinner with Sebastian to do a more thorough examination of these data, but let's not jump to conclusions yet."

"Sounds good, Katya." Terry nodded. "I suggest we be selective about what we tell him, however. Let's stick to the simulations he asked us to conduct. We'd better get cleaned up if we are going to be ready for dinner. I will grab you from your rooms in about 30 minutes."

Logan turned to gather the empty bottles and escorted his friends to the door.

Chapter Four:
Training Day 1

Change in Dinner Plans

Baren arrived back at the hotel early. He entered the lobby and took a seat next to the fireplace. Despite the heat outside, the fire was burning. He held his hand in front of the glass shield, feeling there was little heat coming from the flames, making him unsure if the fire was real.

He sat back, took his smartphone from his jacket pocket, and glanced at the message list while he loosened his tie.

"I WON'T BE ABLE TO JOIN YOU TONIGHT. PLEASE GIVE THE PROFESSORS MY REGRET AND SAY THAT I WILL SEE THEM LATER. SM" Chair Meyer's message was at the top of his message list.

His spouse, Mitchell, sent a message. "LOOKS LIKE I WON'T BE BACK UNTIL TOMORROW NIGHT. ENJOY DINNER. MISS YOU!"

Baren started to respond when TechStaff's message appeared. "I AM ON MY WAY."

Then came the message from emergency services: "WATER SURGE AT RIVER DETECTED AT 15:20. MINOR DAMAGE TO RIVER BANK AND SUSPENSION BRIDGE. NO CASUALTIES."

Followed rapidly by another message: "DATA LINK COMPLETE. SIMULATION RESULTS COLLATED. WILL REVIEW WITH YOU TONIGHT," from Yvette.

Well, this will make for a full evening, Baren thought as he returned his smartphone to his jacket pocket and rose to walk to the front desk. "Is the private dining room ready?" he asked.

"Ah, Secretary Baren, please let me check." The attendant checked a display. "Yes, sir, the room is ready for you. Is it still for six people?"

"Five," Baren replied, "one will not be joining."

"Understood. Shall I have someone escort you to the room?" The attendant prepared to call over a colleague.

"That won't be necessary. I have been there before." Baren pulled his device out again. "Thank you for your assistance."

Baren sent a message to Logan. "I   AM HERE NOW AND READY..." He felt a hand on his shoulder.

"Do you always wear that suit?" Logan smiled. Katya and Terry stood behind him. The trio dressed down from the attire they wore for the Council meeting earlier in the day, all going with shirts and pants. Katya wore a light scarf, anticipating a chill in the dining room from the ventilation.

"I am surprised that you are on time! I am sure this is your influence, Terry. The Logan I knew was never on time."

"Teamwork at its best!" Terry exclaimed.

"I am starving! May we go to the dining room?" Katya looked for a sign to the room.

Baren started walking. "Of course. The room is this way." Baren led them past the restaurant to an adjacent room that had RESERVED: GLOBAL COUNCIL on the door sign. "Here we are." Baren opened the door, signalling for Katya to enter.

The room was larger than Katya expected. It overwhelmed the single dining table in the middle. There were two waitstaff talking near the door to the kitchen. On a small table next to them sat two bottles of unopened wine and a pitcher of water.

"Good evening," one of the staff said as he approached the

group. "Secretary Baren, I am glad you are joining us tonight. My name is Phillip, and I will be looking after you."

Baren smiled and introduced his colleagues, encouraging them to sit. He glanced back at the entrance, to see if there was a sign of TechStaff's arrival. He wanted to hear the trio's report on the simulations.

As the four sat, Baren asked the servers, "I wonder if you could leave us alone for a few minutes? We have some sensitive matters to discuss before we dine. We can serve ourselves the wine."

"Of course." Phillip walked to the kitchen door, motioning to his colleague to follow.

"Sorry I'm late!" TechStaff ran into the room, out of breath. "The preparations for tomorrow took longer than expected." She closed the door and walked to the dining table.

Baren opened the two bottles of wine and brought them to the table. "Great, now that we are all here, please tell us what you have found, Professors."

"Will Chair Meyer be joining us?" asked Katya while reached for the basket of bread on the table..

"Oh, sorry. I forgot to mention. She could not make it tonight but will catch up with us later. I will brief her on what you've found," Baren said as he offered wine.

"Just a little please," Katya said. "Perhaps Logan can start the report, and Terry and I can fill in as needed."

"Okay," Logan started, sipping the wine. "The good news is that your AI system looks intact. There has not been an appreciable change in the system for the last several months.

"We found what looks like a new set of communication nodes that integrate with the AI system."

"If it's integrated, doesn't that automatically change the function of the entire system?" TechStaff asked as she reached for the wine bottle.

"A good question! Let me see if I can explain." Logan took out a pen, grabbed a napkin, and drew a surface. "If we start with your original AI system, you can define its capacity by constructing all the possible decisions it can make when processing information. This is its manifold, number one. If we do that, we can identify how often specific trajectories are considered by reconstructing the data on the manifold. That defines the likelihood of visiting different parts of the manifold, which comes from the interactions between different communication networks. In doing so, we found an area of the manifold that was seldom visited from the data reconstructions."

"Was that number two?" TechStaff asked.

"Excuse me?" Logan asked.

"You said, 'number one' but not 'number two,'" TechStaff explained.

"He's binary. It's either one or nothing," Terry chuckled.

Logan winked, raising his wineglass. "Touché. Anyway, this area of the manifold is a potential for the system but was not accessed until recently. What we do not know is whether flows that go through this area have any effect on the system. It seems to simply represent a parallel communications feed."

Terry added, "The challenge is that there is a lot of uncertainty around this area, so we can't get a good estimate of the effect from the data."

He continued, "I did a network analysis and could identify the location of the nodes related to flows through this area.

"With the uncertainty, I can pinpoint the location within

several kilometres for some, but for others, it's too variable to know."

Baren poured himself some wine. "So, you have already mapped out the locations of these suspicious nodes if I understood you?"

"Some but not all," Terry replied. "The ones I am most certain of are in Southeast Asia and northeastern North America."

"This should work out well." Baren took a sip and sat back in his chair. "Let me make a proposal.

"The Council deliberations on your offer finished on a positive note, with the majority in favour of integrating BrainMaze with our AI system. So cheers to you." He raised his glass to the trio.

"But there was some concern about the reliability of your system and how it would perform once connected with our AI system globally. The suggestion was to conduct a pilot study on-site at one hub of the AI system. It just so happens that one of these is in Southeast Asia near Kuala Lumpur," Baren said with a slight smile.

"So, we are going on a trip?" Katya asked.

"Better than that," Baren continued. "You recall the 'rogue' group I discussed with you earlier during our ride back to the hotel? It may be better to consider them as a Special Operations team, who have been tasked with investigating these anomalies. They would benefit from your expertise. My suggestion is to make you part of this team."

Terry swirled his wine and sat back in his chair. "A Special Ops team? You mean like with guns and jumping out of helicopters and stuff? This is exactly what my Ph.D. training prepared me for." He added a smile to temper his sarcasm.

Baren laughed. "Not to worry, my friend. We have a plan. I do not expect you to become militia , but there is a potential danger since we do not know who has infiltrated the system. We would like to give you a briefing on a few things before we travel to Asia so that you are at least able to handle yourselves if there are problems.

"You are all in good shape, given your running schedules, so we can explore what other skills you may have, work to enhance them, and make sure the Special Ops team can compensate for any weaknesses." Baren took another sip, glancing at the kitchen for the waitstaff.

"Boot camp!" Katya exclaimed. "This is awesome! We will be going to boot camp! When do we start?"

"We can start tonight," TechStaff spoke up, "We are short on time, obviously, so we are ready to start in about one hour if you are up to it."

"Oh! So, we'd better go easy on the wine." Terry looked at his glass.

"I think you can finish what you have, Terry. Let me go to the kitchen and see about our dinner." Baren stood and walked over to the kitchen door.

Katya leaned over to her companions. "This is so cool! Who would have expected such an opportunity when we started the day?"

Terry shook his head. "We're scientists, not soldiers!"

"I doubt we will be in any gunfights, Terry. The team needs us for our brains, not our bodies." Logan tried to soften Terry's concern.

TechStaff nodded. "Exactly. The team is pretty well set for the standard military operations. Some are tech-savvy, but we need your knowledge to help us navigate the AI system problems."

Baren returned to the table. "The dinner is being plated and will be out momentarily. I apologize in advance that it's not extravagant. I want to make sure we get a bit of training in tonight, which would be difficult if we had our traditional four-course meal."

The waitstaff came out with covered plates. Phillip placed his two in front, and Katya, TechStaff, and his partner served the three men. Phillip signalled his partner to lift the covers off the plates. "Tonight we have for you a salad with roasted vegetables and a few slices of duck breast. The salad has a light dressing of olive oil and lime. We've finished the salad with some toasted pumpkin seeds."

"Thank you, Phillip. This is marvellous," Baren commented as he picked up his serviette and placed it on his lap. "Enjoy, my friends." He finished raising his glass to the trio again.

They ate in silence.

Logan was the first to speak. "There is another thing we didn't mention to you, Sebastian. When we were out for our run, there was an unexpected flood along the river path. There was no warning from the water control systems. Fortunately, Terry's Motif got a warning signal in time."

Baren raised his eyebrows. "I saw that there had been a flood but wasn't aware you three were there!"

"It's okay. We're very speedy," Logan continued. "I mentioned this to my colleagues earlier. When I analyzed the data from our run, I saw there was another connection to Terry's device moments before the flood. I haven't had the time to analyze it further, but I assume this was a link from your AI system."

Baren glanced at TechStaff and back to Logan. "I can't be sure. I thought we disconnected it after you left headquarters, but it is fortunate that you maintained the connection." He turned his gaze to TechStaff. "Kim, perhaps you can review this with Logan later to see what happened. I will contact the local water control manager as well to see why the warning system was not activated."

Logan's disclosure surprised Terry, given the conversation the trio just had in Logan's room. And now over the past 12 hours, they had gone from simple scientists to being part of an international special operatives squad.

Logan noted Terry's grimace. "Let's do that in the morning. I want to run a few more analyses, so we have better understanding of the communication source."

Baren stood. "Of course, Logan. We have enough to do this evening. I think we are finished with our meals, so may I suggest we head over to the training centre? We will go on, and you three may wish to change into something more sporty. I don't think we will do anything physical, but you may feel more comfortable in your running attire. I will send a vehicle to pick you up in 15 minutes."

"Do we have time for a coffee?" Katya asked. "It will help offset the wine and the food."

"I will have it waiting for you in the vehicle. See you soon." Baren bowed slightly and walked out with TechStaff but paused at the door.

"I know this hasn't crossed your minds yet, but we will compensate you for this. By now, you should have received messages with an informal contract for our arrangement."

The door closed, leaving the trio alone.

Terry turned to his colleagues, but couldn't come up with anything to say. He stared at Logan.

"What?" Logan tried to break the stare.

"I don't get you," Terry finally spoke. "I thought we agreed to keep the running thing between us?"

Logan sipped wine and placed his glass on the table. "We could debate this for several more hours, but we should get moving, or we will miss our first lesson." He stood and walked toward the door.

"Logan, we really should take a moment here," Terry called out.

Logan paused. "We do not have enough information. We have unfounded suspicions and odd hallucinations. We are scientists, my friend — we work from facts. At the moment, there are few."

Terry stood. "What the hell does that mean? You can't tell me that almost getting wiped out in a flood isn't a fact!"

Logan turned. "But we were not wiped out. How exactly we were warned remains unclear, but there is no benefit for more debate without more data."

Katya felt the growing tension. "I know how you feel, Terry. We have not really had time to evaluate. Let us see how the rest of the evening goes, and then maybe we can set aside time to talk this through. And I would like to finish the analysis, Logan, especially this mystery communication feed that saved us from getting carried down the river!"

"Let's do that then," Terry muttered. "Maybe I'm over-reacting, but the whole thing with the flash flood and the disappearing Councillor tells me we need to be careful."

Katya had seen Terry and Logan argue from similar positions

before. Terry devised elaborate explanations for phenomena that sometimes had no connection to data and even bordered on fantastical. Logan was far more grounded in what the data supported, and would challenge Terry as to how one would test his elaborate explanation. This had an odd effect on how each acted: Terry weighed the possibilities, while Logan acted immediately. Katya often ended up trying to find a middle ground in these scientific debates.

"Okay, boys," she began, "let's make our way out of here and see how things go tonight. It is not a big commitment yet, and we can simply pull out at the end of the session tonight if we are uncomfortable. Is that agreeable?"

"Of course, this is what I was suggesting." Logan displayed a mischievous grin.

"Don't be an ass." Terry walked up to Logan, bumping him playfully. "I'm good with that, Katya."

The trio left the room and took the elevator this time.

Katya entered her room and breathed a heavy sigh. The excitement energized her. The Council's acceptance of the BrainMaze proposal was timely because it would allow them to work out the bugs in the interface before they went to a broad mobilization.

She opened the message program on her Motif and saw the line: "CONTRACT FOR BRAINMAZE TEAM." She opened the first message to see a barrage of statements in legal language specifying the parties that were entering into the agreement. Baren was the contractor for this rather than the Council, which made sense given the clandestine nature of the operation. The details of the agreement were very high level, focusing on 'consulting on AI deployment' and 'investigation of global network integrity.' As expected, the contract absolved any responsibility of the Global Council in the engagement.

She read down to the compensation line.

"Each member of the BRAINMAZE TEAM shall receive no less than 1,000,000 (one million) units each upon completion of the contracted tasks."

"Oh my! That's three million for us!" she said aloud. *This is more than enough to move the BrainMaze to the next level. We won't need to beg for any grants for some time!* she thought. The compensation added to her excitement.

While she changed into some fresh running clothes, she wondered whether they would use the BrainMaze goggles on their trip. She sat and wiggled her toes into her running shoes. She recalled their early struggles with BrainMaze and the breakthroughs during the development of the new computer interface.

Katya's BCI

Several years prior, when Katya was studying brain-computer interface platforms, more commonly known as BCI, there were many challenges scientists faced. One was the emphasis on simple measures of brain function, such as electrical signals from populations of neurons measured with EEG or estimates related to brain blood flow, such as functional MRI. Most BCI scientists believed that brain processes were expressed by changes in signal amplitude, which drove the software. There were more sophisticated measures such as the frequency content in the brain signals. EEG signals, for instance, contain a wide range of frequencies from as low as 1 Hz to 100 Hz or higher. Some BCI applications performed spectral analyses to focus on specific frequencies, using the change frequencies to drive the software. Meditation software, for instance, emphasized slower frequencies.

The problem was that the signals were coincidental. You know that two things tend to occur together, in this case, rhythms of low brain frequencies and meditative states, but you cannot be certain when you see slow brain rhythms that a person is meditating. There were some people, like Terry, who showed changes across a broader range of frequencies when he meditated (though Katya wasn't sure he really was meditating). Personalization was the key, where the system was calibrated to the individual's brain rather than some generic average of several people.

Katya, Terry and Logan agreed that accumulating as much information as possible on an individual's brain would be a better foundation to build a more robust BCI platform. BrainMaze had already moved in that direction, with the capacity to use brain imaging data as the starting point for the model of a person's brain. Katya was the first. They created the simulation of her brain and found some important features in her brain dynamics that were not present from looking at a generic model.

"This doesn't mean you're abnormal, Katya," Logan explained as he showed her the manifold architecture her brain networks created. "It's just impossible to predict the capacity of any single brain based on an average, especially when there are nonlinear actions."

Katya smiled. "So then, I am supra-normal!"

"Without a doubt." Logan grinned.

The personalized brain models were a start but ran into

problems with accurate predictions. The trio trained machine learning classifiers to predict brain and mental states, but the classifiers were only accurate where the new state closely resembled one of the training sets.

"This is where many of the current machine learning algorithms have problems," Terry observed. "Since many use linear operators they construct templates that are additive representations of the examples that were used to train the algorithm. This is great to get an average, but you ignore the unique parts of each example. It's this uniqueness that is central to an accurate prediction for nonlinear systems like our brain."

Katya started by using BrainMaze to form libraries for each brain, beginning with the initial model and upgrading it as new data came in. But rather than creating more robust averages of a brain, she changed the platform to focus on the variations in behaviour, reflecting Terry's observation. The more that BrainMaze learned about a particular brain, the more precise the predictions became.

But they were never perfect.

The trio found that as BrainMaze's accuracy rose above 80%, any departures from the expected distribution severely derailed it. Logan showed this when he trained his avatar to move a ball toward a target, which he hoped would lead to teaching it to play soccer. The avatar learned the range of movements of the legs that could predict how best to hit the ball toward the target. Logan then tested a scenario where his avatar was lying on the ground and used its elbow to hit the ball. And then on another, the avatar headed the ball toward the target. After adding these scenarios, the distributions fell apart giving predictions that were essentially random.

"We need to step back from this," Logan told Katya, "and think of what we want the BCI to do. We have a task, like moving the ball into the goal, and have some constraints on how this can happen. We need a system that can capture these general rules but doesn't get stuck implementing the same solution when others are available."

That solution was more difficult than it sounded.

"This really amounts to constructing extensive manifolds that act to constrain potential solutions and then updating the manifold configurations," Katya suggested.

Logan agreed. "The challenge is to avoid over-fitting the data and then needing to reconfigure completely when errors are identified. It's a delicate balance."

The first interface was cumbersome and fraught with errors. The lab teams worked to develop machine learning algorithms that could update rapidly to improve prediction, but there were often significant failures in new situations.

Terry and Logan were reviewing the data with Katya, noting the complete failure to predict when a person was falling asleep.

"This is because the machine learning algorithms only know what you tell them," Logan commented.

"Yes, of course, Logan. This is why they need extensive data. The more data, the more precise the estimation will become. This is the basis for most machine learning work." Katya signed — this was a familiar argument.

"Let's try a different approach, you two." Terry knew where this conversation was going.

He walked over to the virtual whiteboard. "Logan and I have been working through some new ideas for BrainMaze that we think will help in clinical decision support, especially when we need to predict treatment response.

"What are trying to learn about a nonlinear system by observing it, cataloguing the observation, and creating a dictionary of the observations, almost like a look-up-table. We assume we can use the look-up-table to predict what the response to an event should be. The problem is that we never really learn 'how' the system does it. Only 'that' it does it. Let's take try something different."

Terry drew a grid on the whiteboard with symbols that looked like chess pieces. "I love the analogy that Holland uses about learning chess, in his book 'Complexity, A Very Short Introduction.' You can learn chess by watching a game and tracking the movements of each piece, repeating the observation for the next games, and then build a catalogue of moves and counter-moves.

"But as an approach to learning the game, it's a serious challenge. By rough calculations, there are at least 10 to the power of 50 possible legal move sequences, which is larger than the estimated number of atoms in the universe. That's a huge catalogue!

"A more efficient approach is to uncover the rules that constrain the legal moves. By doing this for chess, we dramatically reduce the problem from an infinite space to one where a dozen or so rules capture all possible realizations of chess. We understand chess by understanding the rules of play. We can build a better BCI by focusing on the rules for the coordination of behaviour."

"I don't follow, Terry. I understand the analogy, but we do not know all the rules that govern the coordination of behaviour." Katya shook her head.

"We don't have to. We aren't trying to build a perfect system. We are trying to build a useful system. That means we need to understand the rules to help the algorithms learn the essential features." Terry made an arrow from the chessboard to a bubble and wrote "AI" in the bubble.

"Of course, chess isn't a perfect analogy, but giving an AI system the rules was how the early computers learned chess and beat the masters. We can use the same philosophy but use the principles that Logan derived for Complex Adaptive Systems to design a better BCI."

Katya looked at Logan. "What do you think, Logan?"

Logan leaned back in his chair and put his hands behind his head. "I believe he's almost right."

"We are talking about trying to make AI more intelligent," Terry continued, "and as Katya said, the way it's usually done is by giving it more data. How about trying different data? We could construct manifolds for a person's brain and train the AI systems with those features. Then it will learn how to predict the navigation of the manifolds and, better yet, the transitions between manifolds.

"Is that better, Logan?"

"Well, it's a little too simplistic." Logan winked.

"Yeah, but it's close enough." Terry smiled.

Katya looked at the drawings Terry made on and turned back to them. "I think I know exactly how to do this."

Let's get you in shape

A knock on her apartment door shifted Katya's attention.

"Ready to go again, Katya?" Terry called out.

"Yep." She stood and opened the door to see Terry and Logan

wearing running shorts and dress shirts.

"Uh, the running shirts were still wet." Terry noticed Katya's expression.

"Well, you two are always trendsetters." She let her door close and led them to the stairs to the lobby.

"Hey, did you read the contracts? We can run our labs for the next 10 years on these funds!" Katya called out in the stairwell.

"Yeah, it is pretty amazing." Terry replied. "It was vague, though. I'm concerned that they could weasel out of the commitment since the deliverables are not concrete."

"I would say this is expected," Logan interjected. "They need to keep this sufficiently vague if they are going to use Council funds."

"They could just say that we are working on the BrainMaze-AI interface and leave it at that." Terry tried to find a middle ground.

"Sure, but I think the extra work we are doing goes beyond the original agreement. The proposed contract terms imply a longer engagement," Logan countered.

"That raises another point," Katya added. "This engagement is longer than we had planned. Did you two inform your labs and families that you'd be heading to Asia?"

"I did. My family is okay with this, though my wife did caution that there is a tendency for us to engage in some mischief when we are together too long." Logan laughed.

"Funny, mine said the same thing," Terry added.

"My family already assumes this," Katya said, seeing a vehicle with "GC" on its door pulling into the driveway.

There was no conversation during the trip, but there was coffee. The route passed the Global Council HQ, taking the freeway for several minutes before exiting to an old industrial complex. Baren and TechStaff met them, both dressed in dark grey uniforms that looked like a combination of yoga and scuba diving outfits.

"Do we get an outfit like that?" Logan asked, eyeing the two.

"Not tonight. We didn't have time to get them ready. I think your, uh, running gear will do for now," TechStaff replied with a grin. She signalled for the trio to follow as she turned to enter a building. The lights were dim, and there were no windows visible. The interior resembled a warehouse with a large open space lined with small offices.

"What is this place?" Katya asked.

Baren turned to respond. "When the Global Council was established, there were concerns about confrontations. Not everyone agreed with the idea of the single governing body for the planet, if you remember.

"Anyway, the Council felt it should establish a strong security force as a defensive measure, so they built these facilities for combat training. We kept them a secret to prevent the impression that the Council had a police force or army.

"The facility is no longer in use, at least officially, so it's a perfect place to prepare our operation."

"I see," Katya replied. "But if it's not officially used anymore, how do you keep it running?"

"Well, Sara and I have enough, shall we say, discretionary funding to cover some of it.

"Perhaps we can get started and give you a better idea of our plans?" Baren continued. "Let us move to the centre of the room." He pointed to a set of mats on the floor that looked like they were used in gymnastics or martial arts.

Baren sat first, followed by TechStaff. The trio sat facing them.

"We don't have a lot of time to train you as soldiers, which also would not make sense given your expertise," Baren continued, "so we will take a few days for some basic skills training, building on what you already have. I know you are in decent physical condition, but do you have any other experience that might be beneficial in combat?"

Logan spoke first. "I was a competitive kick-boxer in my twenties. I can also drive a motorcycle or mountain bikes on trails."

"Good!" Baren turned to Terry.

"Well, I did martial arts when I was a kid, until I was 14. I used to go hunting with my dad and cousins, so I can handle a gun," Terry said with a shrug.

"Let us hope the gun won't be necessary," Baren commented. "How about you, Katya?"

"Well, I have to deal with these two guys daily." Katya laughed.

"That makes you the most qualified!" TechStaff interjected.

Katya continued. "I know technology very well. I built the BCI platform for BrainMaze, so my computer engineering skills could be helpful if there are things we need to develop or disable."

"For certain, Katya!" Baren replied. "What I think we will do is assess your combat skills and decide where to go from there. I know it seems odd to have our Special Ops team contain fighting scientists, but since we have to keep this all quiet, we can't recruit the usual agents for this."

Katya frowned. "Do you expect that there will be combat?"

Baren shrugged. "I cannot be sure since we don't know the enemy."

"We have a small but well-trained team who will be with you most of the time. If there is trouble, they will handle it. I want to be certain, however, that you will be okay by yourselves, as you never know when and where a battle may happen," Baren concluded as he stood.

"It's late, so we won't do anything too strenuous, especially with the day you've had so far! We can do a simple test of your firearm skills and resume tomorrow." Baren nodded toward TechStaff.

"Great!" TechStaff said, "Let's go to the shooting range." She pointed to a room behind her and walked with the trio following. Baren remained at the mats.

"Are you joining us, Sebastian?" Katya noticed he had not moved.

"I am afraid not. I have a video call coming in soon from the Council members in Asia, who want to discuss our travel the logistics. I will see you in the morning," Baren said with a smile.

"Okay," Katya said, "have a pleasant night," she paused and caught his gaze, then ran to catch the others.

TechStaff opened the room to show four makeshift firing lanes with large wooden blocks at the end of each, which served as targets. The blocks had a human outline traced in white.

"This won't take long, but let me show you our weapon first," TechStaff said as she reached for the object on the table. It looked like a small automatic weapon, like a sub-machine gun but with a fatter profile, making it look more toy-like.

"The weapon is a made of Kevlar and metal to make it light but strong enough to be used as a weapon on its own if needed." She held it up as if she were going to hit someone.

"The weapon has a digital control that you can over-ride if

needed and switch to Manual Mode." She activated a small screen on the side of the weapon. The screen read, "SAFETY ENGAGED."

"When it's first activated, it starts in Safety Mode. You can only release the safety with your fingerprint. I set this one up for me. We'll set yours up tomorrow." TechStaff placed her thumb on the safety switch, and the screen changed to: "STUN MODE — COUNT 10."

"The weapon has four settings. I call the one you see now Stun Mode and will fire only rubber bullets. They're blunt and not very aerodynamic, so your target should be within 5 to 10 metres. The count tells you how many shots you have left."

She tapped the screen, and the display changed to: "KILL MODE — COUNT 25." She looked up at the trio. "You can probably guess what this means. The bullets are standard steel-tipped. They won't puncture a vest unless you are point blank. It's a semi-automatic setting, so you just need to pull the trigger and fire. This is also true for Stun Mode, by the way. The targeting on this weapon is pretty good to about 200 metres."

She tapped the screen again, and the display changed: "RCKT MODE — COUNT 5." TechStaff smiled. "We couldn't spell out 'rocket' on the display, so we abbreviated it. This mode, as you might guess, fires small rockets. They pack a wallop on the recoil, so be prepared. It's useful for penetrating walls or doors. It can disable vehicles and some armoured vehicles, too, but I wouldn't recommend using it against combat tanks."

She double-tapped the screen, holding at the last tap. "SELF DSTRCT" began flashing on the screen. "This turns the weapon into a bomb. Once the user releases the weapon, it will detonate in five seconds. If there are rockets left, the explosion will be even bigger!" TechStaff said with a tad too much exuberance. "Sorry, came from a gaming background where blowing stuff up was very, uh, calming." She chuckled.

"Okay, you've made us sufficiently uncomfortable now," Terry said, only half-joking.

"Ha, I get it," she replied.

She turned to the target and said, "For tonight, we'll just keep it in Kill Mode and see how do. I will put it on manual so that any of you can fire." She handed the weapon to Logan.

"Is Self-Destruct Mode still possible in manual?" Logan asked, holding his hand back.

"Oh, yeah, thanks for asking. It's a bit more complicated as you need to push the trigger forward and then press the manual safety button, but it will work. You still have five seconds after it's activated to get out of the way," TechStaff finished, thrusting the weapon toward Logan again. "We'll give you each five shots. The first couple we'll ignore since you'll need to get used to the weapon."

"I haven't fired a weapon in years." he walked to the top of the lane.

"Oh, wait," TechStaff said, turning back toward the table, "please put on these hearing protectors." She handed each of them a pair of earmuffs. "I doubt we'll be shooting all night, but better to be safe."

Logan put on the earmuffs and pulled the weapon to his shoulder. The sighting was simple, with a distance indicator that required lining it up with the target. Logan squeezed the trigger, heard the muffled explosion of the bullet and felt its recoil, but closed his eyes and did not see the bullet hit the ground in front of the target. Logan aimed again, this time slightly higher, and tried to keep his eyes open. He fired and saw the bullet hit the wall left of the target.

He turned around to TechStaff and shrugged his shoulders. Taking off his earmuffs, he said, "I don't think it will get much better than this. I have little experience with firearms."

TechStaff, holding the earmuffs out from her ears, said, "Take three more shots. There's no prize here. We want to know the range of skills you three have so we can get the rest of the team prepared."

Logan nodded once and put his earmuffs back, returning to the firing lane. He aimed and squeezed out three fast shots, one hitting the wall to the right of the target, one just outside the outline of the shoulder on the wooden block, and the last on the outline.

He turned, smiled at TechStaff and handed her the weapon. "Don't worry, Logan. This isn't a contest. We just need to get an idea, that's all," she said.

"I'm here for brains, not my body, right?" Logan said, continuing to smile.

TechStaff looked at Logan somewhat puzzled and said, "Your brain won't work without your body, so we need both."

Logan laughed uncomfortably and handed the weapon to Terry.

Terry stepped into the lane and raised the weapon. He too hadn't fired in decades. Two things came to mind: first was to aim with both eyes open and the second to breathe out just before firing. The first shot hit the base of the woodblock. This suggested the siting was a bit short. Terry adjusted his aim and fired again. The shot hit just above the head on the block outline. He made one more adjustment and fired off three shots in succession. The first two hit the torso in the outline, and the last hit the middle of the head.

Terry turned to his colleagues, smiling, taking off his earmuffs. "It's easier in target practice but not so much in actual combat."

TechStaff looked at Terry and cocked her head. "I didn't know you were in combat, Terry."

"No, no, that's not what I meant exactly. I mean, I haven't been in combat, but when you're hunting, your target isn't just going to sit there while you take careful aim. The context is different. I know the rules of how to shoot a weapon, but the particular realization depends on the context. You shouldn't judge my ability based on target practice. I may be great in here, but a mess in the field," Terry explained.

"I understand," TechStaff said, deciding not to pursue that point. She turned to Katya. "Are you ready?"

"Sure," Katya said, putting her earmuffs back on and taking the weapon from Terry. As she walked to the lane, she carefully studied the weapon to understand how it worked.

She positioned herself in the lane and brought the weapon to her shoulder. Of the three, Katya had the least experience firing a weapon, since firearms were scarce when she was young. The family of her first boyfriend had a farm outside the city and collected guns to help rid the farm of pests. Her boyfriend showed her how to fire when they set up a metal container for the target. The experience was unpleasant. The loudness of the gun bothered her, and the recoil bruised her shoulder. Her boyfriend made this worse by finding it funny. He was no longer her boyfriend shortly after the event.

Katya erased that thought and focused the sites at the target.

She lightly squeezed the trigger, and the weapon recoiled as the bullet exited. Katya saw a puff at the base of the woodblock from the bullet, telling her that the siting was a little off. The recoil was not as strong as expected. She raised the weapon again, but was unsteady with her aim. The bullet hit far to the left of the target.

She frowned and looked down at the weapon. She quickly pressed a button beside the display, raised the gun to her shoulder and launched a rocket that hit the base of the wooden block, blowing it into pieces.

She turned to TechStaff and said with a grin, "My expertise is technology. I can use the technology to find the best solution to a problem."

"Noted, Katya, noted," TechStaff said, still stunned by the extreme but effective tactic.

"You're incredible." Logan laughed as he spoke to Katya.

"This is what I keep telling you," she replied.

"Okay, Professors, let's get you back to your rooms. We'd like to start by 5 AM, which is, oh gee, five hours from now," TechStaff noted with surprise.

When they returned to the main room, they saw three people across the floor talking among themselves. Two were very tall males, and the third was unclear, as the long jacket and hat made it difficult to know the gender.

TechStaff paused and called out, "Hey, we're done now. Shall I bring them over to you?"

One of the large men bent down to the third person and replied, "Sure."

As they approached, the third person turned, revealing her face. When she smiled at TechStaff and the trio, there was no doubt who it was.

"Hello, Chair Meyer!" Katya shouted.

"Here, you can call me Sara, please," Sara Meyer said. "I am sorry for all the cloak and dagger stuff, but as I think Sebastian explained, we are in a tough situation."

Her voice as Sara Meyer had a much less measured tone than as Chair Meyer.

"So, you're part of this rogue group?" Terry was a little less surprised.

"Well, actually, I sort of started it. Sebastian, Kim and I started seeing all the problems in the AI system and the increasing tension on the Council, so we started sidebar investigations. Sebastian knew some guns-for-hire that he trusted from his days in local politics. They did a bit of digging and found that some of the Council were saying one thing and doing another."

"But that's typical in politics," Terry commented.

"At one time, for sure, but when you are on the Council, your first obligation is to the Council, not to special interests. This is why it's an appointed and not an elected position. You have to be elected within your district to be eligible, but that doesn't guarantee a position on the Council. There are annual evaluations, and if someone is not supporting the Council mandate, we can kick them off. It hasn't happened yet, but I think the risk keeps everyone in line.

"Anyway, Sebastian told me about the simulations. It confirms that someone is messing with our system. This is serious because if we can't make a meaningful impact on the water issue and, ultimately, the climate, there'll probably be a full-blown revolt against the Global Council, not to mention the harm to the planet. We can't afford to go back, given all we have achieved. It would be anarchy. Not that I mind anarchy, but only in certain areas of my life," she finished with an odd laugh.

"It seems dangerous for the Chair of the Council to be in the field trying to uncover a spy within her own Council," Logan observed.

"This is true, Logan. If the situation were different, I might have chosen a different strategy. But with the disasters we've seen over the past months, and the perceived inability of the Council to do anything, there really is no other alternative. Sebastian is the only one involved from the Council, so if this goes sideways and I am wrong, the Council can survive. But if I am right, we need to act outside the Council. I don't know who at that table we can trust." Sara's voice trailed off.

One of the tall men spoke. "Perhaps we can continue the conversation tomorrow? I think everyone is tired, and we have an early start."

"Yes, of course," Sara responded. "Don't worry about breakfast and coffee tomorrow. Despite the Spartan appearance of this place, I got an excellent espresso machine and know a place that opens early enough that we can get good pastries."

TechStaff moved in, saying, "Terrific, so let me take the Professors back to their hotel, and we can start fresh tomorrow."

"Excellent, Kim," Sara said, holding back a yawn. "Let's do that. Rest well, everyone."

Chapter Five:
Training Day 2

The drive over

TechStaff met the trio in the hotel lobby. "Sara thought it would be helpful for me to accompany you to the training site this morning so I can give you an idea of what to expect. And, if there is time, maybe we can review the analysis you did on your river run yesterday?"

The vehicle that pulled up as they exited the building was not the Global Council vehicle, but an older personal model.

"Is this yours?" Terry asked.

"Yes. It's a sort of mash-up of different models, but it is basically impossible to track. I've been playing with it for several years, and now that we need a stealth vehicle, I am happy to say I have the very first one!" TechStaff said as she keyed in the destination on the console. The vehicle drove to the end of the driveway and stopped abruptly, opening the doors and announcing they had arrived at the destination.

"Okay, so there are still a few bugs to work out." TechStaff scratched her head as she checked the console.

"Shall we call a taxi?" Katya asked.

"One second, please." TechStaff entered a few commands on her smartphone and synced with the vehicle. "Okay, here we go." The doors closed, and the vehicle continued.

"Sometimes, these machines can be so literal!" she exclaimed, which none of the trio really understood.

Katya spoke. "So, what is our agenda for the day?"

"Well, there will be excellent coffee at the training centre, so we can start with that," TechStaff responded. "Sara and Sebastian want to hold a briefing to introduce you to the rest of the team.

"You all gave us an idea last night about some of your strengths, so most of the training will enhance those. The sessions today will be a mixture of continued assessment of your skill levels and training to help supplement where possible.

"For example, Logan has a background in hand-to-hand combat, so our team will work with him to see what he remembers and give him some pointers if he is rusty. Katya and Terry, you can join in too if you wish.

"Katya, it would be helpful for you and me to talk with the rest of the team about the goggle interface for BrainMaze. It's far more advanced than anything we have, so we'd benefit from a lesson there."

"I can get you devices and goggles for BrainMaze rather quickly. We have many prototypes in the lab, so we could have five or six sent over by tomorrow," Katya offered.

TechStaff smiled. "Thanks! Let's see how it goes. It might be easier for us to figure out how to link your system with ours, so we get the best of both, as you said to the Council yesterday."

"You learn fast!" Logan interjected.

"Have to in this business. Anyway, we'll also do a briefing on the vehicle tech and some tweaks we made on our AI system. Sebastian heard about your impressive accuracy with a weapon last night, Terry, so he wants to give you a bit more exposure to some of the other toys we have if you're interested." TechStaff finished and checked the console to see their progress.

"I think we have another 10 minutes before we get there. Logan, did you want to talk about the analysis of your run?"

"Certainly." Logan removed his Motif and brought up the results, showing the activity of the AI network and BrainMaze during the time of their run. He explained the graphics while the timestamp on the display moved forward to the point where Terry's link to BrainMaze shifted to the AI system.

"Here is where the puzzle comes." Logan paused the playback. "We were disconnected from the AI system when we left HQ, so the source of this new link it is not clear."

TechStaff studied the display. "Can you zoom in on the orbital node?"

She sat back. "That node is not part of the Global AI system. The orbital node is at a different altitude and somewhat more south than the one displayed here. I think this is a different system."

"And one that saved us. We got the warning of the flood just moments after the link was formed." Terry added, "This also connects to other nodes in North America and Asia."

TechStaff shook her head. "I don't understand how this other network could be there without us knowing it."

"I guess it's only linked for certain kinds of configurations, maybe only when there is a need to access the Global AI to change a trajectory. Whatever it is, it knows a lot about communications networks and system flows."

"I am definitely looking forward to meeting its owner!" TechStaff smiled.

Introductions

The trio and TechStaff entered the training centre and were immediately greeted by the smell of freshly made coffee. Off to one side in the large room was a table with a restaurant-style espresso maker, and several people gathered around, waiting their turn to create the beverage of their choice.

Sara noticed the trio enter. "Good morning, team! You're looking well-rested. How about another shot of caffeine in there for reserves?" She smiled as she pointed to the espresso machine.

"Awesome." Terry walked toward the machine. "I should have brought donuts!"

"We have a variety of breakfast pastries on the table." Sara pointed to a large tray. "There are some healthy and some, well, less healthy items on the tray. You may want to tank up here since I doubt there'll be time for lunch today."

Terry examined the tray of pastries. "I like this kind of boot camp," he said and grabbed a 'less healthy' pain au chocolat rather than the low-fat, wildberry muffin. Logan followed, grabbing one of each while Katya decided not to take any. "I had some food before we came over, so I should be okay."

"I will save you one of the healthy pastries for later, Katya. I can guarantee you will want it." Sara wrapped one in a napkin.

Baren stepped forward. "I want to introduce you to your bodyguards. I know that we do not yet know the threat we are facing, but it is best to play it safe in these situations." Three large people stepped forward and nodded toward the trio. Katya recognized one of them from the previous evening when they met Sara.

"These are former Special Forces Officers who have volunteered to help us. I'd like to keep their identities secret, so we won't use their real names. You can call them 'BG,' which stands for Body Guard, followed by the initial of your first name. For example, Katya's would be BGK." Baren continued, "From this point forward, they will be with you day and night."

"BG's," Terry snorted. "Do they sing?"

Baren continued, ignoring the comment. One of the three persons stepped forward. He had the build of a rugby player, with a few facial scars that reinforced the ruggedness. "At your service, Katya."

Katya acknowledged BGK but felt a bit insulted by the perception that she needed guarding. "Is this necessary, Sebastian? I have seen no evidence that there is a physical danger to us."

"Nor have I, Katya. Not yet, that is. Given what is at stake, I doubt our, uh, opponents, will do anything physical until we find them. There is no need to fight until someone knows you are there."

Baren turned to the next bodyguard, who stepped forward. She was as tall as the others, with a slim, athletic build and dark, closely cropped hair.

"Logan, this is BGL."

"Greetings, Professor. I look forward to working with you." She exhibited a professional smile.

"I think you can call me Logan," Logan replied shyly.

"I prefer 'Professor' since we are working together," BGL replied, and walked back.

Baren turned to the last bodyguard. "Terry, this is…"

"I guess that makes me BGT," the last bodyguard commented as he walked forward, extending his hand. He had a slimmer swimmer's build and the broad smile of someone you might expect to meet in a neighbourhood pub.

Terry grasped BGT's hand. "Pleased to meet you. I am sure we'll have," he tried to find a word, but all that came out was "fun."

BGT laughed. "That I can guarantee — that I can guarantee!"

TechStaff took a muffin from the table. "Maybe we can start with the technical parts and look at our Combat System. I also want to make sure I spend some time with you in particular, Katya, so we can figure out a way to integrate our system with BrainMaze."

Tech inspect

TechStaff pointed to a door at the opposite end of the atrium. "Let's head over to the lab, and I can show you what we've done."

Sara grabbed a pastry and coffee. "I would like to join you all, if that's okay. I need to learn more about the guts of BrainMaze, and this seems like a great opportunity."

"Cool." TechStaff turned and began walking.

Katya expected to see a high-tech lab with the latest and greatest computer and combat devices. What met them was a large, open room with tables of scattered electronics, burnt-out silicon boards and cables that appeared from the flooring like someone forgot to connect them. "This looks like a real science lab." She grinned.

"Since we are not officially supposed to be doing this, we kinda have to do it with whatever we can scavenge. Yvette and I collected much of this stuff."

Yvette poked her head up from behind a workstation. "Hi, everyone, sorry about the mess." She walked toward the group, wiping her hands on her shirt, leaving large black stains from the solder and grease.

Logan smiled. "Some things do not change. How are you, Yvette? It's good to see you."

Yvette extended her hand. "Nice to see you too, Logan. I'm looking forward to working with you again."

"It has been too long." Logan extended his hand. He was pleased that there appeared to be no tension from her. She seemed genuinely happy to see them.

"Great to see you, Yvette." Katya stepped up. "I heard you provided us with the critical data to do our analysis of the Global AI system. Impressive work!"

Yvette smiled, glancing away. "I'm glad it was useful."

"Definitely was, Yvette." Terry added, "Great work as usual."

Yvette glanced over to Terry, and then back to Katya. "Okay, we're on a pretty tight schedule. Let me show you what we have so far."

Yvette motioned to her workstation. "Kim, did you set up the patch?"

TechStaff raised her hand to indicate 'wait' and walked over to another workstation. She inserted her device into the port and signalled 'okay' to Yvette.

"Our Combat System is a fully trained AI interface that we have developed over the last five years to better link up team members." Yvette brought up a simulation of a Heads-Up-Display.

Baren interrupted, "Thank you, Yvette. The system looks like a typical HUD, or Heads-Up-Display, but we've integrated the AI system to guide team decisions as it collects the data feeds from everyone. We also use a bit of augmented reality to give the users a better idea of the environment they are in, like the density of doors, the depth of holes and so on. We try not to bombard them with information but rather select and give them the critical information they need to make fast decisions."

"This is your work, Yvette?" Logan rubbed his chin.

"Basically, though, a lot of the algorithms were developed by others. I think my major contribution was to link the best code to get a more robust prediction chain. See, many of the AI systems are built on stuff you give them to learn, which limits their capacity to adapt. I tried to incorporate a more dynamic set of learning rules to deal with novel environments." She spoke quickly so that she was not interrupted again.

TechStaff also spoke up. "We figured we might get an even bigger bang if we could link in BrainMaze somehow to help with the adaptive part. I don't know this stuff as well as Yvette, but from my understanding, the AI systems are fantastic at doing calculations when you give them all the data, but they have more problems learning about data they haven't seen before."

"This is reasonable." Logan stopped to consider the video display more closely. "Using BrainMaze will give you more stability too. We built BrainMaze from Complex Adaptive Systems' principles, so the adaptations it considers are far more subtle than the extreme alterations you see in some AI systems."

There was a slight pause in the conversation as the group tried to interpret Logan's statement.

"Exactly," Katya added. "An AI system that over-emphasizes new information may end up solving the problem at hand but fail when it has to return to more typical cases."

Sara spoke up, "You mean like over-compensation?"

"Yes, effectively." Katya turned to Sara. "The danger with this, of course, is that you may never get back to a reasonable equilibrium. Biology does this sometimes, where it may mobilize multiple agents to a new target, like immunity, which could end up having bad long-term consequences like severe allergies. That is catastrophic, of course, and with combat, an overreaction could be equally catastrophic, not for the battle but for the war."

The group stood looking at the display for a moment, watching a simulation of a reconnaissance patrol through a mountain pass. The display showed the location of the other team members in front and at the rear of the subject. By orienting to the other team members, the data was fed into a portion of the display. At the bottom of the display were real-time indicators of local atmospheric conditions, combined team trajectories, and polls of data feeds from other teams. The system allowed the user to select the key items of focus but could alter it in case of a large shift in conditions.

"TEAM 2 AND TEAM 4 ON INTERCEPT PATH," flashed on the display.

"Is that good?" Terry whispered to Yvette.

"Let's find out." She clicked a few points.

The display switched to show the movements of Team 3, their Team, which was Team 1 tasked to observe and guide the other teams, and Teams 2 and 4. Each was represented as a single trajectory on the mountain pass. The terrain display showed that the pass would close to a narrow valley in a few hundred metres. Teams 2 and 4 would need to move down to join Team 3 to move through the pass or move up to go around along the ridge. The topo-map suggested the ridge ascent would be strenuous.

Yvette paused the simulation. "At this point, the data suggests that Teams 2 and 4 should scale the ridge, rather than joining Team 3 in the valley."

"What are the other variables? Is there a time limit to destination?" Katya asked.

"It will be night soon, so the teams should try to get out of the valley as fast as possible." Yvette hovered her finger over the console.

"If there is urgency, why not push them all through quickly?" Baren suggested.

"Let's try that." Yvette adjusted a few variables and hit the button.

The simulation showed a convergence of the three teams. The pace increased to get through the pass, and the teams clustered. A storm of weapon fire caught the teams as they approached the narrowest part of the pass.

"No one survived." Yvette pressed the 'pause' key on the console, looking away from Baren.

"Okay, let's try the AI's suggestion. Send the two teams up the ridge," Baren grumbled.

In this simulation, Team 3 stayed back until Teams 2 and 4 had scaled the ridge. By the time they had reached the ridge, night had fallen, and the teams all had to switch to Night Vision Mode. Team 3 proceeded along the valley floor with Teams 2 and 4 on opposite sides, moving slightly ahead. A bright flash exploded in the valley, disabling Team 3, and similar flashes happened slightly later on the ridges. Weapon fire ensued, eliminating Teams 2 and 4. Team 3 was left exposed.

"Shall we retreat?" Yvette asked.

"Stop the simulation, please," Baren hissed.

"The tactic of splitting the teams would have worked in daylight, but the need for night vision added a new variable that led to an imperfect prediction from the AI system." Yvette stopped the simulation.

"May I try something?" Katya stepped forward, holding her Motif out to TechStaff.

TechStaff connected it to her workstation. The display showed: "BRAINMAZE CONNECTED."

The icons of the three teams grew and elongated to suggest a longer collection of personnel. The shapes changed to resemble a tadpole swimming down the valley, then an oval, then a teardrop.

The head of the tadpole passed through the narrow part of the valley and reemerged, immediately followed by weapon fire at the tail. The head of the tadpole exited the valley.

Baren was puzzled. "What happened?"

Katya looked at the display, and Terry and Logan. "One moment," she replied.

Terry raised his eyebrows and turned to Baren. "This is cool."

"Because there was sparse data on the enemy's capacity to monitor the team's progress, BrainMaze created a digital mask. The prevalence of tech nowadays means most will rely on what their devices tell them rather than what they see with their own eyes."

"Oh, I like that. BrainMaze set up a digital smokescreen." Sara made a 'poof' gesture.

"Exactly!" Katya replied. "The only way to level the playing field was to insert some uncertainty into the equation and limit the capacity of the enemy to know where the team was.

"This only works because the enemy relied on their digital feed. BrainMaze inserted a random noise mask in the communications channel to make it impossible for the opponents to track specific targets. To them, the teams would appear like amorphous masses."

"But even then, it wasn't perfect." Sara pointed to the tail. "What happened to the team in this section?"

Katya frowned. "Casualties were unavoidable. BrainMaze and the AI system decided this was the best outcome possible."

Baren stepped in. "This solution won't work if we have to decide who lives and who dies."

Sara raised her hand to scratch her cheek. "It's not us who decides, Sebastian. It comes from the math, and the math doesn't have the emotional burdens we do. It knows the task and parameters. That is irrefutable. What we do with the info is another matter." She clenched her jaw as she stared at the display.

Logan tapped on the display. "These are just probabilities based on data. There are other things we can do to make these decisions, well, more humane. We are sending information about the interpersonal interactions of the team, each member's history, their value to the team and their perceived value beyond. These facts can completely change the prediction."

"But how will we know when we have the right answer?" Baren stared at Logan.

"This is the challenge." He moved his hand across the screen pointing to the valley on the display. "We won't."

Tech update

There was another update Sara wanted to include in the Combat System.

"You know that we use vocal communications in our devices at present." She directed her comment to Katya. "I understand you have tech in BrainMaze that reads thoughts and sends them to other people."

"Not exactly," Katya replied. "It's more a system that can translate basic utterances generated in your brain to speech of text. It takes speech just before it's articulated. We call it a Brain-to-Speech system or B2S."

"How do you use it?" Sara continued.

"We set it up for communications between pairs of users. In our BrainMaze network, you request a link to another person and think about what you want to say. The decoders convert the electrical brain signals from the electrodes that surround the goggles to speech, which is sent to the other person. The receiver can see it displayed or hear it through a speech synthesizer."

Baren spoke. "I can see that being very useful in noisy environments and in situations where you don't want to speak out loud. Is it accurate?"

"It takes some training for each user, both the algorithm and the user. The algorithm combines some of the core speech decoding work that uses the syntactic context to determine the complete utterance and aligns that with a library of the person's brain signals related to speech formation," Katya answered. "The user has to learn the interface and to focus just long enough to form an utterance that BrainMaze can decode.

"We would not have been able to do this ourselves were it not for the open science community sharing the code for these decoders and helping us test and debug. We probably saved 10 years by having this as a community project," Katya added.

"I can appreciate that," Baren replied. "When I was still in research, it was a very closed system and highly competitive. We would never share code between labs for fear someone would steal our ideas."

"Fortunately, most of the community now sees more pluses than minuses to open science. Even our industry partners have signed on," Katya continued. "I think they realized they were wasting resources trying to do it all in-house. Now they benefit from being part of the open innovation community but still can keep their company viable through this novel business model.

"Of course," she concluded, "this doesn't guarantee the solutions we get are perfect."

Terry added, "We had some problems in the prototyping days where the system would confuse lexical equivalents, but since we wanted this to work in real-time, we opted to focus on speed over accuracy, knowing that the receiver might figure out what was meant. We were going to have the user edit the utterance before sending, but that was too clunky."

Terry remembered some early test sessions:

Katya thought: SEND ME THE RED BALL.

Terry received: SEND ME THE RED BULL.

Terry thought: ARE YOU TIRED?

Katya received: ARE YOU HIRED?

Katya thought: I DON'T NEED A JOB.

Terry received: I DON'T FEED A SLOB.

Terry said, "Hey, no need to insult my clothing choice."

"What are you smiling about?" Sara asked him.

"Oh, sorry, just old memories." Terry smiled. "Katya, can we set up the B2S system here?"

Katya looked at TechStaff. "We can try to set something up. I can't be certain that the training will be as robust as it is with us. BrainMaze has learned our speech patterns over more than a year. I don't know how much of that knowledge is transferable."

Logan added, "Remember, the major difference with our system is we deliberately tried to teach BrainMaze the rules of grammar and syntax, rather than just trying to understand words or short phrases. Part of the reason we are so good at understanding speech, even when it's severely degraded, is we understand the grammatical rules and can fill in the missing bit to get a pretty good idea of what was said.

"This is like what Katya was saying to the Council, that if you understand the rules that govern the coordination of an output, in this case, speech, you are much more likely to understand an individual realization because you know the rules."

"I get it," Sara spoke, "but these rules are not the same for all languages."

"Good point, Sara," Katya replied. "We focused our system on English so far since that's the most common language in our field. I think that makes the training time a little easier since the grammar does not vary that much between people. The system does have to learn the idiosyncrasies of each person."

Sara turned to TechStaff and Baren. "Kim, maybe you can review the schematics with Yvette and work with Katya on the interface for this B2S system with Combat AI."

Katya interjected, "If you want to establish such an interface, it would be better to create brain avatars for your team, so they can link up in BrainMaze."

"That we can do. This is a research facility, so we have brain scanning facilities similar to what you have in your lab."

"Wow!" Katya's eyes widened. "That is excellent. I would not expect a neuroscience lab in a Council facility. Now we can create avatars for everyone and plug into BrainMaze!"

Her comment hung in the room.

"Does that mean you will be able to read our minds?" BGK furrowed his brow.

"Not at all. The technology and our understanding of the brain is nowhere near close enough to do that. The avatars simply act as a conduit to help you interface better with BrainMaze. You can think of it as customizing a speech recognition application to your voice." Katya tried to assure that nothing dubious was behind the avatar creation.

Sensing the uneasiness, Sara considered a compromise. "Maybe just a few of us can get set up. I don't think we'll have time to train all of us, anyway. Kim, Sebastian and I will have avatars made. If we need to do more, we can consider it later."

"I think Yvette would be a better choice than I." Baren smiled. "My old brain may have difficulty learning new tricks."

Sara pondered, considering a reply to Baren's comment, but opted to continue. "Okay, I think we've done enough here for now. Logan, could you go with BGL and Sebastian? I'll go with Katya to get the avatar factory started."

Logan

"Logan, you mentioned your kick-boxing experience yesterday. Was that competitive or more recreational?" Baren asked as he led the way into a room with large mats on the floor and several punching bags of different sizes.

Logan thought the room resembled the training rooms he practised in when he first learned kick-boxing. "It was competitive. I was on the path to national and European championships when I stopped."

Baren turned to Logan. "What made you quit? It sounds like you were successful."

Logan sounded a little sad as he answered. "In one particularly tough training session, I was hit hard in the head by a kick that came after the end of a sparring round. It did not knock me out, but it spun me around. This is part of the game, but I needed to consider what my future might hold.

"I was in graduate school then and was seriously engaged in the science of complexity. If I wanted to continue to use my brain, I had better protect it. I got a huge rush from kick-boxing, but I noticed the toll it was taking on my body and probably my brain, so I decided to hang it up and focus on my science."

"That makes sense to me, Logan. I could never understand the attraction of fighting for sport. I prefer to rely on strategy rather than brute force." Baren turned to BGL, who followed them into the room.

"Just as we did yesterday with the weapons, we'd like to get an idea today of your hand-to-hand combat skills. This will help BGL and the rest of the team to know our capacity." He pointed to the wall. "There's some sparring gear over there. Please put on the headgear and gloves, and let's get started."

Logan walked over, grabbed headgear, and was looking at the gloves when BGL grabbed a pair. "I will be your sparring partner," she said. "It's better for me to assess your skills if I can test you directly rather than watch you with someone else."

Logan reflected. He was going to say something about never having fought a woman before, but he decided that would not be wise. "As you wish," was his response.

The two walked to a centre mat. Baren stood back and set the small video to 'RECORD.'

"Are there any rules?" Logan asked.

BGL quickly lashed out with a foot sweep that Logan avoided by jumping straight back. She spun with a back kick that caught Logan in the side. "There are no rules in combat, so there are no rules here." She backed away and returned to the centre of the mat, bouncing lightly on her feet.

Logan smiled, tapping his gloves together. "Excellent."

The pair circled each other more cautiously. Logan felt the familiar adrenaline and the scripts he used to review before a match coming back.

"Keep your eyes on your opponent's torso, not their eyes or hands."

"Keep your centre low and do not extend yourself unnecessarily."

Logan tried a sidekick that BGL easily avoided. He followed with a jab that she dodged. He felt a bit stiff still and was reluctant to try a combination at this point.

BGL swept at Logan's leading leg again. This time Logan countered with a kick that BGL blocked, and she returned a right cross that caught Logan on the side of his head. It was not a hard punch, but it was enough to make him notice.

Logan stepped back and then quickly stepped forward with a strong front kick, sidekick combination that caught BGL flat-footed. She avoided the front kick, but the sidekick she took in her abdomen, though she lessened the impact by rolling away. Logan maintained the pressure and threw two hooks. BGL ducked to avoid them, but she momentarily lost focus. Logan swept her front leg, which put her off balance. Another short kick pushed BGL to the mat.

Logan made the mistake of relaxing after he saw BGL fall. Once she hit the mat, she rolled on to her side, sweeping her feet around to catch Logan's legs, sending him backward onto the mat. Logan landed heavily.

"Never let your guard down," flashed into Logan's head as he rolled upright.

"Shall we continue?" Logan stood cautiously. BGL nodded and prepared herself at the mat's centre.

Logan took a more circumspect approach, testing BGL with

jabs as he circled. BGL did the same, but kept a firmer stance, sliding to the left or right to keep Logan in front. BGL tested a few front kicks that Logan easily avoided. Logan noticed BGL left an opening after her front kick. They had several more cautious exchanges, but none that allowed either to gain an advantage.

BGL front-kicked again. Logan parried the kick and slid inside, throwing a hook to BGL's head. In the close quarters, BGL used Logan's momentum, grabbing his arm and unbalancing him enough to push down to the mat. BGL placed her elbow in Logan's abdomen as they fell, knocking the breath out of him. Logan surprised himself, however, and rather than submitting, he mustered enough energy to slide out from under her and get himself upright and in a defensive posture.

"I am impressed," BGL said as she rose. "While you sometimes telegraph your intent, you are fast enough that you can compensate — to a degree."

Logan caught his breath. "I am quite out of practice, but there is a 'like riding a bike' aspect to it."

"Well, we're hoping we won't have to put your skills to a real test." BGL walked over to the wall, taking off her gloves and headgear. "Seriously cool moves, though. You can be our Ninja warrior in a pinch!"

"Ninja scientist, you mean," Logan smiled, putting a towel over his shoulder and removing his gloves.

BrainMaze forward model

"So, how does this work?" Sara asked as she came into the room that housed the brain scanner.

"The data we collect here is to get a measure of your brain's structure: its size, shape, the density of different tissue types and the connections between the parts. This gives us the skeleton for your brain." Katya motioned for Sara to place a helmet on her head for the measurements.

The machine was an older version of the one in Katya's lab but provided a reasonable measurement of brain geometry and connections by measuring the diffusion of water across the brain and tissue conductivity. Brain connections are insulated with a myelin sheath, which is essentially fat, so the water diffuses parallel to the sheaths. The measure of water diffusion gives a rough estimate of the direction and size of connections. The conductivity measure provides estimates for the speed of signal propagation.

"But that can't be enough to get an accurate model." Sara sat down in a chair.

"That is true, but it gets us very close. You remember my presentation to the Council, where I showed you the wiring diagram for the Global AI? We can do a similar thing with the wiring diagram of your brain to tell us which parts have the greatest capacity to interact with each other. Some parts of your brain will have a connection profile that gives them the potential to interact with numerous other regions. We call these 'hubs' like you have hubs at airports for air traffic."

"But not all hubs are the same. There are no hubs that see all air traffic."

"Yes, for sure! And this is the same in the brain. Hubs may interact with many other areas, but there is no one region that sees it all. But hubs tend to interact with each other. For instance, if you need to go to Los Angeles from Moscow, you will likely fly to a European hub and then to a North American hub. We call this the 'rich club' where hubs with high capacity to interact broadly also tend to interact among themselves. It's a very efficient way to send things around a network without requiring all of it to converge to a single site."

Sara's data streamed into the BrainMaze, where it was quickly processed to build the geometry of her brain. The white matter connections and their conductivity soon filled in, along with the unique folding patterns of her cortex.

Katya continued her running commentary while she watched the data feeds. "The anatomical data only tells us what is possible, however. There is redundancy in the system where there are several paths that can get you between two different points. In your brain, the consequence of using one route versus another may show up in a change in your behaviour. You may be able to respond faster with one route, for instance. Over time, your brain will test these possibilities and use some more than others. So, besides the structural measures, we need to get functional measures to map out what your brain can do and what it actually does."

Katya connected another transmitter to the helmet to collect the bioelectric signals for Sara's brain. The information from her brain structure was used to better triangulate the signals, allowing for finer resolution of the location of the signal sources.

Sara performed simple memory tests: reciting back a list of words, trying to recognize pictures, checking to see if she could remember how to navigate between different landmarks in Berlin. Then, using a video console, she navigated through a building, trying to locate her friend's apartment based on real-time clues.

"This is a fun task because it keeps you engaged as you try to solve the puzzle and at the same time, gives us measures of your brain's navigational system and the interactions of sensory and motor systems. We'll need to supplement this when you are moving, but these data give us the foundation for estimation," Katya mentioned in-between tasks.

Sara sat up and rolled her shoulders during a break in the data collection. "I think I clenched my jaw a lot. I hope that doesn't mess up the data!"

"It should be okay," Katya replied. "Our data processing stream is quite robust to the muscle artifacts, and BrainMaze is very good at extracting the key features from the signal to give rise to function from structure."

"This last part will take only 30 minutes but is vital for BrainMaze to be helpful in the real world." Katya placed a pair of clear glasses on Sara's head. "The transmitters in the glasses are sensitive to your brain's electrical signatures, like the helmet, but with slightly lower resolution. The difference here is that we need to get a better estimate of how your brain works when you are free to move about. Even scientists sometimes forget that most of what we do involves moving around in the world, so the data we get from the constrained environment using the helmet and video games can only go so far." Katya reached around behind the eyeglass arms and attached a cable. Then she attached the other end of the cable to a point on the crown of Sarah's head. "This last channel gives us a little better resolution for your brain model."

Sara walked through a virtual environment, picking apples from trees and placing them into a cart she pulled behind her. Her task was to collect exactly 100 apples in 20 minutes. Some apples fell out of the cart as she moved to the next tree, so she had to decide whether to retrieve them or continue grabbing more so she could replace the lost ones. This also meant she had to keep a tally of how many apples fell from the cart.

"Okay, I think we are good for today." Katya came back into the test room.

"I was really enjoying that." Sara removed the glasses. "It's almost therapeutic!"

Katya laughed. "Believe me. You are not the first to say that. We have used this sort of platform for clinical therapies. We have collaborators in Israel that have used this interface to test for memory problems and develop supportive therapies. There are even some versions that help relieve stress and promote meditation. Having the brain link really helps make the personal connection.

"Anyway, we have all we need to set up your brain avatar. It will take an hour or so for BrainMaze to calibrate the avatar, so we should be able to get you started with the interface after lunch."

"That's amazingly fast, Katya. With just these data, BrainMaze will be able to read my mind!" Sara winked, recalling BGK's concern.

"Close but not exactly." Katya wanted to be accurate in her response, mindful of Sara's science background. "What we do here is set up an interface with BrainMaze that reads your potential brain states to help guide you and the device more effectively. BrainMaze doesn't have all your memories and experiences, so it cannot read your mind. It will use the data to create a personal representation of your brain's configuration and help predict which parts you will most likely visit in the current situation. Logan would call these manifolds. Mapping these for your brain can help with the simulation capacity, trying to identify the best outcomes.

"You'll need to take some time to train BrainMaze on your speech patterns, so we can use the B2S interface. You probably should wear those glasses for the rest of the day to do the training naturally, as if you are talking to other people."

TechStaff burst into the lab. "Is it my turn yet?"

"We need to bottle and sell your enthusiasm!" Katya looked over to Sara. "If you want to go check on the others, Sara, I will get her avatar creation started."

Battle simulation

After Katya finished the avatar creations, she went to the main hall to see the group gathering in the centre.

"Next exercise is to see how well you work as a team," she heard Sara say.

With Sara leading, Katya, Terry, and Logan followed the bodyguards to a door that hid a stairway to the basement. They entered a large room that had big crates scattered with what appeared to be transmitters on top.

"This is our combat simulation suite." TechStaff had somehow gotten there before them.

"It's an augmented reality environment where we can project different kinds of battle scenarios. The headsets are comparable to what we have for our Combat AI, though a bit less sophisticated." She pulled out four headsets and handed them out.

"Here are your weapons." She handed them model weapons similar to what they had used the night before.

"You'll need simulation suits as well to get full tactile input." TechStaff pointed to a row of suits hanging on the wall.

"I'd like one, too." Sara walked toward TechStaff. "I need the practice."

"It'll be better than the usual team building workshops you go to, I'm sure," Katya joked.

"Definitely." Sara put the headset on. "Let's try a city simulation. I doubt we're going to be in any mountains or valleys, so let's practise with something we are likely to encounter."

TechStaff moved over to a console and began entering information. She looked at Sara and asked, "Day or night?"

"Day. It'll probably be the only sun we'll see today."

"Coming right up." TechStaff entered a few more commands as the team donned the suits.

"Okay, here's the deal," she continued. "All of you are on the same team. We can put Sara in command since, well, because she is. The task is to navigate three city blocks and recover a black suitcase. The Combat AI has been trained to locate the suitcase, so check the info screen on your headsets for updates. The case belongs to your opponents, who you can't identify until you first encounter them. An analysis script will run when you see someone and run it through the database to ID them. They are dangerous, so don't hesitate if you feel threatened."

"Got it." Sara turned to the others. "Everyone stay put until they activate the simulation. Then we can move."

As the simulation came online, filling the headsets with a modern cityscape. The streets littered, but there were no people. The sky was bright blue, with a sun high, suggesting it was mid-day. People then appeared walking on the sidewalks as more of the simulation came online. Traffic also appeared, becoming heavier to the point of a traffic jam. The audio environment was remarkable at conveying the cacophony of a heavy downtown metropolis in the middle of the afternoon.

She's not making this easy, Sara thought, and then pointed to an alleyway. "Okay, team, let's huddle there. BGK, check that it's clear."

BGK peered into the alley. He turned back to the group, indicating it was clear. The team ran into the alley.

"Far enough," Sara said, crouching down. "Can you all see the schematic of the city on your display? It will help us set our approach.

"BGK and BGT, I want you to take the lead. Katya and I will follow, and, Terry, you take up the rear with Logan and BGL. The suitcase we are looking for apparently has a beacon that is detectable from about 50 metres, so monitor your info screens.

"Even though this is a simulation, we need to act as if it's not. Otherwise, we are wasting our time. You'll note that we are in Manhattan in the middle of the day, so if we walk out there with guns out, we're going to be noticed. I want you to holster your weapons under your jackets, and when we walk out of here, make like we are a bunch of tourists marvelling at the sites.

"Let's move," she signalled for BGK and BGT to go.

The team met a sea of people, which made navigation difficult. The simulation was sufficiently sophisticated that if one of them touched a simulated person, they would feel a bump and sometimes an appropriately colourful comment about paying attention to where they were going.

As they moved forward, they spread out in response to the flow of people coming at them.

"We are getting too spread out," Terry commented over his headset, looking back to see Logan and BGL fall behind.

"Slow down up in front," Sara responded, and glanced back

at Terry.

Katya noticed two people staring at them from across the street. As she scanned, a message popped up on her headset info screen, "IDENTIFICATION CONFIRMED."

"We have company across the street," she whispered into her headset.

Terry looked over at the same pair and received the same information on his headset. "Confirmed here, too."

BGK spoke up, "I have a signal from the case 20 metres ahead to the left."

"I expect there'll be more opponents ahead." Sara looked around. "I think we need a diversion."

Terry started walking across the street, straight toward the opponents. As he got closer, he waved his hand. "Hey, Jeff! How are you? It's been so long!"

"What the hell is he doing?" Sara hissed.

"I think this is your diversion." Katya nodded in Terry's direction.

The simulated 'Jeff' stared at Terry and spoke, "I believe you are mistaken."

"Uh, you're not Jeff? Hell, you look just like him," he said as Terry stepped toward the curb, caught his foot and stumbled.

Or at least feigned stumbling.

As he lurched forward, he reached into his jacket and drew his weapon, firing two quick shots, both of which hit the two opponents.

BGT moved fast, signalling BGK and running toward the case's signal. Katya looked over to see them moving and also noted two more opponents running from across the street ahead to intercept.

"There are two coming to intercept," Katya yelled into her headset.

Sara fired at the two opponents, yelling out to the crowd, "Everyone down!"

The simulated crowd reacted like a normal crowd and began screaming and running in random directions. One ran into Katya, knocking her down. She scrambled to the curbside behind a car to avoid getting trampled. Logan and BGL were tangled in the crowd, struggling to get to their colleagues.

Sara could no longer see any of her team. "Move to the street, to my point now!" She joined Katya behind the car.

BGL called out, "We're behind you about 40 metres. We'll hold here in case they double back."

"Acknowledged." Sara glanced back to confirm their location.

"This is fun!" Katya smiled broadly.

Sara looked at her. "I'm glad you're entertained. Man, we messed that one up! We've lost our advantage in all this chaos."

"Maybe there is an advantage in chaos." Terry came up behind them, holding the suitcase. "Does this mean we win?"

"We're under fire!" BGK called.

Sara checked her information screen and located them. "We'll be there in a second." She motioned for the three of them to move out around the car. "Stay low!"

As they passed three more vehicles, Sara signalled for Terry to go back around the car while she and Katya moved ahead. The information screen showed that BGK and BGT were close.

Terry peered over the car and saw BGK and BGT crouched near a trash can. They were taking fire from a point up the street that he could not see. "I'll draw their fire, Sara. You and Katya can then take them out."

"Terry!" Sara yelled.

Terry jumped out from beside a car and fired several rounds high and toward the opponents. He then jumped back as he heard the fire returned, shattering the glass in the car.

Sara saw the source of the opponent's fire and moved quickly, motioning for Katya to follow. They saw two opponents firing from the back of a pickup truck and then ducking to avoid return fire. Sara and Katya took the opportunity when the opponents were ducking to run closer to the truck. As the opponents rose to fire another volley, Sara shot twice, knocking out both.

"Nicely done!" Katya yelled.

Sara ducked down. "We're not done yet. My info feed says there are two more around still. Can you see anyone?"

"Heading your way from the rear," BGL replied. "We're in pursuit, but the crowd is still heavy."

Katya peered around, seeing Terry crouching with the case next to him. The crowd continued to run around them, but none registered as opponents.

Katya motioned to Terry to come over to them. He ran across the street in a crouch, carrying the case in one hand and his weapon in the other. He stopped looking at Sara and Katy, and he dropped to one knee and fired several rounds toward them.

"What are you doing?" Katya yelled, but then turned to see the rounds hit two opponents who had come up behind them.

"According to my info feed, that was the last of them, and I have the case, so we win, right?" Terry held the case up again.

"End simulation!" Sara yelled, walking toward Terry. "What the hell was that?"

Terry glanced down at his hand. "I got the case, and we're all okay."

Sara tapped his chest with her finger. "That's the problem. You said, 'I got the case,' not 'we.' It has to be a team effort, Terry. This is just a simulation, but if you pulled that shit in an actual battle, we might not have been so lucky. Where did you disappear to when BGK and BGT were trapped? You should have been helping them out!"

"When I saw they were pinned down but well-protected, I went ahead to where the case was and grabbed it before the opponents saw me. I got the case, Sara, and no one died." Terry tried to stay calm.

Sara continued, "I realize you guys aren't soldiers and aren't used to following the chain of command, but you need to at least follow my instructions out here. I'm focused on our goal and how to do it without getting anyone killed. If there had been a slight miscalculation on your part about whether the team had adequate cover, we could have lost them, and probably you, too." Her voice was stern.

Terry looked over at Katya for support, but she shook her head. "Fine, I get it. Pay attention to what the boss says." He dropped the case and walked away.

Katya walked up to Sara. "Please don't be angry with him, Sara. He is always this way. Sometimes, when he has an idea, he will act. This has made him a very successful scientist. I can see how that would not make him a great soldier."

Sara turned to Katya. Her expression was calm. "Damn right. Maybe it doesn't matter. I don't know. We don't know what we are up against, so maybe I am letting my fears get the best of me. I want to be ready in case we end up in a fight. We don't have the resources to pull in an army, Katya. This is all we have." She pointed to the rest of the team.

BGL and Logan walked up.

"I didn't see what happened." Logan removed his headset.

"Our friend's playing cowboy." Katya gestured toward Terry.

"Somehow, that does not surprise me." Logan turned to Terry. "What is that phrase? Yippee ki yay mother…"

"Don't," Terry interrupted. "Just don't."

BGT walked up to Terry, smacking him on the shoulder. "That was awesome, mate! You must have done this before!"

"Nah, I play a lot of video games." Terry chuckled. "This is a good one but follows a typical pattern."

"Oh, really? How about we grab a quick coffee, and you can tell me about it? I'd like to learn more about how we can make these simulations more realistic."

Sara ran up to them. "I'd like to join you for that."

Katya looked over to TechStaff. "Shall we continue with the technical developments while they debrief?"

"You don't want coffee?" TechStaff asked.

"No, I have had too much already." Katya glanced around for a bathroom.

Terry

Sara, BGT, and Terry entered the lounge area and walked toward the water cooler. Terry wiped the sweat off his face before he grabbed a glass of water. BGT prepared three coffees and set them at a table. They started with small talk to cut the tension.

"When's lunch?" Terry asked.

"In an hour or so," Sara replied. "Sebastian and Yvette went out to grab some stuff for us."

"I see." Terry turned his gaze to his coffee cup.

"Despite my initial reaction, Terry, you did quite well in

simulation today." Sara tried to shift the conversation.

"Yeah, I guess it was okay." Terry continued to stare into his coffee cup.

BGT sat back and placed his cup down. "So, aside from being a decent shot with a weapon, maybe a gamer, and, of course, a brilliant scientist, is there anything else that I should know about you that will make our jobs a little easier?"

Terry looked up at BGT and paused before speaking. "Not really. We're not going into war, from what I understand, so I think the combined intellects of my partners and I should be enough for the team."

"Sure." BGT leaned forward. "I was looking at the recording of the target practice you did yesterday. You're an impressive shot. Far better than I would have reckoned, given your background."

"You recorded us?" Terry was a bit surprised.

Sara put her cup down. "We record every training session for us to review, so we can come up with a better strategy for the team. It'll save us time."

Terry contemplated his response. "Makes sense. Are we being recorded now?"

"No, I don't think so. No point in that really."

BGT sat back. "One thing I did notice in the recording and the simulation was that you shoot with both eyes open. That's not something you see a lot in amateurs, and to me, it suggests you've had quite a lot of experience. I mean, keeping both eyes open is something you do in the field so that you don't limit your vision in case you need to respond to something unexpected. It was quite obvious in the battle simulation."

Terry bit his lip. "Well, hunting birds can get quite hairy if there is a large flock."

"Yeah, maybe. You know, I suspect that there's something you're not telling us, Terry." BGT sat back. "Keep in mind that it's my job to watch your back, so I need to know as much as I can to do my job. I'd think you'd appreciate that as a scientist, in the sense that you can do a better job with a collaborator if you know what skills they do and do not have. We need to work as a team here. You're not just a scientist, mate. You've seen battle."

Sara sipped her coffee. "There is another issue, Terry. As part of the planning for getting your team cleared with us, we needed to run background checks. It's standard, of course, especially since you will be privy to a lot of the inner workings of the AI system."

"Yeah, I figured you needed to check our credentials." Terry focused on his cup.

"It's more than that. We needed to do a security check. Your colleagues came through with flying colours, having been basically nerds for most of their lives. But we couldn't get such information on you. Every time we tried to get information before your undergraduate work, we'd hit a wall, or, maybe better, a hole. It's as if you just appeared on the planet and then went to university."

Terry shifted in his chair. "I can't help it if your records are faulty."

Sara leaned forward. "They're not faulty. There is no full record of Terry Chatan from Canada before 20 years ago. It's not an error. Whoever you were before, that was wiped clean. If it wasn't for my insistence, you would not have been cleared."

There was an extended silence as Terry gazed at his coffee cup, swirling the remaining coffee with his spoon. "We are not being recorded, right?"

"Where did you see combat?" Sara asked.

Terry did not look up. "Mainly in rural Alberta."

"I don't remember hearing about a war in Alberta."

"Well, some wars aren't what you call conventional." Terry looked up at Sara, "especially if there are criminals."

"You were involved in a crime war?"

BGT set his cup down. "Nah, he's joshin'. How could you be involved in a crime war and not have been arrested or killed?"

Terry looked up, raising an eyebrow.

"Informant? You became an informant?" Sara's eyes widened.

Terry sat back and collected his thoughts. He felt he could trust Sara, given her position both as Council Chair and the lead of the Special Ops team. Since BGT was under her leadership, he would naturally have to keep quiet.

"Look, I can tell you about this, but none of my friends know about it. My wife doesn't even know! Promise to keep this between us, please. Even though this was over 20 years ago, there could still be some nastiness that'll come back to my family and me." Terry sat forward.

Sara looked over to BGT. "You can trust us completely, Terry."

Terry exhaled. "When we were growing up, the economy in my hometown was not so great. The weather wreaked havoc on the farmland, which not only hit the farmers but also the industry that surrounded it. Food processing plants downsized or closed, farm machinery shops closed, shipping companies downsized; it wasn't a very hopeful environment.

"I was not the best kid in school and was more interested in partying than studying. I had very little trouble with the material they taught us, so I could afford to slack off. There weren't many real jobs, so we found creative ways to get extra money, which ultimately involved moving illegal drugs in from the West Coast through to the US border. Stuff would come in from the interior of BC, and we'd haul it down. The US border in Alberta was easier to cross because there were a lot of farm roads and far fewer customs agents. We started moving pot, and then it expanded to other stuff.

"We made a lot of money that way, but then other groups got wind of what was going down and tried to move in. The gangs in Vancouver started intercepting deliveries and taking the merchandise back to Vancouver, or maybe overseas. Then we started seeing groups from out east moving in.

"We got pretty good at outsmarting them, at first by taking alternate routes and changing our routines. I remember one time when we put a shipment in the middle of a truckload of pigs, it gave the stuff an interesting aroma." Terry chuckled.

"But it got to the point where the gangs stopped playing nice and started attacking. We had to learn quickly to fight, or we were going to end up dead. Having some experience shooting through hunting helped, but we were just kids. One guy we worked for was ex- militia, so he gave us more formal training in the fine art of combat.

"I'm sort of embarrassed to say this now, but we ate this stuff up. We got very effective quickly, and having grown up on the prairie, we knew how to take advantage of the open terrain. There were a lot of nasty firefights that didn't go well. There were more than enough casualties to go around." Terry rubbed a scar on his neck.

"Anyway, one of the West Coast gangs knew they were going

to lose more by fighting us, so they cut a deal with our supplier to share in the profits in exchange for helping fend off the other gangs, both from the west and the east."

"I am really surprised we didn't hear about this," Sara interrupted. "I imagine there was a lot of violence, and in small-town Alberta, that can't go unnoticed."

"True, though with the firepower we had, I think the attitude was that the authorities would leave us alone, so long as we just killed each other. At least that was true for the local cops. There was stuff going on federally and between the US and Canada, but that didn't affect us directly." Terry paused and sipped the last of his coffee.

"At least, not at first. When the merger happened, things really blew up. The Vancouver gangs started fighting on their home turf but then carried the battles elsewhere to do preemptive strikes for the eastern groups as well.

"Then came the retaliations. An eastern gang came to my hometown one evening and tried to burn the whole place down. The battles went from being about the drugs to just being about revenge. We were lucky we fought our way out, but there were some innocents hit.

"That's when the hammer came down hard on us. The RCMP grabbed me from my home early one morning and gave me a pretty hard grilling. I think they realized I wasn't high up enough in the organization to have critical information, but I knew how to get it.

"So, in exchange for protecting my family, I started working for the RCMP. I would give them tips on timing a shipment's arrival and who was likely to be there. They were less interested in taking the merchandise than in getting key figures.

"About two months undercover, I was told about a meeting of some of the key leaders at the distribution centre in BC. The cops swooped in and took everyone into custody. A few had outstanding US warrants and others plea-bargained. This effective stopped the activity from the Vancouver gangs, and with a loss of the shipping capacity, the eastern gangs pulled back.

"They moved my family and me up to Edmonton and then out east, where I decided to go to university rather than fry my brain on drugs." Terry sat back and placed his empty cup aside.

BGT had a skeptical look. "That's it?"

"I don't think I need to go into the details of the battles. I am not proud of those days. Many people got hurt physically and emotionally, and some got killed for being in the wrong place at the wrong time. I'm not a soldier like you. I didn't keep track of my kills," Terry snapped.

"Sorry, man, I didn't mean any offence." BGT stood and walked over to Terry. "I've had a lot of battles myself and lost some good people. I'd like to think we are in a better society now, where that kind of insanity is all but gone. I guess I find some comfort in the possibility that what we did then may have helped move us to where we are today, so those losses were not all in vain."

Terry looked at BGT. "It doesn't make the pain any less, BGT."

"Call me Mick, okay? The BGT thing isn't necessary in here." BGT stood up.

Terry nodded. He didn't appreciate what a burden his history had on him and felt some relief that he could share a bit.

"Okay, Mick. Uh, so as I said, I'd appreciate it if you both kept this between us. I don't think Katya and Logan would be happy to know that I'm not the angel they think I am."

Sara sat back in her chair, smiling. "I appreciate the honesty. I am going to sound presumptive here, but I assume your combat skills are probably a little rusty? I'd like to polish them. We need all the expertise we can get."

"I'm not killing anyone, Sara. That's not in my repertoire anymore."

"I understand and appreciate that. But I think your tactical experience will be helpful. We have Mick and team to do the heavy lifting if needed. We need you for your brains. If your brain can contribute to integrating BrainMaze and helping us tactically, if we get in trouble, I'd say that's a pretty good deal."

Terry wasn't sure how to respond.

Katya

Katya was stretching in the centre room, trying to work out a knot she had in her lower back. She tried several yoga poses and then a few ballistic movements to test the muscle.

"You're in pretty good shape for a scientist." BGK was watching from the side.

"I will take that for what it's worth," she replied.

"No, I didn't mean it as an insult. I've worked with a few scientists in my career, and they would not have been able to handle the action we've given you so far."

"Well, my friends and I do a lot of running. There is a therapeutic effect, but it's also great for fitness, of course. I am actually quite fast, maybe even faster than my friends." She smiled.

BGK was skeptical. "You don't have the muscle mass for that

kind of speed. I can see you being good at endurance runs, but short sprints, no way."

Katya laughed. "But I don't need the muscle mass of a sprinter! I am smaller than you, so the weight I have to move is much less than you. That makes it much easier for me to move fast."

"Katya, that may be true, but there is no way you are faster than me," BGK said, half-joking and half-challenging her.

"Maybe not in a full sprint, but in complicated terrain, I would easily win." She turned to continue stretching.

Baren had been listening and intervened. "This is a good segue to the last training exercise, the obstacle course! We can go to the next floor where we have our training course set up."

Katya laughed aloud. "Was this planned all along?"

Katya and BGK followed Baren into another room, where there was a spiral staircase to the second floor. Terry went with TechStaff and Sara to receive some additional training on the Combat AI's tactical programming. Logan continued to work out on the heavy bag. He found his memory for the movements was better than his muscles would allow.

The obstacle course was in a room much larger than the main floor. There were no additional rooms along the side, and the ceiling was substantially higher. The course contained a series of wooden ramps of varied configurations, with gaps that would require leaping across to navigate. There were several taller structures that a participant would need to climb over and a trough of water about 1 metre deep and 20 metres long.

Baren turned up the light in the room, revealing small flags with arrows that marked the route through the course.

"Normally, we do laps through this for training, but with the challenge on the table, I propose you do two laps. BGK has done this before, so he has a slight advantage, but hopefully, that will be gone the second time through. The starting point is over there." Baren pointed to an orange flag at the far end of the room.

Katya and BGK jogged over to the flag. Katya lined up in a ready stance, while BGK bounced in place.

"GO!" Baren yelled.

The first part was a full-out sprint of about 40 metres, where BGK took the lead for the first half, and Katya closed ground by the end. The course then turned to a 3-metre climbing wall. In her flexible shoes, Katya made up significant time, and the two landed on the other side of the wall simultaneously.

The next was a series of ropes that were used to swing over obstacles, like holes or water. Katya and BGK were even through this until Katya's hand slipped on the last rope, and she hit the edge of a water trap. She quickly regained her footing, noting this problem for the next lap.

BGK was now about 10 metres ahead of Katya and was approaching dangling rope that led up to a catwalk. A safety net was below the ropes and the catwalk, but also added an extra challenge of getting to the ropes. BGK went beneath the net, grasped the edge of it and pulled himself up and around like a circus acrobat. Katya saw enough to know what to do when she got to the net. BGK grabbed the rope and ascended with ease at first, but about halfway up, he felt his back muscles tightening, so used his feet more to steady himself. Katya had almost caught up by the time he got to the catwalk. The catwalk it was shaky as BGK's heavy footstep resonated across the base. Katya tried to match her steps with his to minimize the interference with her progress. The descent from the catwalk was also on a rope. BGK's muscles spasmed again, slowing him down as Katya passed and hit the net first.

The next obstacle was the long water trough. Katya jumped in and was surprised to find it deeper than expected, with a slippery bottom that made footing difficult. The soles of her shoes found some of grip, but she slipped several times when she tried to increase her stride. She heard BGK enter the water, and rather than running in the water, he swam. He would overtake her soon. They emerged from the pool and ran through a series of slalom obstacles before coming to the last wall. This was almost 10 metres and resembled a very steep hill with a rope hanging down. BGK grabbed the rope and used it to walk up the wall, relying on his strength for the climb. Katya tried first to climb with the rope. She mimicked BGK's technique but found the coordination difficult. At the top, there was also a rope for the descent, which BGK grabbed quickly and repelled down. He turned and faced another hill obstacle. As he did before, he climbed to the top and rappelled down the side. Katya struggled with the second ascent but did better on her rappel this time.

When she landed, she turned to see BGK with a 20-metre lead heading in to start the second lap. She sprinted hard, but could not close the distance. BGK was as determined to win as she was. The distance between them remained the same after the first wall. At the rope swing, Katya was closing the gap, successfully navigating the last water obstacle. At the rope climb, BGK's back was less tight, and he scaled to the catwalk faster than in the first lap. Katya also felt stronger on the rope climb and, once at the top of the catwalk, saw the distance between them getting smaller.

She got to the end of the catwalk and saw that BGK was halfway down. She opted for a new strategy for her descent and let go of the rope, falling to the net below.

BGK and Katya hit the net at the same time. "You're crazy!" BGK shouted as he dismounted from the net.

At the water trough, both used the swim strategy. BGK hit the water too hard, so lost some ground to Katya, but they emerged at the end in a tie.

The two final hills came up faster than Katya remembered. BGK had enough momentum to leap up the side before he grabbed the rope to continue the climb. Katya tried to do the same and was successful for the first few steps, but then lost the cadence and her feet slipped. She held on to the rope and got her footing back. She looked up to see BGK clearing the top of the first hill.

Katya got to the top and looked down to see BGK almost at the bottom. She decided she again needed a different strategy if she was going to win this. She gauged the distance and then leaped from the top of the first hill toward the top of the second hill. The strategy was almost successful. She landed only a half metre from the edge but grabbed the rope. She quickly pulled herself to the top.

"That's cheating, Katya!" BGK yelled from below.

Katya rappelled down the side of the second hill and ran as fast as she could through the slalom course and toward the finish line. She felt BGK closing in as she sprinted for the last 20 metres.

She did, however, cross the finish line first.

Katya fell to the floor, laughing and out of breath. "I am so sorry if you think I cheated. I'm a scientist. I simply tested a new hypothesis."

BGK bent over to catch his breath.

"I think she likes you." Baren patted BGK on the shoulder.

Evening Day 2

"Okay, everyone, we can break for the day," Sara called out from the centre of the main room. "The Professors and bodyguards can head back to the hotel. We have a larger vehicle ready for you. We'll reconvene tomorrow morning for our last training exercise and complete the plans for our trip overseas."

Sara turned to Baren and the two engaged in a private conversation.

"I guess we can go?" Terry shrugged, looking over at his colleagues.

"Rest well. Yvette and I have some work to finish up, so we'll see you tomorrow," TechStaff moved toward their patchwork lab, followed by Yvette.

The trio and bodyguards exited the facility to see what looked like a modernized microbus. The side door opened, and a voice said, "Welcome, please come in. I will take you to your hotel so that you may rest."

Logan shook his head while entering the vehicle. "I still can't get used to this. The next thing we know, it's going to make dinner suggestions."

"I am happy to provide such information, but they have instructed me to take you directly to the hotel," the vehicle replied. "However, there is an excellent Lebanese food truck en route."

"Excellent? Now we get food suggestions from something that doesn't eat." Logan rolled his eyes.

The door closed, and the vehicle began to move. For the first several minutes, there was silence.

Terry looked over. "So, how did it go with the brain avatar creation, Katya?"

"I think very well." Katya gazed at the floor. "Yvette and Kim will work on training with BrainMaze tonight, I imagine. Sara seems to have picked up the idea quickly, but I do not know if she will have the time to do much training before tomorrow. Using the B2S system will be a challenge."

"I get the feeling that Sara will forgo sleep to get herself ready." Terry looked out the window as they passed the river and approached the main street.

"Besides talking to each other using brain waves, what else will this interface do?" BGK remained uncomfortable with the concept.

"Well, I know you weren't at the Council presentation I gave, but it also acts to interface with the AI system, providing new information to guide decisions. This is really where I think BrainMaze excels in intersecting our brain networks with AI."

"So then, you can interact with any AI system?"

"In principle, yes, but we may need to work on the interface. Simple AI systems would not benefit from such an interface. Though we could guide their operation, with a limited repertoire, the AI system would not be able to do anything new. Like if we tried to control the lighting system — at the end of the day, it's only about turning lights on and off.

"Other systems that have a broader capacity and may learn new behaviours and thus find solutions to problems that were not previously possible."

The vehicle slowed to a stop. "The food truck is in front of us. Would you like to exit and place orders?"

"You bet. I am starving!!" BGK was the first to jump out of the vehicle.

"Of course, some non-AI systems may also have a limited repertoire, eh?" BGT laughed as he watched BGK run to the food truck.

Chapter Six:
Training Day 3

One last simulation

The next morning, the trio stumbled into the awaiting vehicle, feeling less enthusiastic about the day ahead. None of them slept well.

The three bodyguards were already in their seats.

Logan grimaced as he sat. "Oh, when did I get this old?" He massaged a sore muscle in his shoulder.

"You'll pass me soon." Terry laughed.

Katya was scanning her Motif to evaluate the outcome for the new combined interface for BrainMaze and Combat AI. The simulations she had set to run all completed, but there were some significant delays in responses, especially going from the BrainMaze to the AI system. She considered putting in a parallel stream that would flag the user when there was a delay so that it would not leave them hanging.

"What's up, Katya?" Terry tried to get her attention.

Katya was silent.

Terry reached over and tapped her leg. "Hey, you okay?"

"Oh, sorry." She snapped her attention away from the display.

"Something engaging in *Der Spiegel* newsfeed this morning?" Logan smiled.

Katya chuckled. "No, no. I am concerned about the reliability of the BrainMaze interface. The link between the systems is not working well."

Terry asked, "Is this because the data are unreliable? BrainMaze's output is in terms of likely outcomes, whereas I think the AI system is expecting categorical answers."

"This is a good point," Katya answered. "We didn't consider this when we set up the connection."

"Maybe you can simply put in a filter between the two systems," Logan offered. "This will harness BrainMaze's predictive coding capabilities but distill the output to something the AI should be able to handle."

Katya agreed. "I like this idea, but I am not sure we can get the algorithms trained before we test them today."

"No better way to train them than in actual use," Terry said. "Well, simulated actual use," he corrected himself.

Katya inserted a filter routine, a software library in the connection between BrainMaze and the Combat AI, and set the program to re-compile. "Let's hope this helps."

The vehicle stopped in front of the training facility, and the group exited. Sara and TechStaff had also just arrived carrying two bags with enticing aromas.

"We got there just as the croissants were coming out of the oven." Sara smiled.

"This will be a good day," Logan replied.

Inside, Baren and Yvette were sketching a flowchart on a virtual display.

"Good morning, my friends," Baren said as he walked toward the team. "Let me unpack the goodies that you brought." He reached for the bag of croissants.

Sara handed the bag to Baren, who immediately grabbed a croissant and bit into it. "Sorry, it is a guilty pleasure of mine. I cannot resist," he said with a mouthful. "Mitchell will not bring them home for us anymore because he thinks I am getting too fat." He patted his stomach, smiling.

"What have you got planned for the simulation today?" Sara studied the display.

"I thought it would be good to continue with the cityscape since that's where we are heading. I've put in a few more authentic features to capture the terrain at our destination." Yvette pointed to the schematics of the street grid.

"Nice! How long until it's ready?"

"It's compiling now. We need to reconfigure the simulation space too, so I'd give it about 30 minutes."

"Perfect, that will give Katya the time to brief us on the new interface while we chow down on a few of these lovely creatures." Sara looked over at the croissants that were now on a tray next to the coffee.

Katya was talking to TechStaff when she heard her name. "Sure, I can do that. But only if I get a coffee first. My brain is not quite awake yet."

"You move to the front of the line!" Sara motioned for Katya to go to the table.

Katya took a cup from the table and filled it with coffee, leaving a little space for warmed milk. She walked over to the display and set the cup down next to it. She removed her Motif from her belt and set up a link to the display.

She took a sip of coffee. "We've been able to set up a rough link between BrainMaze and the Combat AI. It basically works by using the AI system's capacity to synthesize massive amounts of data, with BrainMaze's capacity to simulate multiple scenarios as an adaptive system. It will also integrate the user into the scenarios to better direct their next course of action. The merger gets the best of both worlds, similar to what we proposed for the Global AI system."

"Except this one is used for combat." TechStaff sounded a little fiendish.

"Exactly," Katya continued. "We will take the data feed from the AI system and the added information in BrainMaze to run real-time simulations and update the tactics as the mission progresses.

"You should not notice any appreciable difference in the interface output, but we have noted a slight delay sometimes occurs when the two systems are interfacing. I put an indicator on the displays to show you when this is happening, with directional arrows showing data flow direction. If it turns red, that means there is a delay."

Baren spoke up. "How long are these delays? I can see this being a problem in the heat of battle if we are stuck waiting for a calculation."

"No more than a half a second, but most of them have been shorter. I have tried to put a patch in after I talked to my colleagues this morning about it so that it may be negligible now."

"We've also enabled the B2S system for Sara, Kim and Yvette. It only works for pairwise conversation, so you will need to specify who you want to connect with, and then the link will be made. You do that with the menu where you focus on the name of the person you want to talk to.

"I suggest we use this judiciously as it takes time to get used to and may be a distraction for some." Katya remembered walking into a closed door when testing an earlier version of the interface, trying to link up with Logan.

"Can we try it?" TechStaff asked.

"Sure, we have a bit of time." Katya looked over at Logan. "Perhaps you and Logan can test it since you know the system already."

Logan popped the last piece of croissant into his mouth and stood up from the table where he was sitting. "My pleasure."

TechStaff and Logan donned their goggles and connected to Combat AI. They both saw the display come online with "READY" displayed in the upper corner.

"As before, the system uses your eye movements to navigate the menu. If you check the READY icon, you'll see the drop-down menu has a B2S option. If you move your gaze to it and fixate, it will select the function," Katya instructed.

"Okay, got it," TechStaff replied.

"Good. You should now see a list of available links you can make. Since Logan is the only one on the system, you'll see your name and his name."

"Yep, cool!"

"Okay, here is the hard part. Look at Logan's name and think about what you want to say to him. Keep it short and succinct. Once you're done, glance away, and the system will interpret and send the utterance. Try to stay focused while you generate the phrase, so you don't get the wrong word or phrase stuck in."

"Understood," TechStaff responded. She glanced at Logan's name and thought, *Hello, Logan,* and then glanced away.

"UNABLE TO TRANSLATE" appeared on her display.

Katya was monitoring the communication. "Try again. Imagine the phrase exactly how you say it. Don't go too slow or over-pronounce."

TechStaff tried again, thinking, *Hello, Logan,* and glanced away.

"HELLO LOGIN" came across to Logan.

"Not bad," he said aloud, "but I am already logged in."

"That's pretty good, Kim. The system will learn more about your sub-articulation patterns, and with grammar and syntax tools, it will usually be able to differentiate between ambiguous words," Katya said.

"Why don't I see the message I've sent?" TechStaff asked.

"We disabled that for now, but we can put it on if you wish. Once you get used to the system, you'll find it distracting because if it makes a mistake, you'll spend more time trying to correct it, which can clog the system. You'd be surprised how much a receiver can decipher from a misinterpreted message. The human brain is pretty good at getting the gist based on context."

Logan sent TechStaff a message, *Move away from the table and toward Katya.*

"MOVE AWAY FROM TABLE TOWARD KATYA" was transmitted, dropping 'the' and 'and.' TechStaff understood and moved toward Katya.

She looked over at Logan and then glanced up at his name.

"SEXY CROISSANT" came over to Logan.

Logan laughed out loud. "That is a most unique compliment!"

"Sorry, sorry, I was thinking how nice it would be to have a croissant since I haven't had one yet and forgot that I was connected," TechStaff said with slight embarrassment.

"FETCH ME A CROISSANT" came over Logan's HUD.

"BY YOUR COMMAND," came back to TechStaff, followed by Logan handing her a croissant.

Katya called out, "Excellent, you two. I think we are almost ready to go to the simulation now." She looked over at Yvette.

"Yep, ready to go," Yvette acknowledged.

Sara spoke up, "Great, let's get to the simulation suite and test this all." She looked at TechStaff and Yvette. "Can you two monitor the group for this one? I want to make sure we have good data from the headsets on the team's performance."

TechStaff tried to hide her disappointment in not being part of the team. "Sure, it will be nice to see it in action."

"One more item," Sara added, holding up a belt with small black packets attached to them. "Each of these packets contains a small explosive. It's meant to distract rather than destroy. You tear the tab, and toss it hard against a solid surface, and it blows up."

Sara demonstrated, throwing a package hard to the floor in front of her. The detonation was loud enough to startle with a sizable flash and a bit of smoke. "One of these won't do much damage if you hit a person, other than maybe some burns and bruising. Of course, if you toss a dozen at something, then you might be getting too serious. We can use simulated versions of these today to see how it goes."

The group entered the simulation suite. The lights were intense, making the room hotter than the rest of the building. The crates were configured in a wide 'V' with a stacked cluster at the apex.

"Phew, it's hot in here." Terry whistled.

"We wanted to get the temperature up as high as possible to simulate the climate we will encounter there. It gets into the forties sometimes during the day, and the humidity is very high," Yvette replied.

"Maybe we should keep our outings to nighttime." Terry wiped the sweat from his face.

The simulation gear was laid out with the names for each person taped to the back.

"The suits are going to make it feel hotter, so watch yourself that you don't exert too much," Yvette added. "We'll be monitoring vitals in the control booth."

"How long does the simulation last?" Logan asked.

"We have set it up so that you have to attain a goal, so will go on as long as it takes for you to reach that goal."

Logan smiled. "Great, we'll be done before lunch."

"Or maybe even morning coffee," Katya added.

"I'm glad you all have maintained your confidence," Sara remarked.

"Sebastian, did you get the brief on the mission?" she continued.

Baren was still reading his device as he walked up. "Yes. It seems relatively straightforward. There is a communication hub we are to locate. We'll be getting feeds from the AI that monitors the network traffic and will help us triangulate. We are to disable the hub so that we can run diagnostics." He turned to Katya. "The key here is 'disable.'"

Katya responded with a big smile. "Why are you looking at me?"

"Let's roll, folks," Sara shouted out.

Yvette and TechStaff moved to the control room, and Sara motioned for the rest of the team to gather around her.

"For this one, I'd like the Professors to work with the bodyguards to take the lead. Make sure you can see each other's feed. I want you to act as a unit. Sebastian and I will take up the rear and try to provide you with a broader perspective, in case we need to split up. We'll be Team 1. Let's try the interfaces."

Each of the bodyguards checked in with their assignment.

BGT: "Terry, can you see me? We're Team 2."

Terry glanced at his display. "Yes."

BGK: "Katya, can you see me? We're Team 3."

Katya scanned her display. "Very clear, yes."

BGL: "Logan, can you see me? We're team 4."

Logan hesitated. "Uh, just a moment." He tapped his goggles. "It's quite weak. Kim, can you check my link?"

TechStaff look at her display, which registered all eight team members. "You're showing okay on my side," she said over the intercom. "Maybe it's your goggles?"

"They were working just a few moments ago when we did the B2S test," Logan replied. "Maybe it's some interference from the simulation gear, but let's not waste any more time. It will do for now."

"Okay, Yvette and I can check it out later." TechStaff looked at Yvette to confirm.

"Start the simulation," Sara called out.

The scene evolved to a collection of old buildings lining a wide street. As the simulation came into focus, they saw that the wide street was an open-air market. Booths materialized with arrays of textiles, jewellery, produce and breads. People appeared, populating the market to the point where there was a sea of heads for some distance.

Sara turned to look at the control booth, shrugging her shoulders. "Could you make it any harder? All you need to do now is add in some cattle." Before she finished her comment, she heard the sound of livestock. "Great," she muttered.

"Hey, you wanted real," TechStaff responded on the comm channel.

Katya scanned the crowd, admiring the accuracy of the simulation. "This reminds me of the markets we went to in my childhood. I can almost smell it!"

"That's Terry," Logan said.

Terry bumped Logan as he started walking ahead.

"Hold for a sec, Terry," Sara called. "Let's check the network activity and get our bearings."

The group scanned the scene. The AI system collected, analyzed, and displayed the network flows from the group. The collective feeds were combined to provide a composite of the entire scene. There were multiple points scattered around the market space that became focal points, but then quickly dissipated. The most consistent focus was a building at the apex of the market space.

Baren said to Sara, "I think the crowd is too dense for us to proceed together. I suggest we split into pairs and meet at the apex."

"Agreed," Sara responded. "Holster your weapons, and let's proceed. Team 4, BGL and Logan, take the middle section. Team 3, BGK and Katya, do a parallel path to the east. And Team 2, BGT and Terry, do the same to the west. Sebastian and I will move along on the edge and try to track your progress. Make sure you check your displays for the rest of the team's positions. Keep the chatter to a minimum."

The team proceeded into the crowd. *This is amazing*, Katya thought as she reached out and touched a small goat. The teams quickly lost sight of each other as they waded into the crowd.

Logan peered at his display and saw that his colleagues had gotten ahead of him. Sara and Baren kept to the rear position. Logan turned to BGL to motion that they should move faster.

With no enemies in the marketplace, there was no reason for caution.

Terry watched the crowd in front of him, looking for any odd movements. Most of the people were focused on conversations and selling their wares, save for two that were surreptitiously glancing at them. Terry focused on his B2S menu and sent a comment to BGT.

"THINK WE ARE BEING TRACKED. CHECK 10 OCLOCK"

BGT nodded.

TechStaff's voice came over the team's headsets, "Teams 2 and 4 have indicated there may be hostiles. Team 1, can you see them?"

"Yes, we are tracking all three," Sara replied, as she and Sebastian moved to slightly higher ground.

Katya lost sight of the people.

"CAN YOU SEE THEM?" she sent to BGK.

BGK shook his head, pointing forward, indicating they should continue moving. They arrived at the building first. There were four levels, each one slightly smaller than the preceding, giving it a slight impression of a pyramid. The ornate finishings on the exterior gave it the appearance of a museum, or perhaps a temple.

Katya looked back to see Terry and BGT emerge from the crowd. Sara and Baren stood off in the distance, still monitoring the market.

Logan stood in the middle of a collection of tents, staring at four people who blocked their path. BGL had already taken a position in front of him, standing ready to engage.

"What is your business here?" one of the people asked.

"We are tourists and are interested in seeing the market.

We've heard so many wonderful things about it!" BGL replied, trying to sound enthusiastic.

The person stepped toward them. "If you are tourists, you must have a visa. May we see it, please?"

Logan reached into his jacket.

"Slowly, please," the person cautioned.

Logan pulled out a card and offered it.

The person grabbed the card and read it. "This appears to be a coupon for fried chicken."

Logan smiled. "It's all yours," and shot his palm into the person's chest, knocking him backward.

A second person moved toward Logan but was intercepted by BGL, who knocked the person sideways.

The other two people turned and ran toward the temple.

BGL activated her mic. "Hostiles encountered. Heading to the building."

"Copy," Sara replied. "Team 2, heads-up. Hostiles coming your way. Don't let them get to the building. We don't want them to alert whoever is inside."

Terry looked to the crowd and saw the two people weaving their way through the crowd. "See them. We will intercept."

"No weapons," Sara said. "There's a crowd here, and we don't want collateral damage or a panic."

Terry took his hand off his weapon and looked over to BGT, who had moved up one level of stairs in front of the building to watch the crowd.

"They're still running together. I think we can get to them before they get to the steps," BGT moved down and motioned for Terry to follow. They moved parallel to the front of the crowd, watching the two people's progress. Katya and BGK were running toward them.

BGT tackled the first one as they emerged from the crowd, restraining him with plastic handcuffs.

The second stopped and turned to run back into the crowd. Logan and BGL tried to cut them off, but they ran to the stairs.

Terry stepped over to block the person, but wasn't fast enough. He reached for his weapon.

Logan grabbed Terry's arm. "No weapons, remember?"

Terry frowned, looking over at Logan and back at the hostile, who disappeared into the building.

BGK sprinted from the crowd to intercept the hostile, but he was too late.

"Last hostile escaped," BGK called into his mic.

Katya came behind BGK. "I think we better move away from the crowd. We are attracting too much attention now."

Small groups in the crowd were pointing at the team on the stairs.

Sara and Baren came up.

Sara looked around the building. "Kim, what's your assessment?"

"It's hard to get a lock on the comm flow. The hub is definitely inside the building, but I can't pinpoint the exact location."

Sara motioned to the team to move toward the temple. "We need to get that hostile before they get to the comm hub." She pointed to the other handcuff hostiles.

They arrived at the atrium in front of an enormous staircase. The stairs split at the top in both directions.

"According to the schematics, there is only one stairway that connects each level," TechStaff relayed to Sara.

Sara signalled to pause and huddle. "Okay, these stairs are

the only way in and out. I suggest we each take a floor and try to find the hub and the hostile. Team 4 to the top, Team 3 on the next, and then Team 2. We'll check out this floor. Keep your audio muted but active. Let's try to use B2S when we can."

The teams ascended the first stairwell. Team 2, Terry and BGT, stayed at the base of the next, while Teams 3 and 4 went up the next set. Team 3, Logan and BGL paused on the next floor while Team 4 went up the last set of stairs. Katya sprinted up the stairs ahead of BGK.

"TEAM 4 IN POSITION?" Sara asked Katya.

"A MOMENT," Katya replied, looking back to see BGK coming from behind her. "IN POSITION."

"You need to be more careful about pursuits, Katya. Check before running to a location you can't see. The hostile could be waiting for you around a corner." BGK was out of breath.

"You're just saying that because I beat you up the stairs," Katya replied.

BGK frowned at her and looked around the floor. Like the floors before, it split in two directions. A row of windows lined one side, while the other had three doors, and the middle one was open. Railings along the floor looked down to the atrium below.

He motioned to move to the opened door. They approached cautiously. BGK signalled to Katya to stop, and he took out a metal rod with a small camera attached. He poked the rod into the room, looking into the viewer. "Clear," he signalled.

They entered the room, seeing several large tables with chairs lined up at each table, almost like a dining room, but without place settings. Against the wall, there was an additional table with an interface for a display console. Katya walked over to it and connected her Motif.

"KIM, I HAVE ACCESSED THE BUILDING SCHEMATICS," Katya sent.

The display showed the building outlined in three-dimensions with each room clearly indicated. Katya zoomed in on their level.

"ROOM YOU ARE IN IS NEUTRAL. ROOM TO YOUR LEFT MAY BE HUB," TechStaff sent back as she watched the network activity focusing on the space next to Katya and BGK.

"WILL INVESTIGATE," Katya acknowledged. TechStaff typed in a note to the rest of the team. "TEAM 4, LOCATED HUB ON THEIR LEVEL."

"REMEMBER DISABLE NOT DESTROY," Sara sent to Katya. Katya smiled.

Terry saw the chatter between Team 4 and TechStaff. He watched BGT peer down the hallway and then signal for him to follow.

They proceeded slowly, keeping close to the wall. The rooms ahead had translucent glass doors. Terry touched one, finding that it moved freely. The first room was completely empty save for a small window with shutters closed.

The next room was the same.

Terry glanced over his at display and saw that TechStaff had distributed the building schematics to everyone. He reviewed the floor plans, seeing the comm hub on the floor above them highlighted.

He realized the most likely location for the hostile and said to BGT, "We need to get to the stairs — the hostile is probably on the top floor."

"KATYA, YOU MAY HAVE COMPANY," Terry sent.

BGL and Logan were already running up to the next level, assuming, like Terry, that the hostile went directly to the communication hub.

Logan paused and tapped on his goggles. "These are not working. I am getting no comm feeds, only the simulation," he said aloud.

"Let's continue, Logan. As long as you can experience the simulation, we can improvise on the rest," BGL replied.

"Whatever," Logan sighed.

"Hang tight. We're coming up," Terry called out.

Logan approached Terry. "Hey, can you see Team 3's position?"

Terry scanned the floor. "There has to be more than one person in here if this is an important hub. The question is whether they're upstairs with Katya and BGK or elsewhere."

The answer came quickly as Baren came running up the stairs. "Hostiles behind us!" he shouted, with Sara running close behind. "They just came in. There's 10 or so I think," Sara puffed.

Terry held back his first instinct to go on the offensive. "BGT and I can hold them off here while you help Katya."

Sara looked at Terry, trying to catch her breath. "Logan and BGL can stay here to support you. Me and Sebastian will head upstairs. The Combat System predicts there are more hostiles near the hub room, so Team 3 will need backup."

The four took defensive positions at opposite sides of the top of the stairway, while Sara and Baren continued to climb. The sounds of the approaching hostiles below grew louder.

BGK and Katya stood in front of an old wooden door for the hub room. There were shadows moving across the light that peaked out the crack at the bottom of the door. The two crouched on either side of the door, and BGK fed the small camera under the door.

The camera image appeared on their displays and relayed to Yvette and TechStaff. Though distorted by the fisheye lens, the image showed large computer racks lining the walls with two people working on them. BGK slowly panned the view, capturing two more in conversation near a window. One was the hostile that had escaped from them.

Suddenly, a foot stepped in front of the camera. BGK waited rather than withdrawing the lens, hoping the owner of the foot wasn't looking down. The foot pivoted and moved farther away from the camera, but still partially obscuring the view.

Sara and Baren approached, seeing Katya and BGK crouched by the door. Katya glanced over, acknowledging them and sent, "WE CAN SEE INSIDE. THIS IS THE HUB."

TechStaff sent the video feed to Baren and Sara with the message, "LOOKS LIKE FIVE OR SIX INSIDE. FOUR UNARMED AND TWO UNKNOWN."

As Sara and Baren approached the door, the foot came down hard on the camera, accompanied by unintelligible shouting. The door flew open, revealing two heavily armed hostiles facing them. One of them fired a shot that narrowly missed Sara. Baren returned fire, hitting the hostile. The other hostile fired several shots in succession and slammed the door shut, blocking two shots from Sara.

"This isn't going to be easy," Sara said, watching as the shadow of objects being moved to the door was accompanied by the scraping sound of furniture being moved to form a barricade.

"I will go around," Katya said to Sara. "There is a window inside. If the building schematics are correct, we can go out the windows on the other side of the hall, across the roof and access the hub room window from there."

"Good idea, I will come with you," BGK said.

"Go," Sara said, looking around the floor for alternative strategies.

TechStaff sent a message, "TEAMS 1 AND 4 ARE ENGAGED AT THE HUB."

BGL watched as a group of 10 hostiles made their way up the stairs. They appeared unarmed. "Switch your weapons to Stun Mode, and take an offensive posture," she said to BGT.

BGT and BGL rose in unison and stood in the middle of the stairs. BGL fired once at the step just in front of the pack.

"Go back down, or we will fire on you," she shouted.

One hostile threw a knife at her, which flew past, hitting the wall behind her.

"Okay, then. Open fire." BGL fired off two shots at the front of the pack. One was hit squarely in the chest, falling back on top of the others, and the other in the leg, falling forward.

The crowd unsheathed clubs and knives and started sprinting up the stairs.

BGT fire three shots, all finding their mark but having no effect on the surging crowd.

Terry watched as the two bodyguards stood their ground, continuing to fire. By his estimate, five hostiles were disabled, which should have left only five, but the crowd size did not change.

"LOGAN, SOMETHING IS WRONG," he sent.

No response.

"LOGAN, SOMETHING IS WRONG," he sent again.

Still no response.

"Hey, Logan," Terry yelled.

Logan turned and tapped his goggles. "These are not

working; I can only see the simulation and none of communications."

Terry ran across the top of the stairs, crouching toward Logan. "Something's wrong. Whenever we hit a hostile, another one appears."

Logan looked down at the crowd. "Or even multiplies! There must be 20 now!"

Terry turned on his mic. "Kim, Yvette, what's going on with the sim? Hostiles are multiplying."

"Hang tight, checking," came the response.

Terry looked down at the crowd. They were moving more slowly, but now their numbers grew.

Katya and BGK made it up to the roof, and they looked down to the window ledge near the hub room.

"There's not enough space for both of us on the ledge," BGK said.

"I am smaller," Katya replied. "I will go."

She dangled herself over the building ledge, just to the side of the window, and lowered herself. She wasn't tall enough for her feet to touch the ledge, so she released her grip and landed, almost losing her balance.

"You have no fear, eh, Katya?" BGK said.

Katya looked up, pursing her lips. "Shhh," indicating there was a person near the window.

She pulled out her metal baton and swung it hard, shattering the glass. She jumped inside, grabbing a packet explosive and slamming it to the ground. BGK followed with his weapon drawn.

The explosion stunned the hostiles. The two at the computer staggered back, while two more closer to the window went to the ground for cover. One by the door was shielding himself, but then drew a weapon. He was hit immediately by a stun bullet from BGK.

The door shattered from the rocket, followed by Baren. "Stop them from erasing the server!" He pointed to a hostile who was making way to the console.

Katya threw her metal baton at the hostile, who tripped and started falling into the console. Katya ran and grabbed the hostile before they made impact, using her momentum to push them both to the floor. The hostile landed heavily with Katya on top.

BGK had secured the other two hostiles, tying them up in the corner. The last hostile approached the console and began entering code.

"Stop," Sara shouted as she drew her weapon.

The hostile continued.

Sara fired one stun bullet. It hit the hostile's shoulder, but rather than bouncing off, it passed through. The hostile continued entering code.

"What the..." Sara fired again.

The bullet passed through the hostile's torso and hit the server rack.

"Kim, what's going on with the simulation?"

"I'm on it! I'm on it," came the reply.

The swarm coming up the stairs toward Teams 2 and 3 had now swelled to over fifty.

"The weapons aren't working!" BGT shouted, "We need to go to hand-to-hand."

BGL and BGT tried to maintain a front position to keep the surge from ascending, but many were able to get past them. Terry was using his baton to keep the approaching hostiles away.

"We need to move." BGL shouted, 'Packets, everyone!"

Terry grabbed two of his packets and threw them at the feet of the approaching mob. The explosion scattered a few, but only temporarily halted the progress of the crowd.

BGL swung her baton, hitting two approaching hostiles, and threw a packet. "Go," she shouted, running toward the next set of stairs.

Terry started moving and saw that Logan was still fighting.

"Logan, let's go!" he shouted, but Logan continued.

Terry approached Logan, using his baton to keep the swarm away. "Logan, let's go!"

Logan's kick-boxing memories were driving his movements fluidly and effortlessly. He no longer registered individual opponents, but saw the scene as a sequence of movements, with repeating sequences, like motifs. Kick, spin, elbow, then sweep, punch, duck, then kick, knee, elbow. He was neither attacking nor defending. He heard his name, but that didn't stop the flow.

"Logan!" Terry was close now. He swung the baton, knocking a hostile sideway. He reached out to grab Logan, who spun around, throwing a punch at Terry.

Fortunately, Terry moved his head out of the way of Logan's fist. "Hey! It's me! We need to move!"

Logan registered his friend. "Sorry, I was in the zone." Terry pushed Logan, swinging his baton again to fend off two more hostiles. He threw a packet down to give them some space before they ran to the stairs.

They caught up to BGL and BGT at the top. "The rest of the team are over there." BGL pointed to the hub room.

Sara was still staring at the hostile who continued to enter codes, oblivious to her warnings. She moved to push the hostile, who retaliated by pushing her back and then turned to continue.

"Alright, new rules, I guess," Sara said, as she withdrew her baton and slammed the hostile aside. "Stay down, or I will crack you open."

The hostile looked up at Sara, unsheathed a knife and threw it hard, hitting Sara squarely in the chest.

"Sara!" Katya yelled, forgetting momentarily that they were in a simulation.

"Oh, shit," Sara grimaced as she looked down at the knife protruding from her chest. Her interface to the simulation was cut, and her avatar disappeared from the other's displays.

Terry ran in the room just as Sara's avatar disappeared. "Damn it! Looks like we have a different game here. I don't think we are going to fight our way out easily. We'll need to find an escape route."

Katya swung her baton at the hostile, who threw the knife and turned back toward the console. "I don't think disable is an option anymore," and she smashed the main console to disable access, changed the settings on her weapon on Self Destruct and placed it on the console.

Baren held his tongue. "Okay, so mission accomplished. Kim, get us out of here, fast."

TechStaff was trying desperately to see where the simulation was going wrong. The program diagnostics were all showing normal. She checked the log for subroutine and then noticed something.

"Yvette, what is the last subroutine for this sim?"

"If I remember, it's the link to your helicopter program to lift the team off the roof."

"Yeah, that's a problem. It's not there and is calling a different subroutine that clones itself. If you disable a character, the program adapts and creates a new one." TechStaff turned to load her device's code into the sim program.

"Hey, everyone," she continued, "if we want to play this through, you're going to have to do it on your own. The helicopter option is no longer available. I suggest you get out of that room fast."

BGT looked down the hall to see the approaching swarm. "Exit strategy would be helpful here."

BGK called out, "If we round the floor to the other side, we can get to the windows and outside to the ledge."

"Okay, let's move! Katya's weapon will explode in a few seconds!" Baren yelled, and began running.

The rest of the team followed, with Terry and BGT taking up the rear. They watched the swarm maintain the same pace, rather than give chase. "It's like they're zombies or something," BGT said.

The blast from Katya's weapon sent a plume of smoke into the hall, but had no effect on the swarm.

Terry stopped and watched them. The characters all looked alike now, all fixated on the movements of the team as they ran down the hall.

"Stand still," Terry said.

BGT raised an eyebrow. "What?"

"Stand still against the wall."

The lead hostile moved past them, not regarding them at all. The throng continued with none paying any attention to Terry or BGT.

Once the last one passed, Terry said, "I think the program is stuck in a simple routine that fixates on pursuing a target. If the target isn't moving, then it's no longer a target."

"Excellent," BGT replied. "Let's loop around the other side to meet the team."

They rounded the corner and saw the bank of windows with the bright sunlight beaming through. Baren and Katya appeared at the far end, followed by BGK.

Katya ran up to the window and pushed it open. Looking back, she asked, "Where is Logan?"

Logan had taken up a defensive position just before the turn to the window hall and moved forward into the frontline of hostiles, followed by BGL. The small amount of training was enough for them to work well together, attacking and retreating, all the while watching each other's backs.

"If you ever want to switch careers, Logan, I have a job for you," BGL called out.

Logan was immersed in the adrenaline.

Baren called back to them, "Come on, you two."

BGL and Logan continued their tactic.

Terry stepped forward. "Hey! Let's go already!"

Logan yelled, "This is too much fun," not noticing the hostile behind him. BGL tried to intercept, but the hostile stabbed Logan in the back.

"Okay, that wasn't so much fun." Logan's avatar disappeared.

"Move!" Baren called out. BGL and Terry ran to the window and jumped out onto a 5-metre ledge that spanned the length of the floor.

"Stand very still," Terry called out. "The hostiles are attracted to movements."

The team stopped where they all stood. Baren turned to Terry.

"And then what?"

"Hopefully, they will move on, and we can try to sneak down around them."

The lead hostile walked on to the platform, walking to the edge and stopped. Others continued, each lining up forming rows. They continued, and the rows grew deeper, enveloping the team.

"I am suffocating!" Katya called out.

"Don't move!" Terry called back.

More continued to come through the window.

The concrete platform started to creak.

"There are too many! The platform can't hold us all!" Katya cried.

The platform collapsed, sending everyone plummeting down to the market square below.

"SIMULATION COMPLETE."

Evening

The group gathered in the main room of the training facility. Sara was having a side conversation with Baren. The others were getting out of their simulation suits.

Katya continued the banter with BGK.

"What about swimming?" BGK asked. "I'll bet I could beat you at swimming," he was half-joking.

Katya laughed. "As you wish. I have no doubts that I would win in a swim competition."

"Hey, you two, no fighting, eh?" Terry said, as he walked between them.

"Okay, team," Sara called out, getting everyone's attention. "Let's do a debrief and then call it a day. We have a full agenda tomorrow, and I want to make sure everyone's rested. We'll be flying out in 24 hours.

"First, I want to talk about our performance in the simulation. From what I saw, the teams came together really well, despite the computer glitches. Katya and BGK, you two were great in getting into the computer room." She gave them two thumbs-up.

"Yeah, Katya, your window entry was something else, true to your Professor Fearless moniker!" BGT added.

Katya smiled and responded, "And Logan showed off his Ninja scientist moves!"

"Yes, and Terry remains the cuddly pooh bear." Logan turned to Terry with a grin.

"Lover, not a fighter, man — lover, not a fighter." Terry winked. "What happened with the program? It seemed like the simulation ran amok."

TechStaff looked over to Yvette, who was staring at the ground, and said, "I don't know for sure. We were working on a new adaptive algorithm that has some of the same features that Katya mentioned when she was explaining Complex Adaptive Systems."

Yvette looked up. "Yeah, we linked in the feed from Logan's goggles into the program so that it had the same opportunity to get updates on the team's movement as the team had about the program. Looks like the program took an unexpected turn and somehow blocked Logan from seeing anything useful."

Logan was impressed and annoyed. "So what you're saying is you changed the rules that the simulation program followed but didn't tell us?"

"Um, yes, sort of." Yvette was uncomfortable. "And we updated the algorithms to allow more nonlinear optimization of strategy."

"So the nonlinearities made it impossible to predict what strategy it would use." Logan softened his tone, sensing he sounded too stern. "This was a valuable lesson, I believe. Fortunately, it was only a simulation and not a real battle."

"Don't worry, Logan. We'll have your goggles back in shape by tomorrow," TechStaff tried to defuse the tension.

"Thanks, Kim." Sara moved the conversation along. "Despite the program glitch, I still think it worked out okay. I hope we don't have to do any real fighting, but I feel better knowing that we can handle ourselves.

"We'll have time on the flight tomorrow to work out the remaining bugs from the merger Combat AI and BrainMaze. We can try a few simulations and make any adjustments before we land in Kuala Lumpur."

Chapter Seven:
Logan's Bike Ride

Travel to Asia

Sara laid out the travel plans for the team the next morning, emphasizing the dual purposes of their trip.

"Councillor Xi has formally invited to work with his group on a pilot of a BrainMaze-Global AI interface. Xi is very much a play-it-by-the-rules guy, so we'll need to be careful to stick to the boundaries that he defines for us.

"We need to be extra careful not to let out the secondary purpose of our visit before we figure out what's going on." She looked at the trio.

"I know you three are used to working freely, but there is a lot at stake here. If you have even the smallest inkling of something that can help us identify the infiltration, I need you to share it with us. I know we're a small team, but we can be effective if we work together."

It was clear why Sara had become so successful at building unity in the Council.

'This is why we're here, Sara. We're part of this team," Katya replied.

Sara turned to Katya with a look that said, *"Thanks, but I don't completely trust you,"* which underscored another feature that made Sara effective as Chair. She knew where to lay her trust. She felt she could count on Baren and his team, but was less confident about the trio. Baren's suggestion of having bodyguards for each was an excellent strategy for both protection and monitoring the trio.

Sara continued, "Sebastian, can you give us a brief of the schedule, please?"

Baren stood and walked to a display panel, bringing up a calendar view. "We leave for Kuala Lumpur this afternoon. It will be a 12-hour flight, so we will have time to discuss specifics for the days to come. We will arrive in the morning there, so we will have a full day with Xi and his team. I hope we will have time to go to our accommodations and get cleaned up before we meet Xi for dinner. I suspect the dinner will be a formal affair, so be prepared for a large group."

Logan and Katya looked at each other, rolling their eyes. Neither of them liked the small talk that dominated formal events.

"Kim has already arranged to meet with her counterparts when we arrive, so she will work with them tomorrow evening rather than joining us."

Katya spoke up. "May I join her for that? I think it would be more valuable if I were there rather than at the reception. I am sure Terry and Logan can represent me well."

Logan gave her a sideways glance and smirked, knowing the ulterior motive for her request.

"I like that idea," TechStaff spoke up.

"Very well," Baren replied. "I will inform Xi of the slight change in plans. On the following day, we will start early to get the pilot project launched. We hope we can do the integration in a day or two. Would that be a reasonable expectation?" He turned to the trio.

"If their infrastructure is up-to-date, then it would be reasonable," Logan replied, "but we won't know for certain until we see their system for ourselves."

"Understood." Baren continued. "During the time you are working with Xi's team, Sara and I will start digging to see what we can find out about the odd behaviours of their communications hub. We will reconvene in the late afternoon to share notes on what we've all discovered.

"Aside from the dinner, there are no evening plans, but we should keep that time free in case we need to follow up on anything. The next day will follow the same general plan, though I suspect Xi will ask for another dinner event to say his farewells and celebrate our success." Baren finished with a slightly exhausted tone.

Terry asked, "Where are we staying?"

"Ah, good question," Baren replied. "We have two large flats in an apartment on the outskirts. It's close to the facility where we will work on the integration, so it is convenient that way. You three will take one flat and Sara, Kim and I the other. The flats are set up like two suites within one, with adjoining rooms. The front rooms are smaller, with a bedroom and kitchen. The bodyguards will stay there, rotating between them while standing watch. The back rooms are larger, with four bedrooms and a full kitchen. We had these designed for comfort and security, so I think you will like them."

"Um, are there places to run close by?" Terry inquired.

"You guys kill me." Sara laughed. "Yes, of course. We'll be close to a national forest, so there are some great trails nearby. I doubt there'll be time, however."

"There is always time." Terry smiled.

Baren smiled. "Okay. For transportation, we will have a large vehicle that will have space for extra cargo. I understand there have been a few modifications to allow interfacing with BrainMaze. Is that correct, Kim?"

"Yeah, I gave the group there some of the specs for the link. We'll need to tweak it when we are there, but at least, we won't be starting from zero," TechStaff replied.

"How many bathrooms are there in the flats?" Katya asked.

"Bathrooms?" Baren responded.

"Yes, you mentioned the bedrooms and kitchens but not bathrooms."

Baren laughed, and then paused. "Actually, that's a good question. I have not been there, so I don't know."

"She's saying that because whenever we share a flat, she wants her personal bathroom for all her stuff," Terry added.

"Not true!" Katya defended. "I do that because you two hang your running clothes in the bathroom, and the smell is unbearable."

"Tell you what, Katya, if there is only one bathroom, we can hang our clothes elsewhere, like in your bedroom," Logan joked.

Sara shook her head, smiling. "This is going to be an interesting trip!"

The group reconvened on the stairs at the entrance to the Council Headquarters, where a large transport vehicle was waiting to take them to the private airfield.

Councillor Evans was waiting for them. His features were softer outside the Council chambers, giving him a more grandfatherly appearance.

"I wanted to make sure I was here to see you all off." He turned to Katya. "And I also wanted to reaffirm how pleased we are that you will assist us. I'm sure our Chair has told you this already, but I was one of your strongest advocates to the Council."

"We appreciate that." Katya smiled politely and entered the vehicle.

As the vehicle door closed, Katya turned to Sara. "Is what the Councillor said true? I got the impression he was very negative at the first meeting."

"Yeah, it's accurate," Sara replied. "Evans can be very 'old school' and sometimes gruff, but once he is on your side, he can be a potent ally. I'm sure there is no way I would be Chair, were it not for his support. He showed up this morning to make it clear that you can count on him going forward."

The drive to the airfield was brief, and the group transfer to the small private jet was rapid and without ceremony. The plane had several rows of seats at the front and a conference table in the middle.

"We can work around the table once we get in the air. There is a galley kitchen in the back in case we need refreshments," TechStaff threw her bag near the back of the plane.

Once in the air, there was a great deal of turbulence, forcing the team to remain in their seats rather than gathering around the table.

"We're going to be in this turbulence for a while, it seems," TechStaff commented as she looked at the video monitor at the front of the plane that was displaying flight status. Turbulence had become more prevalent in air travel with the volatility of air currents, making storm formation less predictable.

The turbulence triggered Logan's fear of flying. Despite being on many flights, his anxiety about flying persisted.

Logan tried to calm himself by looking out the window and imaging something other than being on a plane. With the turbulence, his mind drifted to a memorable solo mountain bike trip he had taken several months back.

Back on the bike

Logan appreciated his alone time as much as he relished spending time with his family. The solitude provided a chance for unconstrained thought that often helped him crystallize ideas rumbling around in his head.

To do this well, he needed to isolate himself as much as possible, if only for a few hours. In his youth, sometimes, these hours extended when the exhilaration of solitude was too great. One of his most memorable excursions was a motorcycle ride he took through Scandinavia, where he drove north until there was no more road. As he stood at the edge of the road, at the edge of civilization, his mind was as open and as clear as the vastness in front of him.

He didn't have the luxury of such excursions these days, and frankly, the pull to the family was strong enough to dampen the urge for going. Still, there were times when the desire for solitude was palpable. Today, this opportunity came as a mountain bike ride through the hills behind his home. He hadn't been riding for several years (save for a few rides along bike paths with friends and family) but in the past, he would do frequent weekend excursions through the sand dune parks near his previous home.

The present opportunity was ideal. His family would be away for the morning doing errands, and the weather was perfect for a ride: the temperature warm and the air slightly humid but clear. He pulled his mountain biking gear from the closet and assembled the armour that was necessary in the rocky and thorny hills around them.

He took off with boyish joy about 15 minutes later and began his ascent on the first few small hills. The grade was shallow, so that he could make progress without too much exertion. The terrain was such that he could afford to think a bit about the problem he'd been working through without distraction from biking.

He started his internal science dialogue. *Let us consider how we can describe the coordination of behaviour by the brain in terms of flows and manifolds. Flows can be the representation of brain network activity, and the manifolds express the rules on how these flows can evolve.*

When you describe how to dance, you don't typically do it by telling someone each individual movement. Put your foot here, pivot, put your other foot here, et cetera. This may help to get a general idea, but it breaks the dance up so that you lose the essence of dance as a flow of movements. You learn the rules, and then you practise their implementation, the flow of the dance. The rules define the manifold.

The ascent grew steeper.

If you consider the dance as a flow of coordinated continuous movements, it becomes easier to teach and easier to explain at a conceptual level.

His thoughts paused as the ascent became too steep to maintain balance on the bike. He knew that in about 100 metres, he would come to the peak of the hill and could access a trail on the other side that would wind down to a ravine. He dismounted and carried the bike to the peak, pausing to look around.

In front of him was a cattle trail that wound its way down the hill to the ravine, which sometimes contained water for the livestock. The extreme dryness they'd faced this season left the ravine a dusty crevice. Logan looked to his left beyond the ravine and saw his next target — a much larger hill, on top of which were the remains of an old monastery. The approach from his current direction would be more difficult than from the other side, where the trail was more accommodating for tourists, but recalled a few switchback trails on this side would help the ascent. He remounted his bike.

The descent to the ravine was slow at first.

The analogy of a dance is good to convey the notion of processes that are linked in the coordination of behaviour.

Big rock! Logan pulled his bike up and over with little trouble.

You can express these processes as flows along a manifold.

Branch! He ducked.

The manifold gives a general constraint to the flow, but with those constraints, a given flow has great flexibility in how it unfurls.

The trail made a rapid decline, which snapped Logan's focus on the ride. His speed increased dramatically, and his focus turned to the trail about 10 metres in front of him as he released the brake and let gravity have its fun.

The trail took an abrupt turn, and his bike skidded on the smooth stone that formed much of the base of the trail. He maintained the speed but pulled back a little, realizing that going any faster could be a problem.

At the ravine, the grade was shallow, and the trail broadened to enable a more leisurely ride.

It's like if you are waltzing, and you know the general idea of how to waltz, but the particular way you do it in the moment depends a great deal on other factors.

The ride was glorious through the ravine, with the mixture of stunted old trees, flowering rosemary bushes, and massive swaths of grass near where the water sometimes flowed. This, on a background of a crisp blue morning sky, was almost like a painting.

If you are waltzing in your socks alone at home, or at a formal ball wearing a tuxedo and proper shoes, the rules for the waltz are the same. However, one would not judge your dancing ability based only on how you waltz in your socks.

Logan thought about how this expression could be captured in a simple computer simulation to illustrate the point. He could easily build a 10-node network that would have the general rules dictated, but enough variation in specific expression of the rule to make it appear that different systems generated them. This reminded him of the examples from Edward Lorenz, where different initial conditions can lead to quite different emergent behaviours, even though the system architecture was identical.

He got to the top of the ravine, where the trail wrapped around and started climbing the next hill, which would lead to the ruins.

The trail quickly steepened and provided some challenge for traction as the tires slipped on small rocks. Logan down-shifted the gears to keep momentum.

In fact, it's not too different from riding a bike. The rules for riding a bike are simple, and once you get the flow, it can keep going. Each time you cycle, there are variations to adjust for rocks or trees, but the rules themselves are predetermined.

As he rounded another bend in the switchback and ascended, the trail disappeared into a field of rock and scattered brush. The winter rains probably washed away the trail he remembered. He stopped on his bike to plot the best path to get to the peak. The ascent was quite steep, so he had a few options. First was to go back and pick another route for the ascent, but that would take too much time. The second was to continue biking, blazing his own trail to get to the top. Logan scanned the hill and realized that would only get him a few more metres ahead before he would need to walk. The third option was to put the bike on his back and walk the rest of the way.

He chuckled. "This hill is not presenting a very nice manifold."

Logan dismounted and adjusted his hydration backpack with the straps he designed for this purpose. He pushed one pedal down and turned the front fork to create space, grabbed the fork and crank arm, and lifted the bike up and behind his neck. He pulled the straps from his pack, then wrapped them around the fork and tire to secure the bike, giving him some freedom to use both hands if necessary.

We might call this a bifurcation, he thought as he walked up the rocky hill.

The ascent proved a bit more difficult than it looked. Without an obvious trail, it was uncertain what path would be the easiest. Logan paused after a few steps to re-examine the terrain and better plan his ascent. With the steep grade, he could not see the top, but he remembered roughly where it was based on his starting point. He walked parallel to the ridge for a few steps until there was a natural switchback that allowed him to climb a little higher. By now, it was sufficiently steep that he needed to steady himself with his hands. Around the next bend, he needed to start climbing, as walking was no longer an option.

"Rock climbing with a bike strapped to my back! This is perfect!" he cried out.

Fortunately, the top of the hill was not as far away as it seemed. He pulled himself up and saw the grade flatten out toward the site of the ruins. He paused for a moment to sip some water and continued walking to the ruins.

When he arrived, he unstrapped his bike and placed it to the side. He took his backpack off and checked the time, estimating he could rest here for a while to collate his thoughts and catch his breath.

Logan touched the old stone doorframe for the monastery. He admired the majesty of the structure and its perseverance. "Sometimes, the old ways are the most reliable," he said aloud, patting the stone.

He sat on a rock nearby and took a notebook from his backpack. He could have dictated his thoughts into BrainMaze, but for this type of brainstorming, he still preferred the feel of paper and pencil. *There is something more tangible to it*, he thought.

He sketched out a sphere to represent a manifold and drew a few flows as vectors entering the sphere surface. He wrote down notes: *The core idea is to describe a framework for understanding rules that govern how the actions of neural networks are coordinated to produce behaviour. The coordination can be understood as flows depicting the formation and dissolution of network interactions. The evolution of these flows occurs on relatively low-dimension manifolds, which act as a sort of force field, defining a landscape of all possible network configurations.*

One may try to understand a system by looking at the individual flows, or realizations, but this only tells what that system does in that instance. It tells you nothing about its full capacity and limits your ability to predict what it might do in the future.

As Logan finished his last note and packed his book away, it occurred to him that he really hadn't considered the rate of change for different flows. Processes can have fast and slowly changing components that affect each other. While not a perfect analogy, the changes in the terrain he just traversed occur on a different scale than his ascent on the bike. The large scale of the hilly terrain completely constrained his fine scale ascent, but within those constraints, he had extensive degrees of freedom in how he can climb.

Mounting his bike, he looked at the trail that led to the road back home. It looked roughly 500 metres straight down, but the trail probably doubled that to 1 kilometre with the extensive switchbacks. He glanced at his watch and saw it was getting close to noon. He would have to be quick in his descent.

There were two options to get down. The first was the wide series of switchbacks that made for a safer ride down. The second was a steeper and narrower trail that bisected the switchback trail and was basically straight down the hill. This smaller trail was probably carved out by rockslides and water flows from the rains, but over the years, bikers and hikers alike used this shortcut to reduce their transit times.

Logan started down the wide trail.

If there is a separation of scales in space, there must also be a separation of scales in time, he recalled.

At the first switchback, the trail flattened a little, so he needed to pedal to maintain speed.

Time scale separation may be key in considering how the interplay between flows is governed, his thoughts continued.

At the second switchback, he realized that the wide switchback trail was actually slowing him down.

"C'mon, let's do this!" he said aloud as he turned on to the narrow trail.

The change in grade was immediate as he quickly cut across the next part of the wider trail.

ROCK! He turned his wheel to avoid.

TREE ROOT! He jumped his bike slightly and almost crashed when landing.

A thought: *If you have a slow process working that frames how a process on a fast timescale evolves, then modification of the slow process can eliminate the fast one*, popped into his head.

"Not now!" he said aloud.

The small trail took an abrupt turn to the left that required Logan to put his foot down to negotiate the curve.

The trail curved right, and again, he put his foot down to pull the bike to follow the curve.

DROP!

The trail disappeared in front of him. He landed awkwardly on his front tire but recovered.

Slow permits fast, but does fast affect slow? another thought.

"Focus," he said aloud as he zipped around a large rock and crossed the wider trail again.

ROCK! He lifted his front tire over.

SHIFT! The trail took another abrupt turn

BUSH! He tried to go around it, but a few thorns grabbed bits of flesh from the side of his leg.

When the narrow trail merged into the last part of the switchback trail, Logan got off his bike and examine himself and his gear for any serious damage.

His bike was dusty but showed no obvious signs of damage. He, on the other hand, had three nicely coloured red gashes in his left leg where the bush bit him.

Not too bad, though. He smiled, *It's not a good ride unless you have a few scrapes.*

He had gained some time with the shortcut, but still needed

to get moving if he was going to be back in time to prepare lunch.

He rode and came to the intersection of the trail with the road. The grade had a slight incline, which required easy pedalling.

Okay, he thought, *let's see if we can pull this together now.*

Consider a behaviour, like dancing, as a coordinated flow that has a set of rules that establishes the boundaries of the flow.

Logan imagined a diagram that would show these flows on a manifold. Such visuals he felt were vital as they give a depiction that allows one to grasp the concept without needing to understand the equations.

While imagining the figure, he felt his front tire lurch to the side, and he was airborne. He had the presence of mind to roll as the ground came up to meet him.

ELBOW, HEAD, SHOULDER, BACK, ROLL, HAND, KNEE, FOOT.

Stop.

He lay still for a moment on his back. He could hear bird song and the slight rustling of leaves in the trees as the wind pushed its way through. He looked around and saw his bike ahead of him on the side of the road, and the grasses around him covering the stones that likely caused his crash.

As he stood, he felt the painful throbbing in his arm and opposite leg. Despite hitting his head, the helmet cushioned most of the impact, so it had minimal effect.

I am sure someone will comment on this, he thought.

Looking at his arm, he saw the slow flow of blood running down to his hand and turned his arm over to see the large gash around his elbow. His leg had a large scrape from thigh to knee. *This is a nice match to my other leg,* as he compared the thorn marks on the one leg to the scrape on the other.

He limped to his bike and picked it up, seeing that there was minimal damage to it, save for a rip in the seat.

He rode slowly to his house, hoping his family was not yet back from their trip. When he entered the yard, he saw his wife, Almeda, unloading the vehicle, while his two children, Alfredos and Josef, were running into the house. Alfredos, the eldest and smaller of the two, ran into the house first and yelled to his brother to hurry inside so they could see if their friends were online to play games.

"We will have lunch first. Then you can play," Almeda called to them as she unpacked the last parcel.

She turned to see the bloodied, dusty figure approaching with an enormous smile on his face that she knew all too well.

"It's really not as bad as it looks," Logan said, trying to cover the blood that crusted his left arm.

She sighed. "Let's go in through the garage, so the kids don't see you."

A chime in the plane indicating the turbulence had cleared redirected Logan's attention to the present.

"Okay, we're clear to get up." TechStaff stood. "Let me show you what we did with BrainMaze and the Combat AI. I think you'll like it."

Chapter Eight:
Close encounter of the first kind

Cold welcome

Their plane came in for a landing just as the sun was rising over the mountains. Logan scanned the many trails that slashed across the mountain greenery, making a mental tally of their location on the chance that they might get a chance to explore them. Terry tapped his shoulder and pointed out the window. "That one would be an awesome run."

Logan smiled and gripped the arms of his chair as the plane touched down on the runway. "I am thankful that you continue to distract me when a plane lands."

The plane taxied to an awaiting crew next to aircraft stairs and a large vehicle. The team left the plane and descended into the hot and humid air.

"This is probably the best air we will have today." TechStaff was the last to leave the plane. "The air quality is going to get worse through the day."

The ground crew was quick to transfer the luggage and equipment into the vehicle. Sara entered the vehicle first, seeing the three rows of seats. "I smell coffee." She looked around to see a small machine at the front of the cab that appeared to be a coffee maker. "C'mon in, team! Coffee's here, so we're good to go!"

The team arrived at Councillor Xi's complex just as the rush hour began. Sara glanced behind them, watching as the motorway they had just left was overwhelmed with traffic.

"You would think that with all the advances we have made so far, the traffic would be lighter. And look at all the old internal combustion vehicles! They generate so much pollution and waste time and energy," she commented.

"Unfortunately, there are still many who have not embraced the autonomous vehicles, especially those living outside the cities. Less than half the traffic is from people in autonomous vehicles," Baren replied. "People still want to make choices, Sara, and forcing them to use autonomous or electric vehicles is seen as impeding their choices."

"That's so shortsighted." Sara continued, "I mean, you can see the air pollution right here in front of you. They must know that focusing on their own self-interests comes at a cost of the environment, which affects everyone."

"I am not going to argue with that, but remember that despite the successes of the Global Council, there is still a substantial mistrust of politics, so some would claim that the vehicle changes will have no appreciable impact on the environment and come at the cost of their own freedom. Also, not all the pollution you see is from vehicles. The practice of burning trash and scorching fields is still very prevalent here."

Sara was preparing her response when TechStaff interrupted, "Hey, I think that's the Councillor's staff coming out to meet us. Can you two save this discussion for later?"

"Sorry, yes of course." Sara snapped her attention to the approaching entourage and turned to Baren. "Shall we?"

The bodyguards left the vehicle first, followed by Sara, Baren and then the Professors. TechStaff and Yvette stayed in the vehicle, transferring the extra equipment they might need from the travel cases to backpacks.

"Chair Meyer, I extend greetings on behalf of Councillor Xi." The lead person in entourage walked toward Sara. "I am Enrique and will be your chief liaison while you are here." He was a short, stocky man who looked like he hadn't slept for days.

Baren stepped forward. "Thank you, Enrique. May I ask where the Councillor is? It is usually the case that the Councillors participate in these visits."

Enrique frowned. "Usually, yes, but you have seen the traffic here. The Councillor contacted us and said he is in heavy traffic and will try to join us as soon as possible. We haven't quite got our traffic problems under control here."

Sara tapped Baren and turned to Enrique. "I completely understand, Enrique. Let's see what we can do about the water system and then maybe we can make some suggestions on the traffic."

Baren turned to the Professors. "You may know them already, but let me introduce the three members of the BrainMaze team, Doctors Katya Kaliski, Logan Reznick. And Terrance Chatan."

"An honour to meet you, Professors. We are looking forward to working with you." Enrique bowed slightly.

Katya stepped forward. "As are we, Enrique."

"Shall we move inside and get you set up? I expect the Councillor will not be too much longer." Enrique motioned for them to follow.

"We have two more colleagues in the vehicle." Baren turned and looked inside. "Kim Morgan, our main engineering expert, and Yvette Arias, our senior programmer."

The two stumbled out of the vehicle with large backpacks. "Hello!" TechStaff waved as she struggled to get the pack through the vehicle door.

"Let us help you." Enrique motioned to his colleagues.

"No need, thanks," TechStaff replied. "I'm used to heavy loads."

The group was near the building entrance when Councillor Xi's vehicle pulled up. The driver's side door opened, and Xi jumped out, brushing off his clothing as if he were coming out of a dust storm.

"My apologies for being late. The traffic here is very unpredictable."

"Hello, Councillor Xi," Sara smiled. "You don't appear to be using our autonomous vehicles. I am sure you know they are much better in heavy traffic."

"Yes, yes, so I am told. I prefer to be in control. Technology can rob us of our individuality."

Sara glanced over to Baren, raising one eyebrow.

"Nevertheless, I am here," Xi continued. "Let's get inside and get to work. There is much to do."

Where do we go from here?

Xi guided them to a side entrance of the building. "This is a shortcut to the control room for our AI hub. We can avoid having to meet all my staff, so we can get to work right away. We can take care of those other formalities later."

The building was in immaculate condition, even better than the Global Council HQ. "We spent a lot of effort to keep our facility ahead of the technological curve. Our scientists and engineers are among the best, and take a great sense of pride at their achievements since they were all trained here."

"I can appreciate that," Sara replied. "We're here to help them do even better."

"They will be happy to hear that." Xi opened the door to the control room. Consoles that lined one wall displayed the continuous feed of the water flow across the jurisdiction with pop-up windows zooming in on intersections. The staff in the room had not noticed the group's arrival.

Xi clapped his hands, calling to his staff in their local dialect. He continued in English, "Good morning, team. I am pleased to introduce the visitors from the Global Council, headed by Chair Meyer and Secretary Baren. They bring with them the special guests who have developed BrainMaze, a technology that we all believe will help us achieve even better results in managing our local eco-system. Chair Meyer, would you like to say a few words?"

Sara stepped forward. "Thank you, Councillor Xi, and thanks to all of you for agreeing to work with us on this important initiative. I am sure you have been briefed on the goals here, so I will only add that our success here over the next few days will serve as an example for others to follow. I know I can speak for the entire Global Council when I say that we are impressed with what you have already achieved and can think of no other team better suited to help us."

Xi smiled uncomfortably while looking at his own team, who was unmoved by Sara's compliments.

"Tough crowd," Terry whispered to Logan.

The head engineer for Xi's team, whose boyish appearance belied his seniority, spoke. "We are, of course, honoured by the opportunity, Chair Meyer. Please do not take our silence as a negative, but the challenges we are facing seem insurmountable. Our water system is becoming increasingly unstable, and the recent rise in air pollution compounds this. Although these two may not be linked, many of our local population are suffering from some sort of malaise that they think comes from these things. No matter how compelling we wish to make the case that these are unrelated, the local superstitions and mistrust of the Council remain a formidable obstacle."

Sara clenched her jaw and glanced over to Xi. "I apologize. We were not completely aware of the difficulties you are facing. I can assure you that the team we have here represents the best in the world in dealing with complex problems. Perhaps you can give us a bit more detail and we can get started on testing some solutions?"

The engineer continued, "Of course. There seems to be water contamination in our midst that we are unable to identify."

Logan spoke up. "What do you mean 'unable to identify'? I assume you have the equipment necessary to analyze your water content. What does it say?"

"We do indeed have the equipment. In fact, I am told it is the latest technology for such assays. The challenge is that we see the contamination, but the detectors say there is nothing there."

The engineer walked over to a display panel and brought up a schematic of the water distribution system. The system read normal, save for a few intersection points that showed reduced flow. "Normally, we would not pay much attention to these warnings at the intersections since you might expect variations in flow, but it happens too frequently now and different from what you might expect if it were simply two water feeds."

The engineer zoomed in on one intersection and a pop-up window displayed a video feed of the flow at the intersection. Flows from three large pipes converged into a pool. Clear, fast flowing water gushed from two of the pipes, but an odd green ooze flowed from the third. The green appeared somewhat hydrophobic, taking a path different from the water flow.

"It's like it's alive," Katya commented as she watched the green flowing through the water at right angles.

The engineer activated two more pop-up video feeds showing the same thing at each of the sites. "We've seen it get so bad to where the entire chamber at some sites is completely filled with this green ooze, but we can't identify the source. It seems to start from nowhere.

"What's even more bizarre is that it never flows into the endpoints of our distribution, like into business or residences. We can follow it for a while, and then it disappears."

Baren scratched his beard. "So you haven't cut the water supply, I assume."

Xi responded, "We did initially, but our analysis suggested the green substance was not affecting water quality. The substance is pervasive, but it appears inert. You can imagine the problems that would have arisen if we shut down the entire system. Water is a precious commodity."

"Understood. What did the spectral analysis of the green stuff say?" Logan asked.

Xi looked to the engineer to reply. "It has a very high mineral content, like water you might see coming from a mountain river or something. The green doesn't register stably on the spectrogram. The odd thing is that the analyses suggest it's basically water, but if you watch it, well, it's definitely something different."

"Something alien," Sara said half-jokingly. "So there are no toxins in the green ooze?"

"Not that we can detect. Some of our staff have waded into

the green pools unintentionally and have suffered no adverse effects." The engineer looked a bit embarrassed by the statement.

"Unintentionally?" Sara repeated.

"Well," the engineer paused, "some people in the area believe this green ooze has medicinal properties and was brought by mystical beings who dwell in the mountains. Not quite 'aliens' but close."

The engineer pointed to junctions on the periphery of the city. "These intersections are in the open air, above ground, so people have seen it. We've tried to close them off quickly but the locals in the area really believe it is good for them, so they try to extract it as fast as they can. There are, of course, others who take it as a sign that the Global Council has failed them, allowing the pollution to spread from the air to the water. It's been a difficult time for us."

"Maybe we can get started by testing the interface between BrainMaze and your system. It will give us a chance to start some analyses and get a better idea of this issue." Katya wanted to get things moving.

"Of course." The engineer pointed to a console in the corner. "Perhaps the best thing is to interface with the system from here. It's a redundant monitor and will give you direct access while we continue to work."

"Excellent." Katya glanced over to TechStaff and Logan. "Shall we set up the interface?"

Logan began walking to the console when Yvette stepped up. "Logan, I've fixed your device. The problem came from an old chip set that we jerry-rigged but couldn't handle the data feeds from BrainMaze."

"Thank you," Logan said as he smiled and took the Motif

from Yvette. "Great work as usual!" and he continued to the console.

"Perhaps we can use Terry's interface for this first part. He has the most knowledge of network configurations and has been studying the water systems here, so his avatar will be able to link up the fastest," Logan turned back to Terry, "and it will help with the jet lag."

Terry chuckled and stepped forward to interface his Motif. While the hardware for the local AI system was new, the software was less stable, showing signs it had been patched many times and in dire need of an upgrade.

"I see your system is hanging by a thread," Terry commented as his BrainMaze link evolved.

The engineer grimaced. "Yes, I am sorry about that. As I said, we are facing a lot of challenges. We have been working hard, but we don't have the resources to do a full upgrade. We can't afford to take the system down."

"Well, hopefully, we can superimpose BrainMaze to boost your system's capacity. You can think of it as another operating system that will work to optimize your own operating system." Terry's Motif indicated the link was complete. He activated his display and rerouted the projection to the console.

The projection showed immediately many areas of red where the AI system identified unresolvable prediction errors. Some of the red areas then cleared, only to be replaced by others.

"When was the last time the AI's prediction algorithm was updated?" Terry asked.

"I can't say for sure. I am not personally in charge of that, but I assume it is done quarterly," the engineer replied with a touch of embarrassment.

"Yeah, I think the red areas are places where the AI can't figure out what's going on. If I show you the flow diagrams for the water distribution system, we may get a better idea."

Terry's display showed flow diagrams that captured the velocity and volume of water flow through the system. A simple manifold appeared, with flows traversing the surface.

The engineer looked puzzled. "What is this?"

Logan answered, "This is a representation of the behaviour of the AI system in terms of the relationship between variables it uses to predict water distribution. The surface that is created reflects this relationship. It's called a manifold, which you can also think of as a force field that constrains how a system can behave. The behaviour itself at a particular point in time is the flow you see on that manifold.

"What you see on the manifold are the areas, or attractors, that attract or repel certain behavioural flows based on values of the variables, which helps the AI system make adjustments to avoid going too far in one direction."

The flow continued to evolve smoothly. Then the line fluctuated wildly.

"You see, at this point, there is a red indicator on the map, and this corresponds to an unpredictable flow on the manifold. At this point, the system does not know which attractor to bias and any slight change disrupts the prediction even more."

The engineer studied the diagram. "Can we modify the code to deal with these areas?"

"This is what we are here to find out," Katya answered. "The AI system you are using is very robust but does not adapt well to extreme deviations from its predictive model. We designed BrainMaze as an adaptive system, so it can work with your system to help update."

"This is very risky, but I don't know that we have any alternatives." The engineer glanced at Xi for confirmation.

Xi nodded once.

"Let's try something simple," Terry said. "I think I understand this region of your system, and I might know what's happening. I can set up a BrainMaze simulation to test a few configurations."

"Can you explain this more, please?" the engineer asked.

"Sure. The AI system assumes much of the area in the manifold follows a simple linear path, but there is probably a nonlinear component on the edge that throws off the prediction. The nonlinearity could be introduced by the green stuff or by a flaw in the water distribution system that has not been detected. I can set up simulations with BrainMaze and the AI system to evaluate these scenarios and make small parameter changes to test which are more adaptive."

Terry began the simulations, displaying the flows on the manifold. The simulation branched into several scenarios as the flows approached the instability. Most of the outcomes were the same as they had seen previously, with the extreme values as the flow moved across large parts of the manifold. Two outcomes, however, were different. In one, the flow spiralled to a small point on the manifold and did not move. In the other, the flow took an abrupt turn, moving almost tangentially to the surface.

"Damn," Terry muttered.

"What is wrong?" the engineer asked.

"Well, the two solutions that gave us different outcomes are not necessarily the most practical. The first, where the flow spirals down, is where we reconfigure the variables to converge at the same point, called a fixed point attractor. This is effective, but pragmatically, it means we just shut down the system. The second solution is equally effective, but I don't have enough data to know what this new trajectory means functionally."

"If that represents nonlinear behaviour, we will need to recalibrate the system variables to include that in its model," Logan added.

"I know, but at the moment, I can't even venture a guess what that might be," Terry replied.

Xi spoke up, "This does not bode well if something as simple as this perplexes you."

Logan turned. "I wouldn't characterize it as perplexing. I would characterize it as a problem for which we need to derive a new solution. Please remember, Councillor, that when we are dealing with nonlinear systems, we are not dealing with all-or-none solutions. Rather, we are dealing with ways to reduce the uncertainty of an outcome. Your AI system cannot deal with these new nonlinearities it encounters."

"How can we be certain that your system is any better?" Xi replied.

"Please think back to Katya's presentation a few days ago. Our BrainMaze system lives and breathes on uncertainties. It's adaptive and is constantly testing new solutions to yield better outcomes and, in doing so, reducing uncertainty. I am extremely confident that this solution is your best option." Logan was careful not to sound defensive.

"I would add that this is the first demonstration of what we can achieve with your real system. We still have more data to gather, and the green fluid adds a variable to our investigation that we did not know about," Katya spoke. "If we can work with your team to better appreciate this, we will move more quickly to an effective outcome."

Sara looked over at Xi to read his response. She resisted the temptation to interject, which would make it appear she was imposing her will rather than letting Xi draw his own conclusion.

Xi spoke, "Very well. I will have to trust that your science is solid, else you would not have come this far already. I can guarantee my team will cooperate fully with you, but I want frequent updates. We cannot afford any mistakes."

"Thank you, Xi," Sara replied. "Okay, team, I think Sebastian and I can leave you all to work while we go with Xi to discuss council matters. We'll come back in the late afternoon to see how you have made out."

"Uh, what about lunch?" Terry asked.

Katya laughed. "We now know your priorities, Terry."

Karaoke

Despite Katya's attempts to be excused, she joined her colleagues, Sara and Baren for dinner with Councillor Xi. To her surprise and delight, the dinner was very informal, involving only their team and a few of Xi's staff.

"We understand you are probably exhausted from your trip and have put in a full day here, so we kept the dinner simple," Xi explained.

Once the dinner was finished, the team rejoined TechStaff, Yvette and the bodyguards and began gathering their equipment to go to their accommodations.

Terry turned to Sara and suggested, "It's been a tough couple of days for all of us. Unless we have other plans, maybe we can go out and blow off some steam?"

Logan was all for this, as was TechStaff. Katya was a bit more ambivalent, saying, "Don't we have to start early tomorrow? I want to be in top shape."

Sara thought for a moment and replied, "Look, I am getting to know you all a little better and appreciate the camaraderie. It helps defuse the tension when you can laugh with each other. So, Professor Chatan, can you find an activity where we don't have alcohol, where we are relatively safe from crowds and where we can let our hair down?"

Terry smiled slyly and said, "In four words, Kar ee oo key."

The room was silent in amusement. Katya was the first to speak. "I really cannot sing, so if you want to go, I am happy to go back to the hotel and…"

"We are a team on this one, Katya," Logan said with a devilish grin. "We go together."

Terry knew that a dance club would be far too risky. The crowds would make it easy for the team to get separated, and it was very likely that Sara or Baren would be recognized. Karaoke was a perfect compromise because it allowed for the team to have fun in a closed space and keep watch over who was close by.

"I've been scoping out a few places, and there is one that is halfway between here and our flats." Terry made it sound more like a request.

Sara laughed. "Okay, I think we are committed then. Terry, can you forward the coordinates to TechStaff, so she can program the vehicle?"

"Already done." Terry winked.

The drive to the karaoke bar was shorter than expected, partly because a horrible rainstorm thinned out the vehicular and foot traffic. The teams arrived and ran to the bar. Sara pulled her hat down low over her face and donned glasses to hide her appearance from the doorman. As Logan exited, he said, "Sebastian decided to pass. He and Yvette have work to do so will see us in the morning."

"Given his musical tastes, I am not surprised," Sara replied, knowing Sebastian's passion for opera.

Terry slapped his hat on, and he, BGT and BGK approached the doorman. BGK put on dark glasses but no hat. *God, he looks like the Terminator*, Terry thought.

Terry turned to the doorman. "We need a room, immediately, please."

The doorman slowly turned toward Terry. By now, the rest of the group was lined behind him. The people who were already in line were mumbling in protest.

"I see, sir. Do you have a reservation? If not, it is first-come first-served," the doorman said calmly, turning back to the line.

Terry pointed to BGT. "This is DJ Tee. He is setting up a new playlist for Bar Triple-X up the street, and we need to use your facility to test out a mix. You gotta know that if this works, you'll be part of the crew that we will need over there to control the crowd."

The doorman turned his gaze back to the team. "I don't know who DJ Tee is, sir. Please, go away."

Before the doorman could turn back to the crowd, Sara stepped forward and grabbed the doorman gently by the arm. "Perhaps we could speak for a moment?"

Terry watched as Sara started whispering to the doorman. She took off her glasses and made a few more points. As she put her glasses back on and walked back to the team, she said, "and remember, no one will ever believe you."

The doorman immediately opened the door and made a sign to his partner inside. His partner, the escort, said, "Please follow me. We have perfect space for you."

As the team walked, Terry leaned over to Sara and asked, "What did you threaten him with?"

Sara whispered, "Nothing, but I told him who I was, and this was official business. I also said he should keep his mouth shut because no one would believe that Chair Meyer would be going to a karaoke bar on a Wednesday night. I learned this from Bill Murray." She ended with a smile.

"Smooth," Terry said, as the group came to a stop.

"This is our finest room. It is soundproof from the outside and has over one thousand songs to choose from. You have personal servers who can assist you with song selection. As an acknowledgement of your generosity for joining us tonight, I can also offer you one free drink to start your evening off," the escort said, opening the room to them.

The group entered a large and well-decorated room, with plush chairs, two sofas and three microphones on stands set up on a small stage. There was a computer console to the side of the stage. The escort walked up to the console and touched the lower corner of the screen.

"Most of the functions you need are displayed on the screen. The song catalogue is here, which you can scroll through or search by keywords. The lyric control is here, volume here, and playback controls down at the bottom." The escort continued as TechStaff and Terry followed. "If you need assistance, this call button at the top here will activate my comm system, and I will be able to help you."

The escort stepped back from the console and turned to the

group. "Now, may I take your drink orders?"

"Could you just bring us some mineral water and maybe some fruit juice? We won't be consuming alcohol tonight," Sara replied before the others could.

None of the group was eager to start, so Terry went first. He pulled up 'I Wanna Be Sedated' by the Ramones, which was an easy song to start things off. Though their rendition was a bit restrained, by the closing phrase, many of the team were singing along:

"Ba, ba, ba, ba, bu, ba, ba, ba ba, I wanna be sedated."

The song ended with a round of laughter and a deep bow from Terry.

TechStaff jumped up, saying, "I know one," and went to the console. She pulled up 'Paradise by the Dashboard Light' from Meatloaf, and sang the male part, pointing to Terry to jump in to sing the female part. As the song crescendoed, it became more of a team event with Terry and Logan paired against TechStaff, Sara and Katya. The bodyguards sat motionless on the chairs.

"I know one," Katya exclaimed, walking over to the console. She motioned to Sara to join her, and they belted out a powerfully frightening version of 'Oops! I Did It Again' by Britney Spears.

Terry sat back for a moment while the group chatter died down. He turned to the BG's and smiled. "Do you guys know about disco?"

Terry continued. "There was this famous movie from the era called Saturday Night Fever, which had some of the most iconic songs, many of which were sung by," he paused, "The Bee Gees," he ended with a smile.

The three bodyguards were motionless for a moment, and then BGL spoke, "Yes, we know it. It comes up a lot. Fortunately, seldom in a karaoke bar."

"So, this is a special night!" Terry said, walking over to the console. He searched the library. "Ah perfect. 'Stayin' Alive.' Seems very appropriate given our circumstance." Terry selected the song, "Who's singing this one?" he said, looking at the bodyguards.

"I would like to sing this," Logan chimed in. Katya laughed aloud, perhaps louder than she intended. "No, I am very serious. I can do this," Logan stated. "You guys can do backup." He pointed to the bodyguards.

As the song started, Logan got on to the stage and started with his best imitation of a disco swagger. As the first lyric came up, he belted out in a booming, Wagnerian baritone, "Well, you can tell by the way I use my walk, I'm a woman's man, no time to talk..." The room exploded with laughter and applause. The bodyguards stood behind Logan motionless, but when the chorus came in, they did contribute in complementary harmony. "Whether you're a brother or whether you're a mother, you're stayin' alive, stayin' alive..."

"C'mon, you guys. Dance it out! Disco has no shame!" TechStaff called out as she tried to get them to follow her dance moves. "Ah, ah, ah, ah, stayin' alive, stayin' alive." Katya jumped on the stage next to the bodyguards trying to get them to move as well.

Then, ever so slightly, the three bodyguards started to bop rhythmically. "Boogie y'all," Logan called out as the song transitioned between chorus and the next verse.

By the next verse, Katya tried to accompany Logan by providing a soprano line for his baritone. Sensing this was becoming more of a team effort, Terry added a bit of tenor.

TechStaff continued to lead the choreography for the bodyguards, who confirmed that their current career choice was better.

Sara sat at the back of the room, not quite knowing if she was more embarrassed or amused. "I am glad this room is soundproof!" she yelled.

When the song ended, and the laughter and applause died down, Sara spoke up, "Okay, you all. I shudder to think how this would have gone if we had alcohol!" She laughed and continued, "We do have an early start tomorrow, so let's go and get some rest."

TechStaff signalled for the vehicles. "I guess this may be the last fun we have for a while," she whispered to Sara.

Alien Locator

The next morning, the team piled into the vehicle with TechStaff still humming the beat to music from the night before.

"You are far too cheerful this early in the morning." Logan could not suppress a yawn. "Aren't you the least bit jet-lagged?"

"Horribly, but the tea here is fantastic!"

"I'll stick with coffee, thanks." Logan closed his eyes and snuggled up to Katya, who pushed him away.

"Stay on your side of the vehicle." She smiled, pushing him. "What is the plan today, Sara?"

Logan laid his head back and tried to recline his seat.

"You all never stop playing around. I like that," Sara started. "Anyway, I think the three of you will be busy setting up the BrainMaze interface. I got the impression yesterday the AI system here isn't quite ready for the link, so I am guessing it will go slow."

Sara looked over at Yvette, who was busy on her device. "Yvette, what do you think about the local system?"

Yvette looked up. "Oh, sorry. I've been studying their system since we arrived, and there's a lot that's not standard. Not only is their software corrupted, but there are several other routines that get initiated that I haven't seen before."

TechStaff leaned over to look at Yvette's display. "Those are weird. They don't seem to do anything."

"It just grabs data but nothing more." Yvette pointed to the termination of the routine.

The vehicle was slowing down to enter Xi's compound. "Let me suggest the trio work with the local engineers to get the core AI system interfaced, and you two continue to analyze these data flows. We can get back together later this afternoon to see what you've gathered. Sebastian and I will keep Xi occupied for the day."

"Do you want one of us to work with Yvette?" Katya asked.

"Normally, I would, but given the pretense that you three are here to work with the local team, it might arouse suspicions if there were only two of you there."

"Agreed." Katya moved to exit the vehicle.

The day was frustrating for the trio. Although the local engineers were capable, there was resistance or a real misunderstanding of the goal behind integrating BrainMaze and their AI system.

"I get the feeling they think they are being blamed for the problems here," Terry offered.

The tone of the interactions grew more positive as the day went on, particularly when Katya could train some of the local crew on how to access the BrainMaze system.

"I think we are building trust by showing them that our system is helping them and not replacing them."

The trio met up with Sara and Baren later in the afternoon. He motioned for them to follow him outside.

"Yvette and Kim could not make any progress, but they collected a lot more data on the system's behaviour." Baren provided an update as the group left the building and approached their vehicle. The bodyguards, TechStaff and Yvette were already inside.

The vehicle engaged and pulled away from Xi's compound.

"Can you patch in your data feed, so we can have a look?" Terry sat next to TechStaff.

"Some of this behaviour looks similar to what we saw back at Headquarters when we did the network analysis of the global system. If we use the same analytic strategy here, we may get some idea of whether the data extraction you are tracking is part of the local AI system or not."

Terry calibrated his Motif to focus the network reconstruction in a smaller area. "This will help reduce some of the uncertainty we encountered when we did this for the entire planet."

TechStaff patched in the AI data feed, and Terry began the analysis.

"Remind me how this works?" BGT asked.

"The idea is that we reconstruct a network based on the interactions we measure over a period. With a combination of hard-wired and wireless transmissions, you can see interactions that span many hubs, even if there is no direct link between them.

"In the brain, we call this 'functional connectivity' where you can measure the relationship between two parts of the brain, even if there is not a direct physical connection between them. We use this to characterize networks in the brain that we relate to things like memory and language. These networks are not static, though. They can reconfigure who talks to whom and then go back to the original configuration. The thought is that these switches allow the brain to predict what may happen next, so it can respond optimally. It's actually a common feature of many adaptive systems to test out new strategies constantly. The brain does this very well."

"Uh, Terry, back on task, please," Katya said with a smile.

"Sorry, I get excited about this stuff." He turned back to the display to watch the progress of the analysis. The nodes and connections of the AI system changed colour and intensity rapidly as the data were processed.

"Is this real-time?" Sara asked.

"Not yet. It's recalibrating the network we identified globally using the extra details we got from the local servers. The analysis we did before was at a coarser spatial scale to keep the computational overhead down. We can use that analysis to set the prior assumptions for this one, which should get us to a solution faster. It's like we analyzed whole brain areas to identify some of the key interactions that defined the busiest networks. And now we are focusing on the cells inside one of those areas to see what's special in that region, like which cells are most tightly interacting and when."

Logan spoke up, "But we do this by knowing what the status of all the areas are in general, which sets a context for how the local dynamics in an area are influenced by the global ones."

"You guys are serious brain nerds, you know," Sara said, only half-joking.

The display showed a switch to real-time processing, and immediately, the speed of the changes in network dynamics increased. "This will be hard to follow, so let me increase the time step to 10 seconds rather than 10 milliseconds." Terry entered the change in his Motif.

The network dynamics showed a repetitive pattern that revolved around six nodes that were slightly out of sync with each other. The remaining nodes would be engaged only when one of the six would send them a feed.

Then a new pattern emerged briefly and disappeared.

"Ah, there it is." Katya pointed. "It is indeed the same behaviour we saw in the global network dynamics and seems to happen at this scale, too."

"Is that like fractal behaviour?" TechStaff asked.

Katya replied, "In a way, yes. It's multiscale behaviour where a pattern that is used at one scale is replicated at another because it is adaptive."

She turned to Terry. "Can you find out what's driving that pattern?"

"I'm not sure." Terry looked at the display. "It's only a few data points, and there is a bit of ambiguity of what triggered the reconfiguration."

The new pattern repeated.

"Would it help if you used the estimates from the global network to set some priors for the local operations?"

"I already did that, but there's enough difference in the spatial pattern of the nodes that it only helps a little."

The pattern repeated once more.

"I'm going to remove the prior assumptions. They may bias a solution too much." He reset the parameters and fed the two pattern reversals through the algorithm.

The pattern repeated, highlighting two new nodes. Terry stopped the display and looked at the numbers.

"In the first two pattern reversals, this node initiated the switch." He pointed to a node on the periphery of the local network. "In that last one, it was this," he said, indicating a node slightly off-centre.

"My guess is that the middle node is where we want to go. The peripheral one was probably routing a packet from a subnetwork elsewhere."

"Okay, great." Sara stepped toward the display. "Where is it located?"

Terry superimposed the local map. "It's in the middle of the city. I don't know this place well enough to say what's there."

TechStaff looked at the map. "It's one of the older areas and very densely populated. There are a lot of tech shops too, which may be why they set up shop there as supplies would be easy to get, and they could remain hidden in a crowd of electronics noise."

"You've been there?" Sara asked.

"Yeah, when we came out here last time to help with the integration of the AI systems, I spent some time in that neighbourhood to see if I could find some new toys." TechStaff grinned.

"It might make sense for you to guide us, then. I would ask Xi about it, but I don't want to get them involved just yet." Sara turned to BGT. "Can you take point with her on this one?"

"Happy to. I am pretty sure Terry can take care of himself." BGT winked.

The vehicle arrived at the edge of the city district. The late afternoon traffic was building.

"We probably should go the rest of the way on foot," TechStaff suggested. "This area is very congested, so we are likely to get stuck if we bring a vehicle in."

"I can stay with the vehicle and monitor you all. If there is trouble, I can call for help," Yvette offered.

"Great idea, Yvette." Sara pulled the team together. "Okay, this is like the training scenario we did in the simulation. We don't know who the opponent is, but we know where they are. We are going to be quite conspicuous here, so like we did in the simulator, we need to act like tourists. Use the headsets for communications, but we'll have to limit the goggles to a few of us rather than the entire team. Kim and Katya, I think you two should have them, since you know the new interface. Logan, could you and BGL take the rear? Sebastian, Terry, Katya, BGK and I will position ourselves in the middle. BGT and Kim, on point. We'll take in small arms only, but make sure to holster them."

"Sara, may I make a suggestion?" Baren spoke, "Since we don't know what to expect, it would be safer if you stayed here with Yvette and monitor us. You are liable to be recognized in such a large crowd. Also, if we have someone who can link up the video feeds, it could help better coordinate the team."

"You're probably right." Sara frowned. "Ugh, sometimes being the Chair sucks."

"It will be a great help to the team, Sara." Baren tried to console her.

"No problem. I get it." Sara walked back to the vehicle. "Just make sure you keep all channels open. If we get any inkling of a problem, you will need to exit fast." She entered the vehicle, sat next to Yvette, and closed the door.

BGT looked over to TechStaff. "Alright, shall we get moving, then?"

Sara settled into the vehicle and connected her device to the console. She saw the video feed from the goggles and heard the muffled sounds of the city. "I've got you all connected now. I am going to activate the masking protocol so that we can't be tracked." Sara began sending random noise pulses through the comm channels to obscure their location.

"Roger that," BGT responded and directed TechStaff to follow.

Alien encounter

The team rounded the hill that overlooked the city and looked down the main road that led to its centre. The sun was setting in the distance, leaving a deep blue hue on the distant horizon, yet the brown humid air around the city centre persisted, and the shifting air of the approaching night brought the smells of the city.

"This reminds me of home," Katya spoke, breathing deeply.

"This is nothing like your home, Katya." Terry smiled.

"The smell is like the open market in the neighbourhood close to where I grew up."

Sara sent a message, "I KNOW THAT PLACE."

"Ah, good," Katya replied. "I can take you to my favourite restaurant there when we get back." Her stomach grumbled as she realized she had eaten little that day.

Terry looked over and pointed ahead. "Maybe we can get you something to eat down there," he chuckled.

The vehicle and pedestrian traffic grew denser as they

descended into the city. Similar to the first battle simulation, the team felt like they were swimming upstream, which had the effect of stringing them out. However, this time, they noticed it and compensated.

TechStaff scanned the street to translate the network schematics she received from Terry to what she remembered from her last visit. The density of the area meant there was a lot crammed into each building and alleyway. She remembered an electronics shop at the end of one alley that had a collection of vacuum tubes in perfect condition and old transistors she bought to rebuild an old radio.

But that wasn't their destination. TechStaff scanned ahead, noting an intersection that resembled the one on Terry's map. "I think that intersection is close to where we need to go."

"Good. Let's stick together as we approach." BGT increased the pace.

Katya saw a cluster of people who stared in their direction several times as they approached the intersection. She made a note of this to Sara. "Any ID possible here, Sara?"

"NO," came back quickly on her glasses.

"Which way, Kim?" BGK paused at the intersection.

TechStaff scanned the scene, trying to get more clues. "Sara, can you patch Terry's analysis output? There's something that doesn't seem right."

The network diagram came up, superimposed on the buildings in TechStaff's view. She saw some connections went underground, and some that went through the air, suggesting wireless transmission. There were a few weakly connected hubs that formed as communications focused on a location, then dissipated. The middle node that was identified earlier did not map to any of the buildings.

Rather, it mapped to an alley in between. TechStaff motioned to the team to follow her. "The node is not in a building but somewhere in the alley."

The alley was remarkably clean, given its location. The walls of the buildings on each side looked as if someone had recently sandblasted them. The team scanned the alley, but nothing was obvious.

Terry paused and pointed. "Look down." he motioned at the sewer grate beneath his foot. A green ooze appeared at the bottom of the sewer. It flowed but was thicker than water. Terry flashed a light down that was absorbed as much as it reflected.

"Sara, are you getting this?" TechStaff asked.

"YES. I CAN'T TELL AT THE MOMENT WHAT IT IS, BUT THE LOCATION IS DEAD CENTRE OF WHERE THE NODE SHOULD BE."

"Which direction is it flowing?" Katya looked at Terry.

He watched for a moment. "Uh, in and out, I think," he said as he watched the light beam reflection change to show a flow reversing at erratic intervals.

Katya sent a request. "Sara, can you pull up the sewer flow in this area?"

"YVETTE'S ON IT. COMING YOUR WAY IN A MOMENT."

Katya scanned the schematic. "The sewer is supposed to drain the building on the left. The other building is connected to a different drainage system. I think these were built at different times. But how does a sewer flow in both directions?"

Sara sent a set of schematics for the building.

TechStaff studied them for a moment and turned to BGT. "There is no entrance on this side of the alley, and there's new construction blocking the other. The only way in or out is the front."

BGT grimaced. "Not good. Can we go up and in?" He scanned the wall. "Ah, it looks like no." The wall was too smooth and windowing too sparse to make climbing an easy option.

"Okay, everyone, listen up," BGT continued. "We're going to have to enter through the front door. There is no other easy option. What I suggest is that Kim, Terry, Sebastian, BGK and I go in, and Katya, Logan and BGL stay outside. Katya, keep a tight link with us so that you can monitor our progress. I hope the comm is stable inside, but I don't want to take chances. Keep your weapons holstered but your hands on them."

The team walked back out into the crowded street. No one paid any attention to the group as they walked to the front of the building. Logan and BGL stood back while BGK and BGT tested the door.

"It's open," BGT whispered as he pulled on the door. It was silent as it opened to reveal a long, brightly lit corridor. He motioned for the rest to follow.

"The schematics show that there are a few large rooms off the corridor, with the stairs at the back." TechStaff was directly behind him.

"The place looks deserted," Terry commented as he scanned the corridor.

"Which is odd given of the density of this part of town," Baren added.

BGT paused by the first door and signalled to BGK to open it. He slowly opened the door. In the middle of the room, there sat a circle of people facing inwards, sitting in meditation. BGK put his finger to his lips and closed the door. "I think it's a meditation class or something."

BGT opened the next door. Peering inside, he saw a collection of tables and scattered books, with people reading. Some were also writing on paper. There were no signs of modern technology, such as tablet computers, anywhere in the room.

A small woman walked up to BGT, smiling, and spoke in a language that he did not understand.

"Sorry," he responded. "I don't understand," he said as he shook his head.

The woman repeated herself more emphatically.

BGT shook his head again. Many of the room's occupants focused on him. Two of them rose and walked toward him.

The woman spoke one more time loudly. TechStaff stepped forward and replied to her in the same language. There was a brief exchange, and the woman relaxed. TechStaff bowed and backed through the door, pushing BGT back.

As she closed the door, she turned. "We're in a sort of temple. The people in that room are transcribing old documents, and the ones in the other are in a prayer circle. She was asking if we wanted to join them, but I explained we were just tourists and had gone into the wrong building. We'd better leave now 'cause I got the impression she's a bit suspicious of us."

"We need to check the basement first." Baren walked up to them. "The sewer connection is there, and we can't leave without checking it first."

TechStaff frowned and nodded. "We should make it quick then. They're expecting us to leave."

The team quietly made their way to the basement door. BGK took the lead, followed by TechStaff, Baren, BGT, with Terry taking up the rear. Unlike the corridor, the stairwell was dim.

BGK took out a small flashlight and directed it on the stairs. The group descended slowly, careful not to make any noise.

They came to a door at the base of the stairs. BGK found it locked and motioned to TechStaff. TechStaff walked up to the door and held her device to it to scan the lock. It came back as a conventional lock. "I can't do much here. It's not digital."

Terry stepped forward. "Can I take a look?" He pulled out a small pick and metal file, and jiggled the lock with the pick, while inserting file along the door's edge. He found a latch that he dislodged and slowly pushed the door open. "We had a lot of these kinda doors when I was growing up."

"So, you broke into a lot of them?" TechStaff asked.

"No, I just tended to lose my keys." Terry winked.

BGK entered first, looking ahead to see the room open before them.

In the middle of the room stood a large pool filled with the green substance. The team approached it. BGT withdrew his weapon and signalled to BGK to do the same. They walked in opposite directions around the room. TechStaff walked up to the tank, followed by Baren and Terry.

"Sara, can you see this?" TechStaff queried as she scanned the green liquid.

"YES. ANALYZING THE FEED NOW."

Terry scanned the liquid, noticing it had an odd turbulence pattern. Rather than moving together, the liquid had portions that would move in different directions, as if there were multiple independent elements in it.

"IT'S WEIRD. IT COMES UP AS A RANDOM FLOW, BUT EVERY SO OFTEN, IT MOVES IN UNISON LIKE SOMETHING IS MOVING IN IT. CAN YOU GET A SAMPLE?"

TechStaff repeated the message to Terry. "This is what you might expect if it was not a pure fluid," he replied.

Terry reached his hand toward the liquid, dabbing the surface.

"Not smart," TechStaff whispered.

"Impressive, it's mesmerizing" he spoke as he noticed more cohesion was forming in the green.

"Oh, we'd better step back a bit," he said to TechStaff.

A humanoid, coloured black and white, emerged slowly from the tank. Parts of its body formed out of the green liquid. Two more humanoids emerged, with the same black and white colouring but in slightly different configurations. They had no clothing, but their sex was not obvious.

Baren drew his weapon and stepped back to the wall next to BGT. Terry and TechStaff remained where they were, staying still so as not to appear threatening.

"KIM, YOUR VIDEO FEED! IS THAT REAL?"

"As far as I can tell."

Terry noted a striking resemblance of one humanoid to the pale Councillor he encountered on his run a few days earlier. He felt a wave of excitement. "I think we've met before."

The humanoid did not respond. It reached into the green, and, as it withdrew its hand, another humanoid emerged. The others did the same, also resulting in another humanoid emerging from the green.

"Okay, this is starting to get uncomfortable," BGT spoke. "Terry, you'd best back away now."

The humanoids remained next to the tank, but all turned to face the team.

Terry stepped toward the humanoid he recognized with his

hands wide. "Hey, we meet again, eh? Perhaps we can introduce our teams to one another?"

The humanoid remained motionless, with a fixed gaze except for slight motions of the black and white elements, which moved across its skin like small waves.

Terry squinted to see the elements in motion to make sure he was not hallucinating. The humanoid made a motion toward him.

"Back away." BGT, sensing a threat, raised his weapon.

The humanoid reached for Terry. Terry remained still.

BGT took aim. "I won't warn you again. Back away."

Terry looked back at BGT, then again at the humanoid. He extended his hand toward the humanoid when he heard a weapon discharge.

A rubber bullet hit the humanoid in the upper chest. But rather than propelling it back, the bullet disappeared inside it. The humanoid stopped and turned toward the direction from which the bullet came — toward BGK. It extracted the bullet and threw it back at BGK with such force it knocked him back against the wall.

"Ah, shit!" BGT exclaimed. "Up the stairs, everyone. Move now!"

BGT stood his ground as Baren and TechStaff ran to the stairs. Terry remained where he was, studying the humanoids.

BGK rose slowly. "I'll go after the others. You get Terry."

"Terry, buddy, go!" BGT moved forward and grabbed him. A humanoid grabbed Terry's arm. Terry looked at the hand that grasped his arm, but despite seeing it, he could feel nothing. He tried to touch it just as BGT pulled them into a run. As they ran up the stairs, Terry turned back to see two of the humanoids merge into one.

Baren was the first out of the stairwell and was immediately greeted by a crowd of people from the library. They were yelling at him.

"They say we've violated their sanctuary," TechStaff said as she pulled Baren back from the crowd.

BGK stepped in front with his weapon holstered. "Kim, tell these folks we are going to leave now, and we made a mistake and took the wrong exit."

"They are saying something about disturbing the holy ones and that it's a serious offence."

BGT and Terry heard the commotion at the top of the stairs and paused. They looked behind to see two of the humanoids walking up toward them.

"We need to move — no time for negotiations," BGT yelled ahead.

BGK removed a packet bomb and threw it hard to the ground, making a small explosion that startled the crowd. He used the opportunity to plow ahead into the crowd, dragging Baren and TechStaff behind him. He ran into another crowd that came from the mediation room, armed with sticks. BGK pulled out his weapon and fired two stun bullets at the front of the crowd and threw down another explosive packet as he plowed ahead. TechStaff pulled out her weapon, holding it to protect her from the approaching crowd. Baren extended a telescopic metal baton, which he held ready as he followed BGK.

BGT and Terry met the first crowd, who were disoriented from the explosion. BGT held his weapon high and moved quickly, pushing Terry ahead of him, but mindful of what was coming up from the stairs. A man from the library crowd grabbed

Terry, trying to pull him to the wall. Terry spun to force him to release his grip and then shot his palm into the man's nose. Another one grabbed Terry from behind but was hit by BGT.

"Keep moving!" BGT yelled. He turned to look at the stairs. There was no sign of the humanoids.

Katya could see the battle inside and reported to BGL and Logan, "They're not in a good situation. The corridor is narrow, and there are too many people. We need to get help!"

Logan tried to get a comm feed from Terry, but his goggles only showed his status. "Dammit, Katya, these things are still not working! I can't see what's going on in there!"

BGL move to the door. "I'll go in. You two stay put. Keep monitoring Kim's feed." She disappeared inside.

Logan tried to follow, but Katya pulled him back. "We need to stay here in case more come this way, Logan. I can't do it by myself!" She looked around to see if any of the crowd took notice of them. Thankfully, the crowd remained indifferent.

BGL kept low as she entered the corridor. She saw smoke clearing from the packet bombs and heard BGK barking out commands, but could not see them. She took the offensive and attacked the crowd from behind, disabling them with baton blows. The crowd panicked.

"They're calling for someone," TechStaff yelled. "They're calling for help."

BGT and Terry got through the first crowd with only a few bruises and without seriously hurt anyone. "The last thing we need is to be seen killing a local," BGT reminded himself. Just then, someone grabbed his hair from behind, pulling him to the floor. BGT rolled away and grabbed his weapon. His assailant raised a weapon at him but hesitated. BGT did not, hitting the person with two stun bullets. He glanced over to see Terry making his way to the second crowd. BGT rose quickly and ran after Terry.

Baren could protect himself with the metal baton, parrying blows and striking back. He felt the crowd pulling back and heard TechStaff saying something about asking for help. The crowd to his right dispersed to reveal the doors to the mediation room. Baren saw the flash of a weapon as a bullet whizzed past his head. "We have live fire here!" he yelled, ducking to grab his weapon.

Almost in slow motion, the crowd dropped to the floor, leaving the team standing. Four guards in combat armour ran out from the meditation room with weapons drawn. They fired shots at BGT and Terry, and then toward Baren. BGK heard the shots and spun to return fire, which forced the guards back inside the room. He motioned to TechStaff and Baren to get behind him, and BGL came forward with her weapon drawn.

"We have no cover," BGL hissed to BGK.

"I am aware of that." BGK looked around for options, firing a couple more rounds to keep the guards occupied.

BGT saw the guards duck back into the room and motioned for Terry to run. Terry looked ahead and sprinted and dropped to the floor, looking around to signal BGT to move ahead. BGT moved as a guard stepped out, firing two bullets. One hit the wall. The other hit BGT in the side, knocking him against the wall. The Kevlar vest he had on wasn't enough to stop the bullet as a spray of blood appeared on the wall where the bullet exited. Terry spun to face the guard, firing one shot that went through their jaw. Another guard stepped out with a weapon ready to fire, only to receive two bullets to the neck from Terry's weapon.

BGL and BGK set a volley of fire back at the room entrance. Terry used this opportunity to grab BGT. Baren ran back to assist. The crowd became more emboldened by the presence of the guards and followed. Terry turned and yelled, "Stay the hell down, or I swear you will not see tomorrow," and sent a volley of bullets into the ground in front of the crowd.

The team got outside. Katya saw the wound on BGT and hurried over to assess. "I have medical training!" she reminded everyone. BGT was semi-conscious but bleeding heavily.

"We can't stay here, Katya," TechStaff spoke, anxiously watching the door. The team moved closer to the alley as the remaining guards burst through the doors. The guards spun to see the team moving to the alley and fired at them. The indifference of the crowd outside changed to panic, with some scattering and others running toward them.

A screech of tires broke the weapon fire as Sara drove the vehicle at the guards. The vehicle door opened.

Sara looked at the injured BGT. "Get him inside fast."

Yvette jumped out and helped Katya and Terry get BGT inside.

The rest of the team crammed into the vehicle and sped off.

Katya kept pressure on BGT's wound and said, "His vitals are low, and he has lost a lot of blood. I can't do much here."

They placed BGT on the floor of the vehicle. He had lost consciousness, and his breathing was shallow.

TechStaff bit her lip, looking back at BGT. "Is he going to be okay?"

"I hope so. It appears the bullet passed through, but I do not have the tools here to know if there are fragments inside. I am concerned that a major artery was cut, so we really need to get the bleeding under control."

TechStaff opened a long case in the back of the vehicle. "We have some basic medical equipment in here, Katya. Maybe it will be useful."

Katya directed BGL to maintain compression on the wound while she looked through the case.

Baren spoke, "We can contact Xi, and he can expedite medical attention."

"We can't do that right now. Xi can't know we've been poking around here without his permission. And with the things we just encountered, I don't want Xi to call out his forces, and we end up in a street battle," Sara replied sternly.

"Sara, if we don't get him attention fast, he will die," Baren replied.

"I am quite aware of that and don't intend to allow that to happen." She clenched her jaw. "Kim, were you able to identify alternate solutions?"

TechStaff was still looking at her device. "Yeah, there are a couple. When we came through last time, we connected with the Dean of the Med school. She seemed cool. Another option is to contact the tech group I know and see if they can direct us. They are well-connected but still under-the-radar."

Sara thought for a moment. Given it was very late, the likelihood the tech group would be contactable at this hour was high, while the Dean would be lower. But by contacting the Dean, they might get medical attention right away.

"I will contact the Dean right now," she said aloud. "Vee, open a link to Dean Shen."

In a few moments, an audio feed was established. "Chair Meyer! I am surprised to receive a call from you. It's very late here, and I hope you understand."

"Hello, Dean Shen. I apologize for the inconvenient hour. We have an urgent matter and could really use your help."

"Of course, I am more than happy to help the Council. What do you need?"

"It might be easier if I just showed you. Can you open a video feed?" Sara turned to TechStaff.

A window of Shen popped up on the console. Sara held the camera to show BGT on the vehicle floor, still unconscious and bleeding.

"Oh, my," Shen responded. "Where are you? Who is the injured person?"

"We are about five kilometres from the medical school," Sara replied, adding, "the man on the floor is one of my staff. We are here investigating a potential sabotage of the local AI system and got caught in a scuffle where my team member was injured. Doctor Shen, this is a very sensitive political matter, so I am asking for your help to take care of him at the med school."

Shen was silent, staring ahead without blinking. She glanced to one side and then back directly ahead. "I can take care of him myself. I will meet you at the medical school. I can be there in 10 minutes and will recruit some of my staff to assist."

Sara breathed a sigh of relief. "I am very grateful, Doctor Shen."

"Come to the side entrance of the building where the medical imaging facilities are. We can take him in there without attracting too much attention. There are likely to be a few biophysics students who could help get some imaging done if we need it."

The comm link ended. "Vee, activate over-ride option emergency. Fastest route to the medical school." Sara sped up the vehicle.

They pulled up to entrance of the medical imaging facilities about 15 minutes later. The Dean was standing in the entryway with two others dressed in hospital scrubs.

The vehicle doors opened, and Sara and Baren were the first to jump out. Katya looked over at the Dean, then back to BGT, who was weak but stable.

"Thank you again for helping us, Doctor Shen," Sara greeted her.

"I will do what I can." Shen motioned for her colleagues to follow. They brought a hospital gurney with them.

Katya stepped out of the vehicle. "Doctor Shen, my name is Katya Kaliski. I am a neurologist but did a lot of work in the ER. Our friend was shot in the abdomen. The bullet appears to have exited completely, but I can't be sure there were no fragments inside. He is currently stable, but very weak. You can see that he has lost a lot of blood." She motioned to the blood-stained floor of the vehicle.

"Thank you, Doctor Kaliski. If you can transfer your medical record to our system, we will attend to him immediately. We can take it from here."

"I can assist you, Doctor Shen," Katya offered.

Sara touched Katya's arm. "I think they can handle it, Katya. We also need to limit our exposure here." She turned to Shen. "I'll set up an alert system for you so that you can contact us whenever you need to."

"Very good, Chair Meyer. We will do our best. And you'd best get your team out of here now," she motioned, "Once this has all blown over, I expect that you will share the full story with me over some nice tea." Shen gave the team a much-needed smile of comfort and assurance.

"I consider that a date." Sara motioned for the team to get back into the vehicle. "Let's get back to the flat and try to get some rest."

Brief debrief

The group arrived back at their accommodations.

"Yvette, I had problems with the goggles again," Logan said as they walked from the vehicle.

"What do you mean? I am sure I fixed them." Her tone was defensive.

"Like I said, there was a problem. There were no signals being sent to me other than my status. I felt completely helpless. It is fortunate things did not get more serious, else there could have been more casualties."

"The problem is you, Logan. I fixed them. If you had paid attention to the interface, you would have seen they were working just fine!"

"There's no need to get upset, Yvette. I am merely pointing out…"

"Piss off, Logan! Don't give me your condescending attitude. You messed up again, and you won't admit it. You always do this! You take all the credit, but when something goes wrong, you deflect the blame to someone else!"

Baren stepped in front of her. "Yvette! That's quite enough. I suggest you take Logan's feedback seriously and look at his goggles immediately. If you cannot be civil, there is no room for you on this team! I can easily replace you."

There was silence for several moments.

"Hey, everyone. It's been a very intense day for us, so let's try to dial it down and get some rest. There's a lot to process." Sara broke the stillness. "Sebastian, could you and I meet for a bit and decide how best to proceed tomorrow? We will see the rest of you all in the morning."

The trio entered their flat, followed by BGL. "I will be in the front room tonight, keeping watch. BGK is with the other group."

"Don't you need to rest?" Logan asked.

"I will, but not now. We've already encountered more than we bargained for, so I am pretty tightly wound up. I may do some yoga to clear my head while you all are sleeping."

The trio silently acknowledged her, shifted into the back part of the flat and closed the door behind them.

Katya excused herself. "I need to wash the blood off." The statement was both a matter of fact and poignant.

"This shit is getting real." Terry sighed.

Logan stared at the floor. "Those creatures from the sewer — what were they, Terry?"

"I don't know. They looked extremely artificial in their construction, but very alive when they formed. Some kind of alien maybe? I will say that they looked a hell of a lot like the Councillor I saw on our river run the other day, though these were a lot less animated."

"What about the one that BGK shot?"

"Well, yeah, that counts as animated, I guess. It all happened so fast, Logan. I really didn't have time to process what was going on. Maybe we can get the video feed and push it through BrainMaze."

Logan removed his jacket and shirt, walked over to a large chair, and collapsed into it. He removed his shoes and put his feet up. "I am exhausted."

Terry was still standing, lost in thought.

Katya emerged from the bathroom, having changed into tights and a t-shirt. "There was blood all over everything. Fortunately, the material is easy to wash." She pulled her hair back and sat down on a chair next to Logan.

"Terry, sit down," Katya suggested. "You just went through hell to get BGT out of there. You should rest."

Terry glanced at her, then looked down at the bloodstains on his jacket. "I need a beer," he said and walked into the small kitchen. "Do you want anything?"

"I'll do the same," Logan responded.

Katya thought for a moment and changed her automatic response. "Just some water, please."

Katya said to Logan, "Terry did an amazing job in the battle. Wait until you see the video. I swear you won't recognize him."

Terry reemerged with drinks in hand. "Recognize who?" He had taken his jacket off in the kitchen.

"You," Katya replied, "you were amazing in there today. BGT would not have made it out of there if it wasn't for you."

"I think you may be exaggerating, Katya. You only saw what was on the video feed, so it may have looked like I was doing a lot. The real credit should go to BGL, who distracted the crowd long enough for us to make our way out."

"You're going to say it was a team effort," Logan added.

"Well, it was." Terry handed Katya a glass of water and an open can of beer to Logan.

"Yes, but not all team members contributed in the same way, I'd say," Logan continued.

Terry stepped back. "I don't see where this is going, you two. One of our team almost got killed today. It could have been a lot worse." He sat on the sofa.

"I meant nothing by it, Terry. It's just that we haven't seen this side of you before. You're usually more reflective, so to see you like some latent warrior was a bit of a surprise."

Terry opened his beer and took a sip. He gathered his thoughts before he spoke. "I guess the stress of the situation empowered a strong fight-or-flight response in me."

Katya felt it was time to change the subject. "So, these things you saw, are they behind the communications hack in the Global AI?"

Terry was silently grateful for the shift in conversation. "Well, they were at the location of the hub we identified. It's impossible to know whether they specifically are the ones, or maybe it was the group we fought."

"I didn't get the impression the people in the temple were technically sophisticated. It looked to me like more of a religious cult or something."

"Unless that was a facade," Logan added. "The guards that showed up were certainly adept enough with modern technology."

"True." Terry sighed. "And then there's the green stuff we saw. It may be a conduit of some sort." He surprised himself with an enormous yawn.

"You are tired?!" Katya exclaimed.

"Seems so." Terry blinked. "That fight-or-flight thing may have drained my reserves. Maybe I'll try to get a few hours of sleep." He set the beer down and stood up. "Good night."

Katya and Logan both replied, "Sleep well," and watched as Terry moved to his room.

Katya looked over at Logan, who was staring at the door to Terry's room. "What's the matter?"

"Oh, it's probably nothing, but our friend is not himself right now. It could be the stress of the situation, but when was the last time you saw Terry leave a full can of beer?" Logan smiled slightly.

Katya laughed a little. "Good point. We're all at our limits, but it's probably best to focus our efforts on the things we discovered today rather than trying to second guess each other."

Logan closed his eyes and nodded. "Right, as usual, Katya. I think I will follow Terry's lead and excuse myself. See you in a few hours."

"Rest well, Logan," Katya replied. "Oh, you didn't finish your beer."

"As I said, I will follow Terry's lead." Logan smiled, rose, and walked to his room.

Katya watched as Logan closed his door. She stood and walked over to the small window next to the sofa. It was the only window in the room, giving the impression that you were staring from inside a prison. She regarded the flicker of streetlights over the empty streets. Her gaze moved up as she scanned the buildings. The sky above them was black. *The air is so dense here, you can no longer see the sky.* She frowned. The stars always brought her comfort; she really needed that now.

She moved to the sofa, grabbing her Motif, and lay down as she reviewed the activity logs and current status of BrainMaze.

A video message from her daughter, Ileana, came up, showing a clip of her in a small aircraft.

"Hi, Mummy. Grandma's friend is taking us flying. I want to learn this so I can come with you on trips!"

Katya watched the video, feeling tears forming in her eyes.

Ileana asked the pilot if she could try the controls. The pilot obliged, asking her to sit in the co-pilot chair and use the stick to guide the aircraft.

"You're a natural pilot," Ileana's grandma said from outside the camera view.

Katya stored the video so she could reply later. She did not know what to write in reply.

She sighed and tried to focus on the activity logs. The data they had collected over the day was incredibly rich, occupying much of the computational capacity of BrainMaze's system. The difficulty in linking different scales of data — the global data that led here and the local data they were currently integrating — presented some challenges for the algorithms.

It is good we updated our analyses to be more mindful of uncertainty of the relationship between scales, she thought. It would still take time for the analyses to finish, but what they sacrificed in terms of calculation time, they gained in precision and reliability.

Katya switched to review the video feed from TechStaff during the battle. The jarring video as the group ran from the basement to the main level gave Katya vertigo. She blinked her eyes and placed the Motif down. She looked at the ceiling, and her sight defocused as sleep finally came to her.

Musically dynamic

Katya's dream began with her sitting next to her piano. Not in front, but next to it. She had started lessons five years ago, so that she and Iliana could practice together. In this dream, she was initially alone, hearing the melody and chords for an Italian aria, "O Del Mio Dolce Ardor." She was learning the piece so that the next time Terry was in town, she could accompany him on the piano as he sang.

She heard the voice of her piano teacher, "This is the genius of the great composers. See how the melody line stays the same in the last stanza, but with the subtle change in the chord structure gives the last part a different sense of urgency."

"But isn't this just swapping out motifs?" she heard herself respond.

"Yes, exactly. The motifs are selected to fit the constraints of the piece. But consider that in the context of the faster melody, the slower changes in chord progression affect the overall feel of the song," her teacher replied.

"So the interacting timescales are the key to the song's progression?" she asked.

"For sure! This is how you know a great composition. The composers had an intuitive sense of this, and even if the ideas of complexity weren't around then, they were writing pieces that encapsulated some of the key principles."

She was surprised to hear her piano teacher describe principles of Complex Adaptive Systems, but the link of flows and timescales to music made perfect sense.

The image of the piano faded slightly. The melody and chords moved in different time scales, yet the points where trajectories changed affected the emergent feature of the song. *If we were talking about the brain, this could be considered "plasticity" but is simply a recombination of existing motifs producing a new emergent feature*, she thought.

"So, what you are saying is that new rules are emerging from a recombination of existing motifs?" Now the speaker sounded like Logan.

"I don't think it changes the rules. It's a recombination of existing repertoires that may shift the system to a different part of a manifold," Katya replied, looking at Logan's face.

"Like crossing a separatrix?" Logan replied.

"That sounds like some weird S&M thing," she heard Terry's voice now.

"Well, math can be sexy," Katya laughed, "though in this case, it separates the manifold into distinct regions, like a barrier."

The scene came into focus, and she realized the three of them were sitting up to their necks in a hot tub.

Terry continued. "The interacting flows idea also pertains to music improvisation, where coordination of musical improvisation between players can be understood from the perspective of recurrent flows. A simple drone line can set the general rules, and the players are free to test out various motifs within the rule set, which comes across as 'improv, but can also be cast as reordering of motifs. Sometimes they sound great, but sometimes they sound like fingernails on a chalkboard."

"That is very interesting," Katya replied and began to rise from the hot tub, but stopped when she realized she was completely naked.

She looked across at Terry and Logan. She prepared to speak, then saw that the tub was not full of water but the green substance they had seen in the water systems.

What are you guys wearing? she thought, pressing against the edge of the tub.

Logan and Terry rose from the green. Their skin looked normal, but she saw an odd black and white ring on the surface of the green around their bodies. She felt herself jump.

And heard a loud knocking.

"Hey, Professors! Time to wake up! We need to get moving in

about a half hour," BGL called out.

Katya opened her eyes, feeling her heart pounding. "Ack, my dreams can really freak me out sometimes," she whispered to herself.

"We'll be ready," she called out.

End of Book 1.

An introduction to Book 2:
Sewer Chase

Jumping in deep

The initial pace for the run was slow, with Terry taking the lead, scanning the surroundings to identify the water distribution network. Terry remembered a paper on old architecture for water distribution, which warned of a weakness in the system. He had pulled the paper up on his Motif and used this new information to build another simulation. Within seconds, BrainMaze had pinpointed the single point in the system that was most vulnerable.

Terry signaled a turn and ran to a nondescript building that had the sewer system access point. The door was unlocked.

The trio descended the stairs among the enormous steel pipes and rusting turbines. Terry spotted the weak point several flights of stairs below.

"You see?" he said. "Where that green sludge comes in, the filters only deal with large particles. It's easy for it to diffuse through the system here without detection."

As Logan watched the rising green tide, his heart raced, as he knew what might be coming. "Let's get back up the top," Terry said. "This green stuff will flood the chamber soon, and we don't want to be swimming in it."

As the three emerged, a large Alien in white clothing ran toward them.

"I see a gun!" Katya shouted.

The trio ducked behind a fence, but not before the Alien had fired a warning shot.

Terry looked over the fence to see the Alien jump into the sewer. "It's going in!" he said.

Logan acted. "I will go in after it." He stood up. "We were going to have to go in anyway, and I did some bog diving when I was a Ph.D. student. It took me a year to get over the trauma and at least that long to clean my glasses." With that and a smile, Logan leaped over the fence and ran into the sewer after the Alien.

When Logan came to the first landing, he paused, kneeling to get his goggles out and rearrange his gear. The dim light from the sewer was enough for him to do this without needing more light and attracting attention. As he knelt, he scanned around to see any signs of the Alien. Other than the sight and sound of the green sludge pouring into the chamber, he could detect nothing. He put the goggles on and waited. *Katya, how do I look?* he thought.

The trio had discussed a routine for situations like this. They were vulnerable, with one person separated from the group, but the goggles provided an interface with BrainMaze that allowed them to continue to work as a team, even at a distance. Terry and Katya watched Logan disappear and proceeded with their duties. Katya immediately put on her goggles and recalibrated her BrainMaze interface to link with Logan's. Terry stood watch in case other threats emerged.

He glanced at the B2S icon in his goggles and thought again, *Katya, how do I look?*

Katya scanned her display. She saw her avatar sync up and then the feed from Logan's link: "KATYA, HOW DO I LOOK?" The B2S converter was on silent text-only mode, given the precarious situation they were in.

Katya scanned the readings from Logan's avatar, smiled and thought, *Logan, you look hungry and a little hungover.*

Soon the response came: "KATYA." Even without sound, she could image the drawn-out vowels feigning disapproval of her comment. Of course, the B2S converter was not perfect, so who knew how her thought was actually translated?

"LOGAN, YOU LOOK HAIRY AND A LITTLE HAWAIIAN," was the read-out Logan saw on his display and chuckled under his breath. *I guess that means I am okay*, he thought to himself.

He stood and saw a shadow behind him. He knew this was in a dangerous position, but rather than turning, which would waste precious milliseconds, he stayed low, kicked his leg out to the side and swung it around behind to trip the shadow. As he turned around, gratified that his body allowed this defensive move, he swept the legs from under the Alien. The leg sweep was enough to unbalance it, sending it tumbling sideways toward the edge of the walkway. This gave Logan enough time to get himself upright and face the Alien. For now, at least, he felt he had the advantage.

Terry had not been paying attention to Katya while he scanned the area. He resisted putting on his goggles, knowing he would feel tempted to follow Logan through the sewer rather than keep watch, but his attention snapped immediately to Katya when she let out an audible gasp. He backed closer to her, keeping his ears open.

"He turned quickly and now is fixating in front. I think he engaged the Alien," she whispered.

Logan didn't know what to do next. He could attack, which is what his training compelled him to do, or he could wait and see. The best approach was to capture and contain the Alien, so that they could figure out their intentions.

The Alien did not rise. Instead, it rolled off the walkway down to the green sludge below.

Damn, I wasn't planning on a swim tonight, Logan joked to himself. He glanced at the B2S icon and thought: "Katya, it's gone into the green. I am going after it."

Logan ran down to the next level, where the green sludge had risen. Fortunately, his neoprene boots would work well here, so he locked his weapon and holstered it as he entered the green. He fitted a mask over his mouth and nose to shield against any toxins in the green sludge.

Rather than sludge, in the typical sense, it was more like slightly thick green water. It was mostly translucent, so Logan could make out the motions of the Alien as it moved deeper into the green. Its motions were erratic; perhaps Logan's leg sweep had injured it.

"LOGAN, WE MAY HAVE TROUBLE READING YOU IN THE GREEN. BE CAREFUL, AND KEEP YOUR CAMERA ACTIVE."

Logan acknowledged the message to himself and slipped into the green. It was deep, requiring using some techniques his wife taught him about free diving and breath control. He tried to relax his diaphragm and keep relaxed as he sunk farther down. About 10 metres away, he could see the Alien, still showing the same erratic movements.

Logan drifted forward slowly, but stopped when he saw the Alien's body split into pieces. Each piece morphed slightly in the green to become mobile and began moving toward Logan. Dirty buggers, he thought as backed away and tried to ascend to the walkway.

When complex systems face a challenge, they send out multiple agents to try different solutions to address that challenge. The immune system is a perfect example of this, where numerous antibodies can be mobilized to face a new intruder, and the ones that are more effective are reproduced. Through this, the system can adapt to the new intruder and have an effective defence the next time an intruder is encountered.

"Terry, Logan is in trouble. You need to get down there fast. I will get help," Katya said aloud as she turned to see that Terry had already gone.

Terry turned on his goggle display to see what Logan's camera showed. When he saw the Alien roll into the green rather than standing to face Logan, it occurred to him that the green might provide access to a regressive state for the Aliens — a sort of "safe place". When the Alien split into segments, this reminded him of a bifurcation, wherein the system hits a trigger point, and then new configurations are accessible. The green may provide that stable state from which the Aliens could try new configurations.

Rather than going into the sewer, Terry decided the best way to combat them was to eliminate the stable state and thereby eliminate the options. He ran to an access door down from the sewer where the controls for water flow were housed. There, he reversed the flow, hoping that it would pull the green out of the sewer.

Terry activated his goggles, glanced at the B2S icon, and thought: *Logan, hold on to something quickly.* Within a few seconds, "OKAY" appeared on Terry's display, and he started the reverse flow procedure. He glanced at Logan's camera feed to see the Alien's progression toward him had stopped. Terry ran to the sewer to get down to Logan.

Logan saw the message from Terry and was holding tight to the submerged stair rail, all the while watching the pieces of the dismembered creature drifting toward him. Their flow stopped, and Logan felt the reversal of the green sludge as it was pulled into the drain. As the fluid continued to drain, some of the Alien's segments moved randomly in different directions, as if testing an alternative path. The last of the green drained, and the segments slowly reformed until all that was left was the intact Alien body on the sewer floor.

Acknowledgements:

The inspiration for this story came from my dear friends and collaborators, Petra and Viktor. There's a lot of us in here. I am also grateful for the encouragement and ideas from Helena and Jessica. Many of the characters in this book were inspired by other colleagues, whom I won't list in case they don't want to know. Finally, thanks to Nancy for giving me the space and support to pull this together.

Title: *A Complex Journey*
     Book One Brain Maze
- Author: Randy McIntosh
- Publisher: TotalRecall Publications
- Paper Back: ISBN:
- eBook ISBN:
- Pages 264
- Publication Date: 2022

Three scientists (Katya, Logan and Terry – aka the trio) have developed a brain simulation platform based on principles of Complex Adaptive Systems, called "BrainMaze". The trio have made great advances in medicine by developing the platform that can use a person's own brain to create an avatar lives within the BrainMaze platform. Simulations done in BrainMaze test potential treatments first in the avatar before going to the patient. The success in the medicine leads to an even greater success for BrainMaze as a tool for people to interact through a Brain-Computer Interface.

Title: *A Complex Journey*
     Book Two The Next Day
- Author: Randy McIntosh
- Publisher: TotalRecall Publications
- Paper Back: ISBN: 9781648831348
- eBook ISBN: 9781648831355
- Pages 200
- Publication Date: 2022

Brain-Computer Interfaces, Virtual Reality, Science and Espionage come together in a story about three scientists who work together to prevent a global climate disaster that appears to be caused by extra-terrestrial intruders.